ALSO BY SHANNON WORK

*Now I See You*
*Everything To Lose*
*The Killing Storm*
*Murder in the San Juans*

# DEATH IN A HARSH LAND

A NOVEL

SHANNON WORK

This is a work of fiction. Names, characters, businesses, organizations, places, events and incidents are either products of the author's imagination or are used fictitiously. Any resemblance to actual persons, living or dead, or actual events is entirely coincidental.

ISBN: 979-8-9869376-2-5 (paperback)
ISBN: 979-8-9869376-4-9 (large print paperback)
ISBN: 979-8-9869376-3-2 (eBook)

www.shannonwork.com

"There is evil everywhere under the sun."
Agatha Christie

# CHAPTER 1

*Thursday, May 19*

HENRY ROSE WAS itching to shoot somebody. It had been that kind of week. Hell, it had been that kind of life.

The night was quiet—too quiet. The type of quiet Henry found unsettling. Like the silence after the dentist says *this might sting a bit* before he sets your mouth on fire. Or worse, the milli-second of silence between a nod and the moment they swing open the gate, releasing a ton and a half of raw muscle and hate, snorting and twisting, before the beast slings you from its back, slamming you to the ground.

Henry sat in the dark, perched on the tailgate of the truck, holding his Remington 700, the civilian rifle he found most closely resembled the one issued to him as a sniper in Afghanistan. He caressed the long steel barrel and stared up at the night sky. He'd been doing it for over an hour.

The desert night was warm, and his shirt stuck to the sweat on his back, a feeling he was used to. It was only late May, but the temperatures on the ranch had already soared past a hundred several times. It was going to be another sweltering summer.

Henry prayed the rustlers would show. He wanted to bust the sons of bitches who'd been stealing sheep, peeling them off area ranches a handful at a time. Never enough to put any of the ranchers in financial straits, but enough to piss Henry off royally.

The ranch had been in his family since the first Roses came to the area in covered wagons in the 1880s. It was thirty minutes northwest of Del Rio, a small town in West Texas known for its history of hard-scrabble pioneers and outlaws.

Henry had been born and raised in Del Rio. And except for a short stint living in Lubbock, riding bulls for the Texas Tech University Rodeo Team, and his three tours in Afghanistan, he'd lived his whole life there. The people who lived in Del Rio were mostly good. But it chapped him raw thinking about the few that weren't.

He sat in the dark, his boots swinging several inches above the rocky ground. If his father had still been alive, he'd have been there with him. Thinking about his father made Henry's heart clench, and he pushed the thoughts aside.

Thomas Rose would be the first to remind him this wasn't the time for being sentimental. Henry had a job to do.

Sheriff Odell Gardner and his handful of deputies had spent months trying to catch the rustlers, but it didn't seem they were any closer to catching them than when they started. Henry had decided it was time to take matters into his own hands. It's what his father would have done.

Henry searched the night sky littered with stars and easily found the Big Dipper. He followed the line from its cup to Polaris, the North Star. Next, he found the Little Dipper and Orion's Belt.

He knew the constellations well. Growing up, he would often sneak out of the house and stay the night in the yard, spending hours staring up at the heavens.

But tonight wasn't the time for stargazing. Henry scanned the dark horizon, visible by the light of the half-moon. He was parked just beyond a flock of sheep on a part of the ranch that more than a century of his ancestors had called the River Pasture because of its proximity to a wide riverbed that dried up centuries ago and now only flowed after torrential storms upriver.

It had been nearly a month since rustlers stole over a dozen sheep off the ranch, and Henry knew it was only a matter of time before the thieves returned. But this time, he would be ready for them. He wanted a few minutes alone with these ol' boys to teach them the error of their wrong-living ways before he handed them over to the law.

He checked his phone and saw that it was almost midnight. He decided to wait another hour. If no one showed, he'd head back to the house.

Clouds like stretched cotton floated slowly across the moon, dimming the arid landscape. After several minutes, Henry surrendered to his growing fatigue and reclined into the truck bed, laying his back against its cool metal ridges and closing his eyes. He would rest for only a minute, he told himself before falling fast asleep.

He wasn't sure how long he'd been out when a gunshot exploded the silence and rolled over the rocky landscape like thunder. It sent a cold chill through him that instantly jolted him awake.

Henry bolted upright, then off of the tailgate, his heart racing. He swiveled left then right, furiously searching the dark moonlit countryside for the source of the blast.

Although the shot had been loud, it had come from some distance away. He quickly ran through the possibilities. Large caliber. Probably a 300 Ultra or Win Mag, a rifle used for big game hunting. But why was someone shooting it in the dark? And why on Rose land?

He grabbed his rifle from the bed of the truck, then held his breath, straining to hear anything that would give him a hint about where the shot had come from. But the night was quiet again.

He took a flashlight from the truck's console and used it to pick his way among the rocks and cacti up a nearby ridge that overlooked the expansive riverbed that gave the pasture its name. Several thousand yards away, high up the slopes on the riverbank's opposite side, a beam of light swept the ground, briefly illuminating the harsh terrain to one side and then the other as someone stumbled among the rocks. They were coming down from the cliffs on the far side. They were on Henry's uncle's ranch. But Jordan and Henry had leased the land from him for years.

He quickly shut off his flashlight, then squinted into the distance, trying to make out who it was, but the person was too far away to see. He watched as the sweep of light made it down the last of the embankment and finally dropped below the gnarled mesquite trees that bordered the riverbed's edge.

The mystery person had been on the trail a few yards from where Henry's father had fallen into a chasm only three weeks before. The path wasn't much more than a rock-strewn split in the steeper slope of the mountain, bordered on both sides by boulders and thorny vegetation.

He strained again to listen and heard the faint sound of an engine starting. A minute later, taillights emerged in the distance on the road that bent up and away from the riverbed as it wound its way toward the highway. Henry knew the road well. It ran between their ranch and his uncle's land.

Something stirred uneasily inside him as he watched the taillights, clouded in swirling dust, disappear over a rise on the horizon.

Henry couldn't make sense of what had happened. A rustler wouldn't have climbed the rocky cliffs on the riverbank's far side where there were no sheep.

Who had been on the ranch? And what did they shoot?

# CHAPTER 2

*Friday, May 20*

THE FOLLOWING DAY, Henry was up before daybreak. What had happened the night before still had him rattled, and he was determined to find out what had happened.

The shot had come from somewhere above the riverbed on his uncle's land. There was no reason for anyone to be out there in the middle of the night, much less firing a high-powered rifle.

He dressed, not bothering to shower, then grabbed his boots from beside his bed and took them with him to the kitchen.

"Where are you headed this early?" his mother asked as she poured herself a cup of coffee. There was a sadness in her eyes that Henry hoped wasn't permanent. It had only been a few weeks since the accident, but he worried she would never be the same.

Henry had moved back onto the ranch following his divorce the year before. It had made sense at the time. The ranch house was enormous, and he'd never liked living in town. Moving home had eliminated his thirty-minute commute from Del Rio every morning.

Henry set his boots on the floor, pulled a chair from the table, and sat. As he pulled the boots on, he told his mother what had happened the night before.

"What do you think it was?" she asked.

"No clue. But that's what I'm going to try and find out."

"Have you talked to Roy?" she asked, referring to Henry's uncle. "Maybe he knows who it was."

"I called him when I got up. He said nobody should have been out there."

Kate Rose had a worried look on her face. She followed him out of the kitchen and to the back door. "Don't you want to wait for Jose," she asked, referring to the ranch foreman. "He could go with you."

Henry grabbed his cowboy hat from a hook and put it on. "I'll be back before he gets here," he said, opening the door.

There was no easy way to get to where Henry had seen the person the night before. He took the road from the house to the highway, then turned west. After a quarter of a mile, he turned back onto the ranch, taking the gravel road that ran between his father's land and his uncle's.

The morning was still dark, the truck's headlights illuminating the way as the road cut across a rolling pasture for several miles before it dipped down into a draw and continued alongside the dry riverbed.

Henry slowed the truck when he got close to where he thought the person had parked the night before. He squinted up at the dark slopes to his right, and stopped the truck when he spotted the gunsight notch in the cliffs where the trail crested the mountain. He shut off the engine, then leaned over and pulled a Colt revolver from the glove box. He checked the cylinder, saw it was fully loaded, then got out of the truck.

The sun, although still below the horizon, cast the sky in an orange glow. Henry stood in the road a moment and listened. But the only sounds were the soft whooshing of a breeze through mesquite trees and the early morning calls of a handful of canyon wrens perched in their branches.

Henry stuck the Colt into the waistband of his jeans, then

picked his way around scrub brush until he caught the trailhead that led up the mountain. He was so close to where his father had died, but he forced the memory aside.

It was a challenging climb. The narrow trail was not much more than a goat path. After several minutes, he slipped and reached out to keep himself from falling, scratching his hands on the rocky boulders on either side. He cursed at the pain but kept going.

Jordan would have said he was nuts for doing it alone, but Henry plowed ahead anyway. Although Henry loved his brother, most of the time, he didn't understand him. They had never been much alike. Jordan handled life methodically. He would have called the sheriff instead of taking matters into his own hands.

Henry stopped climbing when the trail crested the notch in the ridge and took a moment to enjoy the cliff-top views before the path began its descent down the other side. He caught glimpses of the Pecos River in the distance and looked north, toward the river's headwaters a thousand miles upstream, somewhere in Colorado, then swept his gaze south where it emptied into the Rio Grande.

An eagle screeched, circling overhead.

He looked far west, across the expanse of his uncle's land to where it bordered the Moran Ranch, blocked from view by a sheer wall of gray rock that rose hundreds of feet from the ground below. He studied the similar cliffs beside him, then turned and looked back the way he'd come.

He searched the slopes beside the trail but saw nothing. There were no signs anyone had been there the night before, so he decided to go further.

He stood a moment, studying the trail as it dropped over the mountain's far side. It was an area that sloped steeply down about a hundred feet, then leveled out to one side. Part of the ledge was tucked beneath a deep rock overhang. Beyond the shelf, the ground fell sharply to the valley below. There were similar rock formations all over the Lower Pecos River Valley, and Henry knew that many of them had provided shelter for indigenous tribes a thousand years earlier. He wondered if someone had been in *this* one the night before.

The trail to the overhang was steep and narrow. One wrong move, and he would fall hundreds of feet to the ground below. He picked his way slowly down the slope, cautious of rattlesnakes that might be warming in the morning sun.

When he reached the ledge, he turned and looked into the rock shelter. A small clump of sage and mesquite blocked the view of the far side. But closer to him, the ground had been disturbed, rocks strewn this way and that. He noticed a large hole dug close to the shelter wall. And there was evidence of an extinguished campfire.

Henry made his way across the ledge as the gray wall of the shelter loomed high above him. He stopped near the cold embers and looked around again.

Nothing.

There wasn't anything that gave him a clue why someone had been there the night before. He stuck his hands on his hips, frustrated.

He made his way around the clump of mesquites to get a better look at the far side of the shelter. But what he saw had him immediately recoil back again.

Henry felt bile rise in his throat as he took it all in. For a split second, he imagined being back in Afghanistan.

There was blood. A lot of blood. Pooled and spattered over the ground. And fanning several feet up the rock wall.

At the center of it all was the body of a dead man.

# CHAPTER 3

*Saturday, May 21*

JACK MARTIN SAT at the small table bolted to the floor of the Airstream trailer, his Glock 9mm disassembled in front of him. He had meticulously cleaned each part.

In the old days, while working at the bureau, he could reassemble the thing blindfolded. For fun, he would often time himself to see how fast he could do it. But today's cleaning was all business. He hadn't fired the pistol in over a year—not since Aspen. But he was about to head somewhere he might have to use it.

Earlier that day, he had received a call from Jordan Rose, his friend and college roommate. Jordan had told him about his father's accident several weeks earlier. It sounded horrible—a fall on the ranch into a hidden chasm. Jack was upset by the news. He'd always liked Thomas Rose.

After a few minutes, Jordan had gotten to the point of his call. "I'm stuck in D.C. and can't get home," he said. "I didn't know who else to call. The body's got everyone spooked."

"What do you know about it?" Jack asked.

"Not much. Henry found him in a rock shelter on Uncle Roy's ranch not far from ours. Twenty-something Hispanic male with a snake tattoo that wraps one side of his neck."

"Gang tat?"

"Not sure. But the sheriff's a friend of mine, and he thinks the murder could be cartel related."

"Cartels on the ranch?"

"There're rumors they've started coming across the border."

Jack detected a hesitation in his friend's voice. "But you're not sure they're responsible for the murder."

After a brief pause, Jordan replied, "I don't know what to think. But the sheriff seems convinced they are. I'm afraid he might use it as an excuse to close the case before any real investigation is done. They're in over their heads with all the border issues right now. Thousands cross every week in our sector." He paused a moment. "And Mother's nervous. She says Henry's carrying a pistol and ready to shoot whatever jumps out at him. I'm worried he's going to do something foolish. You know how he is."

Jack *did* know. Through the years, he and Jordan's brother had never gotten along. The two brothers couldn't be more different. Where Jordan was calm and deliberate, Henry would go off half-cocked, looking for a fight. Jack hadn't seen him in years, but it sounded like he hadn't changed.

"I don't know," Jack had said. "I don't know what kind of a reception I'd get. Especially if you're not there. I can see Henry thinking I was butting into something that wasn't my business."

"Leave Henry to me. I'll talk to him. I know for a fact that Mother would like to see you. She told me so. Too much has happened in the last few weeks, and it's got everyone on edge." When Jack didn't reply, he added. "I know it's a huge favor to ask, and I wouldn't be asking if there was any way I could get home myself. But the congressional hearing is this week. If I'm not here to testify, I'll miss the whole damn thing. There's too much at stake for ranchers all over the country. I've got to stay."

Jack knew that Jordan was an officer of the American Sheep Industry Association and took his job lobbying for his fellow ranchers very seriously. But Jordan loved his family more. And if Jack refused to check on them, he knew Jordan would pack up and head back to Texas, missing whatever business he had in D.C.

Jack had planned to spend the summer camping with Crockett in the San Juan Mountains above Telluride, Colorado. But plans change. Jack's almost always did.

He would go to Del Rio.

# CHAPTER 4

*Sunday, May 22*

THE FOLLOWING DAY, Jack was up early. He threw the duffle bag he'd packed the night before into his truck, then locked the pistol in the glove box.

Crockett danced at his feet, expecting to go with him. "I'm sorry, boy," Jack said, bending to pet the dog and checking that his collar was secure. "Not this time."

Crockett seemed to understand. His tail drooped, and he stood still, staring up at his master.

"Next time." Jack took the steps back into the trailer and grabbed a sack of dog food. "Let's go find Otto and Red."

The two made their way through the trees that separated campsites twenty and twenty-one.

Jack found Otto on the banks of the creek that bordered the campground. He was sitting on a large tarp whittling an aspen branch. A red hound lay peacefully beside him.

Jack had met Otto Finn several months earlier when he had moved to Telluride to solve the case of a missing author. He hadn't planned on staying as long as he had, but once again, his plans had changed.

In the ensuing months, Jack had grown fond of Telluride and the locals. And Otto, in particular, in whom he had found an unlikely kindred spirit in his octogenarian neighbor. The two had grown close in the few months Jack had been there.

But Jack would have to move back to Texas soon to find

a job. The last case he'd worked, finding the killer of a congressman whose plane had been blown out of the sky over the snowy peaks above town, had paid well. But Jack's savings would only last so long. In the meantime, he was enjoying his time in the Rockies, and would put off moving as long as he could.

Otto sensed Jack behind him but didn't look up. He spoke in a deep and gravelly voice. "You're up early this mornin'."

"I've got to leave town for a few days."

Otto stopped whittling. "Everything alright?" He wasn't one to pry and must have sensed something in Jack's voice.

Jack cleared his throat. "A friend from Texas called yesterday. There's been a—an incident. He can't get home and wants me to check on his family."

Otto remained silent.

"I've got a favor to ask," Jack continued. "I should only be gone a few days, but would you mind watching—"

"Crockett." Otto finished for him.

Jack sighed. "I know it's a lot to ask—"

Otto struggled to stand, and Jack helped him to his feet. The old man brushed some invisible dirt from the back of his pants, then carried the pocketknife to the picnic table and laid it down. His movements were slow and methodical.

Jack was afraid he would refuse the request when he said, "Red and I would love the company, wouldn't we, boy?"

The red hound had followed Otto from the tarp to the table. The two had become inseparable in the few days since Otto received the dog. Jack thought the bond had been unusually quick but was glad since he was the one responsible for the dog being there.

"Is that there his food?" the old man asked, pointing at the sack. "You can set it inside."

Jack carried the bag to the Army surplus tent and laid it on the canvas floor inside. "Thank you," he said. "I shouldn't be gone more than a few days."

Otto held up a hand. "No need to worry," he said. "The boys and I will get along just fine."

Jack glanced toward the creek where the dogs were frolicking in the water. He stood and watched them a moment longer, then, with mixed feelings, said goodbye to Otto and got in his truck. As he drove out of the campground, he glanced in the rearview mirror in time to see Crockett run to the edge of the campsite. The dog stood still, watching him go.

Jack felt a lump form in his throat. Although he didn't have a choice, he hated to leave Crockett behind.

In the few months since Jack met Otto, the two men had spent hours sitting together on the banks of the creek that bordered the campground, Otto regaling him with stories from decades spent alone in the Rockies. There had been stories of bears and snowstorms, explosions and rockslides. It sounded dangerous, but the old man's eyes never sparkled more than when he talked about his time in the mountains.

The location of Otto's mine was a well-guarded secret. As far as Jack knew, no one in town had ever been there or even knew where it was. And although Jack had tried numerous times, he could never coax its location out of the old prospector.

As soon as enough snow had melted in the mountains above town, Otto would hike to his mine and spend the summer prospecting as he had every summer for the last fifty years. But this time, he would take Crockett with him.

He tightened his grip on the steering wheel as he exited the campground. A few blocks up Main Street, he pulled into a parking spot in front of Pandora Café.

Judith Hadley looked up when he stepped inside.

"You're up early," she said, wiping her hands on her burlap apron. She pulled a pen from behind her ear and pointed to Jack's usual table next to the river rock fireplace. "It's open for you. Have a seat."

"I'm not staying. I just wanted to come say goodbye."

She suddenly looked stricken. "You're leaving us?"

Jack had only known Judith for a few months but had grown as close to her as he had to Otto.

"Just for a few days," he said and watched her face relax. "I'm leaving Crockett with Otto."

"Best get back before the eccentric old coot disappears for the summer. Could be any day now."

"That's what I'm afraid of."

She reached out and laid her hand on his arm. "Now don't you worry. If Crockett goes with him, he'll have the time of his life. Especially now that Otto has Red." She smiled, trying to reassure him. "Is your trip business or pleasure?"

Jack thought about it for a moment. "A little bit of both," he said. "I'm going to Texas to help a friend." She waited for more, but he remained silent, not sure how much he wanted to tell her.

The door to the café opened, and a couple of locals stepped inside.

Judith turned to them. "Take a seat wherever you like. I'll be with you fellas in a second."

She looked again at Jack; her smile gone. "Hold on a minute," she said, then disappeared behind the swinging door into the kitchen. She emerged a few seconds later, folding down the top of a paper sack, and holding it out to him, searching his face for clues he wouldn't reveal. "A few things for the road," she said. "When you get hungry."

For a moment, Jack had a sinking feeling he would never see her again. But the trip to Texas would be only a few days, he reminded himself and pushed the ridiculous thought aside.

"Thank you," he said, reaching for the bag.

Judith held onto it. "You be careful, Jack Martin," she said, then let go. "I'll have you a hot meal on the house when you get back."

In the truck, Jack leaned over and double-checked that

he had the pistol safely stored in the glove box, then started the engine and swung away from the curb. As he left town, he couldn't shake the feeling that he was headed toward danger.

# CHAPTER 5

AT THE INTERSECTION outside of Telluride, Jack turned south. He had put the ranch's location into the GPS on his phone. It would be a fifteen-hour trip. Under normal circumstances, he would make the drive in a single day. But not this time. The reception from Henry was going to be tense enough in daylight. Jack wasn't about to make it worse by getting there in the middle of the night.

He looked at the route suggested by his phone. It took him south into northwestern New Mexico, through Albuquerque, then finally Roswell before he would reach the Texas border. He had been through the country before. Although it was a harsh and desolate landscape, it didn't compare with the country outside of Del Rio.

West Texas was wild and rugged, settled by hard-scrabble pioneers determined to make a life in an unforgiving land. Jordan had told Jack stories about when the Rose family first moved there from central Texas. At the time, Del Rio wasn't much more than a frontier outpost with small bands of Native Americans still roaming the area.

Jack couldn't imagine having roots anywhere that ran that deep. The longest he'd lived in one place was the years spent as an FBI agent in Houston. But Houston was enormous and had never felt like home.

He thought about his hometown of Baton Rouge and wondered what life would have been like if the grandparents who had raised him hadn't been murdered. He might have moved back to Louisiana after college. But that was a long time ago, and he pushed the memories aside.

As the highway dipped and twisted through the mountains, he glanced at the empty passenger seat beside him and thought of Crockett. A year and a half earlier, if someone had told him how much he would miss a dog, he'd have said they were crazy.

On the outskirts of the small town of Rico, the urge to turn around was strong. But Jack accelerated.

He thought of Thomas Rose and wondered what had happened. Jordan said it was a fall on the ranch, but Jack wanted to know more. The last time Jack saw him was nearly a decade earlier. And although Thomas had been nearing seventy, he seemed strong and healthy. Learning of his death had come as a shock.

Jack's thoughts turned to Kate, Thomas's wife. She would have been devastated when he died.

Guilt swelled inside Jack when he realized how long it had been since he last saw them. Jordan had called the past Christmas and left a message, inviting Jack, as he did every year, to spend Christmas with the family. Thinking about it now, Jack wasn't sure if he had called him back.

He ran through the last conversation with Jordan again in his head, wondering about the murder. Who had died on the ranch, and why? And was it a coincidence that Thomas Rose had died only a few weeks before?

There were too many unanswered questions.

Jack accelerated.

Was the murder drug-related like the local sheriff thought? The Mexican cartels grew more powerful and brutal every day. Had their violence spilled across into the U.S.? The Rose Ranch wasn't far from the border.

Or was the motive for the murder more sinister? Something closer to home?

# CHAPTER 6

*Monday, May 23*

JACK WAS ON the road before daylight the next morning after a restless night spent in a flea-bag motel in Fort Stockton.

It had been a twelve-hour drive from Telluride and only nine o'clock when he pulled into the Best Western. He could have driven for several more hours but was afraid he'd end up sleeping in the truck if he did. Towns were few and far between this far west in Texas.

He drove for an hour before the sun finally broke the horizon. The landscape was exactly as he remembered. It was wild and desolate country in varying shades of gray and green. There were vast stretches of land cut deep by canyons and covered with gnarled mesquite trees and rock. Rugged mountains rose from the desert floor, peaks not as tall as the Rockies but imposing, nonetheless.

Jack went several miles without passing anyone headed in the opposite direction. He set the cruise control at the speed limit and took his foot off the gas. The early morning light cast everything in a deep orange glow. *The fires of hell*, he thought. And the asphalt highway stretched out before him like a gray serpent leading him into the unknown. This was harsh country.

Forty-five minutes from the ranch, he crossed the Pecos High Bridge. It was a site to see. Perched a thousand feet above the river, it spanned the wall of cliffs on each side. He looked down at the sun-flecked water and watched the river flow slowly to the south, toward its confluence with the Rio Grande.

Several minutes later, he slowed the truck as he rolled through the tiny town of Comstock, an outpost for the surrounding ranches. There wasn't a single traffic light. But he noticed a small diner with a crowded parking lot, and his stomach rumbled. He was tempted to stop but pressed on. He was almost there.

Outside of town, set on a rise to the north, was a barn, its roof painted with the Texas flag. Jack had seen it numerous times before and knew the Rose Ranch was only a few miles farther. He felt something inside him stir and wondered if this was what it felt like to come home.

For a moment, he didn't worry about the reception he would receive from Henry. He was glad to be back.

When a large iron gate on the south side of the highway came into view, Jack slowed the truck and turned off the road. The gate was powder-coated black, with the name ROSE in block letters welded near the top. An American flag flew on the fencepost to the left, a Texas flag on the one to the right.

Jack pulled the truck to a solar-powered keypad, wound down his window, and punched in the code Jordan had given him. It was just past 8:30, but the sun already blazed like fire in the morning sky. The heat radiated up from the ground and through the sleeve of his shirt, quickly warming his exposed arm. He wound up the window as the heavy gate swung slowly inward.

The gravel road from the highway led deep into the arid countryside. Jack slowed several times, crossing the occasional cattle guard that separated one pasture from another. After several miles, there were sheep scattered in clusters in the distance. The road dipped, crossed a dry creek bed, then climbed a rise when, finally, the house came into view.

It was a sprawling adobe hacienda painted the color of the land. It was a single story, but the walls soared nearly twenty feet. Symmetrical rows of barrel-shaped terra-cotta tiles covered the roof. A short stone wall circled the house and enclosed a bright green yard that sat in stark contrast with the bleak landscape.

The setting was beautiful, the house surrounded on all four sides by a handful of cottonwood trees and distant horizons.

A hundred yards to the west, there was a cluster of smaller buildings including a barn, where an empty stock trailer sat baking in the sun. Nearby, two horses were tied to a hitching post, swishing their tails.

Jack parked the truck at the house and got out. He opened the gate in the stone wall and took the rock-paved sidewalk to the porch, where he wiped his boots on the woven mat set before two gigantic carved wood doors. He held his breath and knocked, then stepped back and waited for someone to answer.

Overhead, a hawk screeched, and he looked up, shielding his eyes from the sun. He watched the hawk circle several times, then fly away, and had the sinking feeling it was a warning. Something didn't feel right.

Someone spoke Spanish inside, then one of the doors swung open.

A stout, hatchet-faced woman stood staring up at him. She couldn't have been much over five feet, with an olive complexion and close-cropped black hair streaked liberally with gray. Her eyes were black and bored into Jack like she was warding off the devil.

Jack recognized her immediately. "Ado. How are you?" His smile wasn't returned.

Ado had worked for the Rose family for years, cooking and cleaning. It had been a decade since Jack had seen her.

The woman's frown deepened. "Who are *you*?" she asked in a heavy Hispanic accent.

"Well, look what the cat drug in." Henry appeared behind her and stood just in the doorway. His hands were on his hips. "Back in town to butt your nose in where it doesn't belong again?"

Henry was a good three inches shorter than his brother, with a stocky build, sandy-blond hair with a hint of red, and penetrating blue eyes that made him look ready to fight. His volcanic temper was notorious and could transform his face from contented one moment to red with fury the next. Jack held his breath to see which one he'd get.

Ado stepped back from the door, watching them.

The two men stared at each other in silence.

Jack started to speak—to explain that Jordan had asked him to come—when a grin slowly spread across the other man's face.

"How the hell are ya?" Henry asked. He stepped outside and gave Jack a bear hug that nearly lifted him off his feet.

Jack released the breath he'd been holding. "Hello, Henry."

"Come on in and get out of the heat." He held the door open. "Ado, get Jack something to drink. Jack, you want something to drink?"

"No, I'm fine."

"Get him something anyway," Henry told the housekeeper.

But she stood there, staring. "*Es* Jack Martin? *El amigo de* Jordan?"

Henry laughed. "In the flesh. After all these years. Looking a little worse for wear, mind you—that's probably why you don't recognize him. But I guess a long road trip will do that to someone of his advanced age."

Henry was teasing, but Jack smoothed the back of his hair self-consciously. He hadn't thought about how much a decade had changed him.

"*Hay, Dios mío.*" Ado's eyes had grown like saucers. "*Es su amigo como* James Bond? *Cero, cero, siete?*"

Henry laughed again. "You're famous now," he said, slapping Jack on the back. He turned to Ado. "*Si, ahora es un detective,*" Henry replied. "*Pero es sólo Jack.* It's only Jack!" He rolled his eyes and shook his head. "Drinks, Ado. Go get Jack something to drink."

Ado crossed herself, then lifted an imaginary crucifix from her bosom and kissed it as she scurried from the room.

Henry shook his head, chuckling. "Afraid of her own shadow," he said. "And dumb as a box of rocks."

"I hear you," she called from the other room.

"Quit spying, Ado," Henry hollered back. "Or I'll have Jack arrest you."

The woman muttered something in Spanish that Jack suspected included a few curse words.

"Does she know why I'm here?"

"Everyone does." Henry's face went suddenly grave.

"Jack." Kate Rose stepped into the room. "It's so good to see you."

Kate was a petite woman, early 70s, with more gray in her hair than what Jack remembered. But she still had a quiet elegance that instantly put him at ease. And, although her eyes showed a hint of sadness, her smile was warm and welcoming.

When she hugged him, Jack realized how much he'd missed her. "It's good to see you, too, Kate."

She searched his face a moment, and her smile faded. "I just wish it were under better circumstances."

# CHAPTER 7

ELENA TORRES WAS running late for work but worried she shouldn't be going at all. It was too soon.

She pushed the pangs of guilt aside as she finished making the bed—her third bed that morning. She then picked up a hand towel from the bathroom's linoleum floor, the only bathroom in the house, and hung it neatly through the small ring mounted on the wall next to the sink.

She hurried through the small, three-bedroom home with the efficiency of a master sergeant, straightening the couch cushions and scooping up a stray sock. Taking care of the house and her elderly parents had become second nature to her.

"Fernanda will be here any minute," she told her mother as she walked past her into the kitchen.

"*Mija*, you don't need to go today," Sabina Torres said. "You look so tired. You have not slept."

It was true. Elena's reflection in the mirror that morning had surprised her. She was just over thirty, but her normally olive complexion was sallow, and the dark circles under her eyes made her look decades older.

Although the family needed the money, that wasn't why she would go to work that morning. She was doing it for selfish reasons. It was too soon, but she had to get away, even for just a few hours.

"I can do that," her mother said as Elena washed a coffee

mug in the sink. "You do too much. You should be cleaning for a family of your own, not for us."

Elena dried the cup and placed it in the cabinet. "You and *Papi* are my family," she said with a wan smile, then kissed her mother on the cheek and slid past her into the living room.

Miguel Torres was propped up by pillows and seated in his tattered recliner. Elena watched for a moment as he stared blankly through the window overlooking the backyard.

They used to have grass. And flowers. Elena grew sad thinking about the pride her father had once taken in meticulously maintaining their tiny front and back yards. "The prettiest yard on the street," her father had often exclaimed with great pleasure. But those days were gone. The grass had quickly shriveled in the Del Rio heat after her father's stroke six years before.

Miguel sat staring at the baked soil in the yard. Elena leaned across him, took a tissue from a side table, and dabbed at a spot of drool at the corner of his mouth.

He turned to her and smiled but said nothing. Some days were better than others. She searched his eyes for recognition but couldn't find any. Did he know who she was? Did he recognize *mi* ángel, as he'd called his youngest daughter since she was a baby? She suspected today he thought she was a kindly stranger.

Elena kissed him gently on the forehead. "*Adiós, Papi,*" she whispered. "I will see you after work."

The front door opened, flooding the room with morning sunlight and heat. At the exact moment, an air-conditioning unit in an adjacent window kicked on.

"Just in time," Elena said to her sister over the humming sound.

"I can stay until the kids get out of school," Fernanda told her, setting her purse on the floor.

"That will be great. I shouldn't be home much later than that."

Fernanda walked over and kissed Miguel. "Good morning, *Papi*."

Sabina padded into the room. She wore house slippers and a thin cotton dress Elena had seen her in a million times before. The once vibrant sunflowers had faded to a pale yellow.

In a handful of steps, Fernanda crossed the room and kissed their mother. "*Hola, Mami*."

The two women looked sad or tired. Probably both, Elena decided. She felt a stab of guilt and turned away. She grabbed her cell phone from the coffee table. "Don't forget *Papi* needs to take his medicine after lunch," she told her sister. "It's on the counter next to the refrigerator. I gave him water, but he's not drinking it. You should help him. And the hummingbird feeder is almost empty. Please fill it so he has something to watch besides the talk shows."

"I'll take care of it," Fernanda said, trying to reassure her sister. "We will be fine, won't we, *Papi*? Now you go. The deli's customers can't wait on themselves."

Fernanda walked Elena to the door and held it open for her.

Elena hesitated. She should stay. There was still too much that needed to be done, plans to finalize. Her sister had a husband and children—her own family. She should be with them. Elena didn't have children. And now, as the only unmarried Torres sibling, Sabina and Miguel were her primary responsibility.

"We will be fine," Fernanda repeated as if reading her sister's mind. "It's only a few hours. Besides," she continued, "I *want* to be here."

Elena stood there a moment longer, then kissed her sister on one cheek and then the other. "Thank you, *Nanda*."

"Light a candle on your way home," Sabina called out, her voice cracking slightly.

Elena swallowed the lump in her throat. "I will, *Mami*."

She stepped onto the front porch and closed the door behind her, then stood a moment, pushing down the guilt that swelled inside her. It was too soon. But she needed to get away. She needed the distraction of work, or she'd be suffocated by her grief.

It had been only three days since her younger brother was found murdered.

# CHAPTER 8

THE SUN WAS directly overhead, and Jack's shirt had soaked through with sweat. He felt the heat penetrate his jeans and even the soles of his boots as he and Henry climbed the front side of the mountain.

Henry had called the narrow path they were on a "trail," but Jack thought that was stretching the word's meaning. The path wasn't much more than a winding notch up the steep rock slope. It didn't resemble anything like the trails he had hiked in Colorado.

By the time they reached the top, Jack was out of breath. He stopped and leaned against one side of the notch to keep his balance while he wiped sweat from his forehead. The rock was surprisingly cool on his shoulder. He watched Henry pick his way carefully down the trail on the mountain's back side. One misstep could send him tumbling hundreds of feet to the dry gulch below.

Jack turned and looked back the way they had come and marveled at the cliff-top views that stretched for miles. Henry's truck looked like a tiny Matchbox car in the distance, parked just off the road next to a dry riverbed strewn with boulders and scrubby vegetation.

Jack checked the time on his phone and saw that it had taken them twenty minutes to reach the notch in the ridge—a *gunsight* notch, as Henry had called it.

"Let's keep moving," Henry said, heading down on the far side. "We're almost there."

Jack pulled the back of his soaked shirt away from his skin and flapped it several times, trying to dry it, before giving up and letting it fall, where it stuck to his back again. He pushed off the rock, then grabbed a handful of branches from a nearby sage bush to steady himself before he started the descent.

A few minutes later, Henry stopped in front of him. They had reached a spot where the mountain wasn't as steep. It fanned out to their left, providing a natural shelf twenty feet wide before dropping to the gulch below. A great slab of gray and black rock loomed thirty feet overhead and protected a part of the shelf. It was an area of solid stone, like someone had taken a giant scoop out of pure rock, leaving a smooth face and deep overhang that provided a patch of welcome shade in the brutal morning sun. A rock shelter, Jack remembered. Jordan had shown him several on the ranch before.

"The body was over there," Henry said.

Henry dangled his feet over the edge of a boulder for a second, then dropped to the ground below.

Jack did the same, then brushed the dust off his jeans and followed Henry to where the mountain flattened out a bit.

They stood just outside the overhang. There was a large hole dug near an old campfire, and the ground was torn up in several places. Jack noticed a rusted shovel tossed to the side, partially hidden by a mesquite. Although the shelter would provide some protection from scouring winds and rain, it was a brutal spot in the harsh countryside.

"That's where I found him," Henry said, pointing to an area on the far side of the ledge. "Behind the mesquites."

Jack made his way around the trees and was immediately struck by an area of rock and dirt covered with dried blood. There was blood everywhere.

Jack stepped closer, careful not to fall into another gaping hole that someone had dug. He squatted, touched the blood-soaked earth with his fingers, then looked back at the trees.

Henry read his thoughts. "I figured he was trying to hide behind the mesquites when he was shot."

There were only a few feet between the mesquites and the sheer rock face of the shelter behind them. Jack stepped carefully around the trees, avoiding their thorns, and saw blood spattered up the shelter wall.

He turned his gaze south and caught a glimpse of Amistad Lake through the haze in the distance where the reservoir straddled the United States and Mexican borders. "The sheriff thinks this is cartel-related?"

"He thinks it was either the cartels or that a drifter killed him. Maybe an illegal. They walk through the ranch all the time."

"You don't sound convinced."

"I'm not," Henry said, shaking his head. "A drug deal gone bad?" He lifted his hands and looked around. "Up *here*?"

Jack had to admit the remote location was unlikely.

Henry continued talking. "We've heard rumors that cartel violence has spilled across the border, and that the feds aren't telling us about it. But this here wasn't done cartel style."

"What do you mean?"

"The Narcos hang their bodies from bridges. They brag about their killings." Henry shook his head. "They don't leave them on the side of a cliff."

"Tell me again about the victim."

"Odell—he's the sheriff. Anyway, at first, Odell thought the dead guy was an illegal. Probably dropped here by a coyote and killed. Or died by natural causes." Henry stuck his hands on his hips as he thought about it. "Never made sense to me. But then they found out he *wasn't* an illegal but a local. Diego Torres. An amateur archeologist of sorts. Out here digging on Uncle Roy's property."

"Digging for what?"

"Artifacts. We got archeologists scattered all over this country." He jerked his chin toward the rock overhang. "If you get close, you can see the old rock paintings. Done by Indians a thousand years ago—or so they say. These paintings aren't as visible as a lot of them in the area. But archeologists come take photos and measurements every now and then. Some of them hang around longer, looking for things that belonged to the Indians—old tools, shoes, stuff like that. Anyway, the dead guy was digging here on Roy's land."

"By himself."

"As far as I know."

"Why would someone kill an archeologist?" Jack thought aloud.

"Not just an archeologist," Henry said. "Odell said Diego used to be into drugs—using it, dealing it. That's why he thinks the killing was drug-related. Which, around here, usually has some sort of connection with the cartels."

"But you don't think so."

"No. I figure it was either a drifter or he caught the sheep rustlers in action. Instead of risking going to jail, they followed him down here and shot him."

"Jordan mentioned someone's been stealing sheep."

"Yep. They've been taking a handful here and there every few days. They hit us a month ago. I figure we're about due to be hit again, and when they were out here, they ran across this guy."

Henry pulled his phone from the pocket of his jeans. "See here," he said, pointing to the screen. He had pulled up a satellite image of the ranch. "This is the road we used to get here. It runs directly between our ranch and Uncle Roy's but doesn't go by either house. It mostly runs adjacent the old riverbed, out of site. You wouldn't see anyone driving on it unless you were in one of the pastures off the road. In some spots, not even then—the road's hidden in the cottonwoods and mesquites lining the creek bed in spots. It wouldn't be hard for rustlers to get in and out on this road without being seen."

"Where were the sheep they stole a month ago?"

"In a pasture just off the highway. But we moved the rest of them back off the road. The rustlers will have to come deeper into the ranch to find any now."

Jack thought about everything. It was a stretch to think someone stealing a few sheep had graduated to the ranks of murder. It was more likely the killing had been drug-related. Jack agreed with Henry that it probably wasn't the work of cartels. But it would almost be better if it *had* been. The murder would be a single incident, not likely to pose a future threat to any of the Roses.

And if the cartels were responsible, Jack's hands would be tied. He was no longer with the FBI. There would be nothing for him to investigate, and he could head back to Telluride.

But he didn't think the murder was the work of organized crime. And the alternative was worse. It meant the killer was local. Someone closer to home.

# CHAPTER 9

THE CLIMB BACK to the truck was as challenging as any hiking Jack had done in Colorado. By the time he and Henry reached the arroyo where they had parked, he didn't think he could take another step.

His legs were weak and shaking, his jeans stuck to them from sweat. He was sure he'd lost ten pounds. The last time he remembered being as hot was at football practices back in college, where the artificial turf on Kyle Field could reach over 140 degrees some days.

The two men sat on the tailgate, sharing water straight from the plastic gallon jug. Jack was relieved to see that Henry seemed equally wiped out.

"Someone's coming," Henry said, squinting up the road.

Jack saw a cloud of dust swirling just over the horizon. A few seconds later, a white truck crested the rise, headed in their direction.

"Sheriff's office." Henry set the water jug down and hopped off the tailgate.

Several minutes later, the truck rolled to a stop, and the driver got out. He was in a deputy's uniform and rested his hand on the butt of the firearm strapped to his belt. He couldn't have been much over thirty. He was tall and lanky, with a loose, swinging gait as he walked toward them.

He had a skinny neck with an Adam's apple that bulged in the center and bobbed as he chewed on a toothpick. When he reached them, he pulled the toothpick from his mouth and flicked it aside. "Howdy, Henry," he said without smiling. He glanced at Jack, then back at Henry again. "I came out to check if you've seen anything out of the ordinary."

Henry shut the tailgate. "Like another dead body?"

The deputy scoffed. "Let's hope not. Been two too many of those out here recently."

Jack thought first of Diego Torres, then realized he was also referring to Thomas Rose. The statement had been crass, and Henry had bristled when he said it.

"No, I mean anything—or anyone—that looks suspicious." The deputy glanced behind him at the flock of sheep bleating in the distance. "We've got a lead on the rustlers, and I'm making the rounds, checking it out."

"I have the men do a rough count every morning now," Henry replied. "We haven't had any go missing lately, but you'll be the first to know if we do."

The deputy nodded but eyed Henry suspiciously. "I'd advise you to leave the investigating to us. Let us know if you see something instead of trying to take care of things yourself."

"You mean no more going vigilante? Sorry, Bert, no promises."

The deputy didn't look happy with the answer.

"Bert, this is Jack Martin," Henry said, changing the subject. "A friend of the family. Jack, Deputy Bert Lynch."

Jack shook the deputy's hand.

Lynch frowned, turning back to Henry. "What are you fellas doing out here? Looks like you've run a marathon."

"I showed Jack where I found Torres," Henry said, pulling off his hat. He wiped his forehead with his sleeve. "Probably should have waited until morning when it wouldn't have been so hot."

"Now, why would you go and do that?"

"Do what?"

"Climb over to where you found Torres?"

"Jack's law enforcement, too, Bert."

"Was," Jack corrected him.

"Is—was—doesn't matter." Henry waved a hand dismissively. "Jordan asked him to come for a visit. He wants him to check out what's been going on."

Recognition showed on Lynch's face. "You're that detective," he said. "From Colorado."

Jack nodded but kept quiet and saw the deputy stiffen.

"You here to investigate something?"

Henry cut in. "Now, don't go getting your panties in a bunch, Bert. He's just going to look into a few things for us. You know we've lost our share of sheep. And now this." He jerked his chin at the mountain, referring to finding Diego Torres dead.

Lynch hitched up his pants and shifted his weight from one boot to the other, looking agitated. It was too early to pass judgment on the gangly deputy, but something about him rubbed Jack the wrong way.

"Don't know why he needs to bother," the deputy said, looking from Jack back to Henry again. "We're already investigating both cases. We'll find the rustlers. And Torres's murder was a drug killing. Seems to me like your friend is wasting his time."

Jack didn't like being talked about as if he wasn't there but knew better than to pick a fight with law enforcement.

"I've got plenty of time to waste," Jack replied, trying to sound friendly. "And it's been years since I've been here. It was a good excuse for a visit."

Lynch locked eyes with Jack a moment, then finally shrugged and looked away. "Suit yourself. Just as long as you don't interfere with any official investigations."

Henry broke in. "Anything new on Torres?"

Lynch shook his head. "Everything points to drugs. My guess is it's going to be an open and shut case."

Jack knew that murder cases were rarely "open and shut."

"What about the rustlers?" Henry asked. "Odell doesn't think they could have done it?"

Lynch was quick to shake his head. "Sheriff's convinced it's drugs, likely something to do with the cartels."

Jack wondered what evidence they had that made them so certain.

A hawk screeched overhead.

"Well, I best get going," Lynch pulled a toothpick from his shirt pocket and stuck it between his teeth. "Got several more ranches to hit before I head back to town."

Henry and Jack stood watching as he climbed into the truck and left.

"They're going to sweep Torres's murder under the rug," Henry said.

Jordan had said something similar.

Although Jack was usually quick to defend law enforcement, he now feared the same thing.

# CHAPTER 10

THE SUN HAD dropped low on the horizon, casting the countryside in a dusty haze.

Jack drove toward Del Rio and couldn't shake the feeling that something was wrong. Although there didn't seem to be an immediate threat, he felt Kate and Henry were in danger. Probably fatigue, he told himself. Two days of traveling, then a harrowing climb over jagged rock and cactus to where Henry had discovered Diego Torres's body.

He twisted in the seat one way and then the other, trying to stretch the kinks from his lower back, several of his old football injuries aching in protest. It was early evening, but his body was screaming that it was midnight.

Kate had insisted he stay at the ranch. With six bedrooms, the house had more than enough space, but Jack had grown accustomed to being alone. He wanted to focus his thoughts on the case and was wary of the distractions that came with staying with others. He needed privacy.

When it became clear he wasn't going to stay, Kate had called someone and arranged for lodging in town. Henry had seemed relieved that Jack wouldn't be staying, and Jack wondered why.

The truck settled into a slow rolling bounce as Jack drove across the bridge that spanned a wide section of Amistad Lake. He gazed across the water, its surface sparkling in the waning sun. Patches of dry grass and scrub brush lined the shoreline.

Jack slowed when he hit the outskirts of town. Although it had been years since he had been in Del Rio, nothing seemed to have changed. And for some reason, he found it comforting. The fond memories came flooding back.

Downtown, he turned onto Main Street, and after several blocks, the building Kate had mentioned came into view. He found an empty parking spot along the curb, shut off the ignition and grabbed his duffle bag from the back.

On the sidewalk, he glanced around, checking his surroundings. To anyone watching, he would look like a stranger getting his bearings, but it was something more. He scanned storefronts of bustling businesses, locked doors of abandoned shops, and gaps between the buildings, side routes to the alleys behind them. He took note of the location of parked cars and trucks and scanned the faces of pedestrians. Within a few seconds, he'd made a mental note of everything. A habit engrained in him during his days with the Bureau. And one that would now stay with him forever.

Further up the sidewalk, someone opened a door, and laughter and country music drifted out onto the street. Jack read the sign overhead. Mesquite Creek Outfitters, a craft beer and wine bar. Just the place he was he was looking for.

He took the door held open by a stranger and stepped inside. It was an old building with double-height ceilings and a planked floor. There were rows of tables, this way and that. A bar ran along the wall to one side. And an assortment of racks and display cases offering an eclectic mix of merchandise ran along the other. People were everywhere, talking and laughing to be heard over a Toby Keith song being piped through an invisible sound system.

A woman holding a tray of drinks scurried past him. "Order at the bar," she said. "Then help yourself to a seat wherever you can find one."

Jack approached a woman standing behind a register at the back. She had short dark hair with tips dyed a bright shade of blue. A small gold hoop hung from one side of her nose.

"What can I get ya?" she asked.

"I was told I could find Wanda Donaldson here."

The woman raised her brows, smiling. "Someone not like you?"

Jack was confused.

She laughed and waved a hand. "Just joshing. Hold on a minute." She disappeared behind a swinging door. A while later, she returned with a petite, elfin woman trailing behind her.

The woman was tan and shriveled and wore glasses that magnified her eyeballs to the size of chicken eggs. She wore tight jeans, a flannel top, and pointed cowboy boots. A lit cigarette dangled from her lower lip, the smoke curling lazily skyward before disappearing into her nostrils when she breathed.

"I'm Wanda," the woman said in a voice that sounded like it had been drug over asphalt. The cigarette danced on her lip as she spoke. Jack was sure it would drop, but it hadn't. "And who are you?"

Jack started to speak but was interrupted.

"Never mind. I know who you are. You're the fella Kate called me about." She turned toward the swinging door, not waiting for a reply. "Let me get the key." She reemerged seconds later, holding a large brass key aloft. "Got it. Follow me, sonny."

They walked out of Mesquite Creek and took an immediate left. A foot away was a nondescript-looking door. Wanda unlocked it and threw it open, revealing a set of stairs covered with crimson carpet. She switched on the lights, and they climbed to the second floor.

Upstairs, tall doors with frosted glass inserts lined both sides of a long hallway. The doors were sturdy and old, several with the names and office hours of doctors and attorneys now long gone still painted on them.

"Some might call us a B and B," Wanda said, her boots clomping on the wood floor with each step. "But we only offer the bed. You're on your own for breakfast. We don't provide the food."

Jack assured her it wouldn't be a problem. He followed her to a large wooden door with *Dr. Donaldson* painted in black letters on the opaque glass.

"Your last name is Donaldson," he said, then felt like an idiot informing the woman of her own name.

Wanda turned to him and grinned, the cigarette still hanging precariously on her lip. "He was my daddy." She unlocked the door.

"You own the building?"

"The whole thing." She had unlocked the door and handed him the key.

Jack detected a sense of pride in her voice. And with good reason. He thought the old building was magnificent.

"It's the finest room we have," Wanda said. "Kate said to give you the best. And she said she was picking up the tab."

Jack opened the door and stepped inside.

The ceiling soared overhead. The room was spacious, bright, and airy, even in the waning daylight. Furnished with a handful of tasteful antiques that made it look comfortable instead of stuffy. A large oval rag rug laid next to the bed on the wood floor. There was no television, not even a digital clock on the bedside table—a complete absence of technology. Jack felt as if he had stepped back in time. And he loved it.

He turned to thank Wanda, but she had disappeared. For a moment, he considered the idea that maybe she had never been there at all, that he'd been led into another realm by a specter from an era long ago. Now that he thought about it, the whole day seemed surreal.

But a faint hint of Wanda's smoke still lingered, bringing him around. Damn, he was tired.

He closed the door and tossed his duffle onto the bed, then walked to the window and pulled back the lace curtain. The sun was going down. And, except for the small pools of light from security lamps, the alley was quickly growing dark.

Jack stood at the window, listening to the soft drone of country music below, occasionally broken by muffled bursts of laughter.

His gaze slid mindlessly over the shadows, the darkened doorways, and blind corners in the alley below. There were plenty of places for a person to hide before ambushing an unsuspecting victim.

Jack's thoughts turned to Kate and Henry. Then, to the blood-soaked earth where Diego Torres had died.

Someone in Del Rio *was* hiding. Maybe not in the alley below, but somewhere close.

And they were a threat to the people Jack considered family.

# CHAPTER 11

*Tuesday, May 24*

JACK DIDN'T WASTE any time the next morning. He was back on the highway early, headed to the Rose Ranch. Not to Kate and Henry's this time, but to Roy's.

Jack had heard of the reclusive uncle for years but never met him. He knew that, although Jordan and Henry called him *uncle*, he was actually Thomas's first cousin. He also knew that Thomas and Roy had been particularly close.

Their ranches were adjacent to one another. And at one time had been part of a single ranch that, for years, was the largest in the county. But, like many original homesteads, it had been fractured through generations of inheritance.

As with any case, in the beginning, Jack had lots of questions. And since Henry had found Diego Torres on Roy's land, he thought it would be the best place to start.

Roy's house was what Jack considered a typical ranch style. Not nearly as large as Thomas and Kate's hacienda, but still a good size. It looked old—a single-story, built of rock, with a deep porch that ran the length of the front, shading its facade from the brutal Texas sun.

Jack pulled the truck to a wood gate in a short, chicken-wire fence that bordered the yard, then killed the engine and got out. The air was so dry, he could smell the dirt.

It was early morning, but the sun was already on fire in

the sky. The deafening buzz of a hundred cicadas warned of the rising temperature.

"You're Jordan's friend, aren't you?" a man asked, stepping off the porch into the dusty yard. "The one from A&M." He spoke in a thick Texas accent, and his voice was deep. His gait was stiff and favored his right leg.

"I am." Jack stuck out his hand. "Jack Martin."

"He told me you'd be coming. Roy Rose," he said, taking Jack's hand. "Nice to finally meet you."

Roy was tall and lean, with skin long ago weathered by the desert sun. But his handshake was firm. He stood pulling at a long mustache that drooped and fell close to his chin. His thick gray hair curled from under a hat stained with sweat. Every inch of Roy Rose was a throwback to the Wild West. Jack glanced down at his worn boots and was disappointed he wasn't wearing spurs.

Two goats came running from around the side of the house, and Roy kicked them aside. "Let's get outta this heat," he said, turning for the porch. "Want some coffee?"

Usually an avid coffee drinker, at that moment, in the searing heat, Jack couldn't think of anything worse.

"Thank you," he said, then added reluctantly, "I'd love some." He knew better than to refuse the hospitality of someone he was about to question.

Inside, the house was spacious and clean, with wood-planked floors that creaked underfoot. The walls were sheathed in beadboard and painted white. Everything, including the brass light fixtures and door hardware, looked antique and were probably original.

Jack glanced into the study as he followed Roy to the kitchen and noticed a sizable leather-topped desk near the far wall. Stacks of books set in neat rows covered the top, with an old Colt revolver set between them. Behind the desk, a tall, upholstered chair faced the door, indicating Roy Rose was another man who preferred not to sit with his back to the room.

As if reading his thoughts, Roy turned around briefly, then started for the kitchen again. And Jack stole another glance of the room.

The walls were floor-to-ceiling bookshelves, with not an inch of space to spare. Books, old and new, were crammed onto every one. There were small cabinets around the room that held even more, and others were stacked on the floor.

In the kitchen, Roy pulled a mug from a cabinet and poured coffee into it. "How do you take it?" he asked.

"Black."

Roy nodded his approval, then handed the mug to Jack and refilled his own.

They sat down at an oak table that Jack suspected was as old as the house.

Roy set his mug down and turned it in his hands. "Jordan said you'd be coming." He shook his head, looking into the dark coffee. "It's a crying shame what happened to that boy. He was a good kid."

"What can you tell me about him?"

"I hear the sheriff thinks his murder was drug-related." He stopped twisting the mug and looked at Jack. "It's an easy conclusion."

"You don't believe it?"

"I think Odell is being lazy. He's got too much on his plate." Roy lifted a hand to his mustache and twisted it. "I don't buy the theory."

"I heard he was an archeologist of some sort—digging on your property."

Roy sipped his coffee. "Diego wasn't technically an archeologist," he said, setting the mug down. "More of an *amateur* archeologist, I guess you'd call him. He wasn't schooled in it, is what I mean." He thought some more. "As far as I know, all he had was a high school education."

Jack wondered how someone with so little education could have been an archeologist, even an amateur one. "Did he have help?"

"He *was* the help," Roy replied. "Diego did grunt work for the boss until he moved on."

"Who was his boss?"

"David Hansen," Roy said. "He's an archeologist. Legit one, as far as I know. Anyway, Hansen dug for a while on my land and Diego worked for him for a time. Then Hansen left. My guess is that they didn't find enough to keep him interested in my place. But Diego wanted to stay."

"Do you know why?" Jack asked. "What was he looking for?"

Roy hesitated before he answered. "I guess what they all look for. Indian paintings—pictographs are what they call them. And old artifacts, tools, and old clothing. Stuff like that. Archeologists have crawled all over this country for decades."

"Arrowheads?" Jack was curious. He didn't know anything about archeology.

"Some arrowheads," Roy replied. "But they're mainly hunting for things a lot older than what you're thinking. They're studying the tribes that lived here thousands of years ago."

So that was what Diego Torres had been doing when he was murdered. Jack exhaled, thinking about the research he would have to do to talk legibly on the subject. He didn't know a lick about archeology but suspected he was about to learn.

"You said the archeologist moved on from your place. He didn't find anything?"

Roy took his time to answer again. "I don't think he found much. We've got a few faded pictographs. Hansen and his group came out and took photographs and measurements of them. But as far as I know, aside from the rock paintings, they didn't find anything significant to speak of. Just some old bones."

"Bones? I would think that would interest an archeologist."

"Not these," Roy said. "They were all excited at first. But then they had them carbon-dated, and it came back that they were from the 1800s—not nearly old enough to be of interest to them. Soon after that, Hansen moved on. I hear he's digging on the ranch that borders mine now."

"But Diego Torres stayed."

"He did."

"And you don't know why?"

"Sorry. No."

"How often was he out here?"

"Practically every day. I'd let him park his car in my barn to keep it out of the sun. Then he'd ride his bike as far as he could, hide it just off the road behind some trees in the draw, and hike the rest of the way on foot."

"He'd do that every day?" Jack remembered the arduous climb over the mountain.

Roy shook his head. "No. He'd be out there three or four days at a time, then come back in when he needed supplies. But he'd come right back the next day or the day after. Except for Sundays. He always spent Sundays in town with his family."

"Where is his car now?"

"Sheriff impounded it."

Jack made a note to ask the sheriff if anything of significance was found inside. "Did Diego ever bring anyone out here with him? Family, maybe? Or friends?"

Roy shook his head. "Never. After Hansen and his group left, Diego was out there alone."

Jack thought about it a moment. "You said his old boss is working nearby?"

"That's what I heard," Roy answered. "I believe he's over on Frank Moran's place now. Frank's ranch borders mine."

Jack wanted to talk to the archeologist next and hoped he would be able to shed some light on what Diego had been doing on Roy's ranch. If the trained archeologist had moved on, why had a kid with only a high school education stayed?

Jack stayed a while longer, and the two men talked about college football and the weather. On the way out, Jack noticed a shotgun and an old rifle propped against a hall tree, partially hidden by a coat. He hadn't seen them when he'd come in.

"A Winchester 70," Roy said when he noticed Jack looking.

A sniper rifle popular in Vietnam. Jack wanted to ask more but didn't. Something in the look on Roy's face told him not to. It would likely dredge up painful memories, so Jack reluctantly let the subject drop. This time.

Outside, the heat had grown more intense. Roy didn't seem to notice, but Jack broke a sweat as he stepped off the porch into the yard.

The goats showed up again, bleating with excitement. Jack suspected they were friendly or hungry, but he wasn't sure which.

Roy shooed them away again. "They keep snakes out of the yard," he explained. "It was nice to finally meet you, Jack," he said, extending his hand. "I hope you find out what happened to Diego. Like I said, he was a good kid."

Jack glanced in the rearview mirror as he drove away and saw Roy watching him go. The goats were still at his feet. A minute or so later, just before the road dipped into a draw, he rechecked the mirror and saw that Roy was still standing there.

Jack was happy to finally meet Jordan's notorious uncle, but something about the encounter had been unsettling.

On the way back to the highway, he ran through everything Roy had said. There hadn't been enough on the ranch to hold an archeologist's attention, yet Diego Torres had stayed. And for some reason, he was murdered. Was there a connection? Or was there something in Torres's nefarious past that had come back to haunt him?

The thought brought back something else Roy had mentioned. Old bones. A skeleton discovered in the very spot where Henry found Torres. A coincidence? Maybe. But Jack's gut was telling him there was a connection.

# CHAPTER 12

JACK PULLED UP to the hacienda but noticed a flurry of activity at the barn. A handful of men and sheep were milling about in an enclosed pen, a cloud of dust swirling around them.

Jack got out of the truck and started for them. Two jets from the nearby Air Force base buzzed overhead but were nearly inaudible over the bleating of sheep and calls and whistles from the men. The sounds of ranch work were loud.

Henry noticed Jack and hopped the fence. A layer of dust clung to the sweat on his face. "Come to help?" he asked, hollering over the commotion. He pulled off a worn leather glove with his teeth and shook Jack's hand.

"Would I need my sidearm?" Jack nodded at the pistol hung low on Henry's hip.

"If you were smart, you would." Henry grinned. "I've got extras if you need one."

"I met Roy."

"Well, it's about damn time." Henry slapped Jack on the shoulder. "Let's go up to the house. I could use a drink. And you can tell me what you think of our crazy uncle."

Henry hung his cowboy hat just inside the back door, then took off his holster and hung it next to the hat.

"*Tus botas tambien*," Adoncia demanded, scurrying past the men and scowling. Your boots, too. "The house is not the barn."

Henry blew out a breath. "Don't you have laundry or

something to do?" He stuck a heel into a boot jack and yanked the boot off, letting it fall to the floor, then did the same with the other. His socks, stained with rings of sweat and dirt, left sweaty footprints on the floor.

In the kitchen, Henry put ice in two glasses and filled them with water from the sink. They pulled out chairs from the table and sat.

"Did you catch Uncle Roy on a good day or bad?" Henry asked. He took a long drink of the water.

"Good day, I guess. He wasn't surprised to see me. Jordan told him I was coming."

"You ask him about Diego Torres?"

"I did," Jack replied. "He filled me in on what little he knew about what Diego was doing on the ranch. Then he mentioned something interesting. Did you know they found an old set of bones in the same spot you found Diego?"

Henry set his glass on the table. "Human bones?"

Jack nodded. "Diego was working for an archeologist when they found them. But Roy said they weren't interested in the bones since they only dated back to the 1800s. How long have the Roses owned the ranch?"

"Since the 1880s."

"Who owned it before that?"

"The Comanches."

Jack took a moment to think about it and wondered if the bones were Native American.

"Seems a strange place to bury someone," Henry said. "Must have been killed there like Diego. No one would have carried a body up there."

They sat in silence a while.

Jack took in a deep breath, steeling himself before he asked the next question. "Where was it that your father was killed?"

Henry's face went long, and he took a moment to answer. "Not far from the trail we took to the shelter where I found

Torres. There's a chasm about fifty yards west of where we headed up the slope."

Jack hadn't noticed it. "Is it hidden from view?"

Henry shook his head. "There's all sorts of hidden gaps and crevices out there, but this one is wide. You could have seen it from the trail we were on yesterday, if I'd have pointed it out to you."

Jack hated to press the issue, but he wanted to know more. "How did you find him?"

"His truck was parked a few yards west of where we parked yesterday."

"I'm sorry to ask," Jack said. "It's just that I—"

"No need to apologize. It's natural to want to know what happened." Henry twisted his glass in his hand, looking down into the water.

Jack felt a pang of guilt for having brought up Thomas. He wanted to know more but let the subject drop. "Tell me about Roy."

"Uncle Roy?" Henry perked up. "What do you want to know? He's Dad's first cousin, but they grew up like brothers. They were in the same grade in school, played sports together, worked on the ranch together."

"Did they remain close through the years?"

"To the very end. Dad had coffee with Uncle Roy every Saturday morning. Roy doesn't get out much, so Dad would fill him in on what was happening on the ranch. They'd talk sheep, the weather, local gossip—you name it. He's been sort of a recluse since Aunt Evelyn died. It messed him up pretty bad."

Henry shifted in his seat before he continued. "I was young when she passed, but I always heard he lost interest in the world after she died. At least the present world anyway."

"What do you mean?"

"Did you see his study? The books and all? He's practically a historian. In fact, he's written a few articles for magazines.

These days, I don't know if he does much else except read or write. Texas history stuff, mainly."

"There were sheep on his property yesterday. Were those his?"

"Those are *our* sheep," Henry replied. "Roy has leased his pastures to us for years. Dad offered to buy the land from him outright several times, but he always refused. Sentimental, I guess."

"Roy mentioned the archeologist had moved to a ranch owned by a man named Frank Moran. Do you know him?"

Henry leaned back in his chair. "Unfortunately."

"That bad?"

"Let's just put it this way. If you can avoid Moran, you'd be doing yourself a favor. Cranky old bastard."

"I need to talk to the archeologist who's working on his land."

Henry raised his eyebrows. "You need to get on his ranch?" Jack nodded, and Henry sighed. "Get back on the highway and head west. Take the first road after the one you took to get to Uncle Roy's. But stay to the left. After a quarter mile or so, there's a fork that leads to Moran's house. Don't take it. You don't want to run into him at home. Although he's rarely out there anymore. He's lived in town for years."

Jack finished the water and stood up. "Thanks for the drink," he said, setting the glass in the sink.

At the back door, Henry pulled on his boots, then grabbed his hat and the holster. "You talk to Odell yet?"

"Not yet." Jack wanted more information before he questioned the sheriff.

"Well, when you do, find out how close he is to catching the rustlers." Henry closed the door behind them and walked with Jack to his truck. "My two cents is Torres caught them red-handed. You find the rustlers; you'll find who killed him."

Several minutes later, Jack pulled onto Highway 90 and headed west. After the road to Roy's, he crossed a bridge that spanned the gulch that ran below the rock shelter where Henry found Diego.

He scanned the horizon and thought about the rustlers. Unlike Henry, Jack didn't believe whoever was stealing sheep had killed Diego. It was a massive leap from theft to murder.

Then, he thought of Thomas and reconsidered. Although the ranch was thousands of acres, Thomas had died in nearly the same spot.

Had Thomas encountered the rustlers, too? If he had, his death might not have been an accident.

# CHAPTER 13

AFTER THE BRIDGE over the gulch, a gravel road came into view on the left, and Jack took it. He eased the truck through a bump gate, then accelerated, sending clouds of dust swirling behind him. Unless it was raining, sneaking up on someone in this country would be impossible. You could see the dust coming for miles.

The gravel road stretched out in front of him. At the fork Henry mentioned, he stayed left. As he drove, he glanced in the direction of the gulch that was hidden from view by a mountain ridge similar to the one on Roy's.

Like the Rose Ranch, Frank Moran's land was covered in rock and mesquite and scrub brush, most of it not even waist high. There weren't many places for a man to hide.

The road dipped and twisted another mile or so, then Jack noticed an early model truck in the distance, an old camper set in its bed. He drew closer and realized it was parked at the end of a short junction in the road, a spur with a dead end near the mountain ridge.

Jack turned toward the truck and scanned the area but saw no one. Although he was counting on it belonging to the archeologist David Hansen, the truck looked abandoned.

He circled in front of it, then parked several feet away in case there was trouble. There was no evidence of a threat, but he'd spent enough time in law enforcement to be ready just in case.

He shut off the ignition and got out, then walked to the truck and looked through the driver's side window. There were papers and fast-food trash strewn everywhere—on the seat and on the floorboard. A spiral notebook was shoved between the dash and the windshield, with the word *Inventory* scrawled across the front cover in black marker.

Usually, Jack would have felt the truck's hood to check if the engine had recently been running. But the heat from a hot motor would be imperceptible in the scorching temperature. Instead, he peered through faded curtains into the camper set in the truck's bed and saw that it was filled with an assortment of tools and boxes. A large orange beverage cooler sat to one side. A layer of dirt covered everything.

There was a loud screech overhead. Jack shielded his eyes from the sun and saw a hawk circling, likely hunting for his next meal. Ensuring the hawk didn't think he was it, he decided to get moving.

He walked back to his truck and pulled the Glock from the glove box, then stuck it into the waistband of his pants and pulled his shirt down over it. He started toward the mountains, heading for the faint markings of a trail that climbed the gentle rise, zigzagging around boulders and clusters of mesquite before disappearing on the other side.

When Jack reached the trail's peak, he looked down and saw the dry gulch he had crossed while on the highway. One of the mountains on the far side would be the one he had climbed with Henry on Roy's land. He shaded his eyes from the sun and searched the caves and rock shelters on the Rose ranch but didn't recognize the one from the day before. He made a mental note to check the satellite images on his laptop's GPS sometime later. He was curious how close he was to where Diego Torres was murdered.

He looked down the trail and saw that it veered sharply to the right, bending around a cliff face of solid rock a hundred yards or so ahead. If there was anyone out here, that's where he'd find them.

Jack started down, relieved the descent wasn't as steep as the day before. He took the bend in the trail and saw two people standing over a hole in the rocky ground with various shovels and tools scattered around them. Nearby, a wheelbarrow was lying on its side.

Jack quickly assessed the two twenty-somethings. Both Caucasians. One female—thin, medium height, with dirty blond hair pulled into a ponytail. One male—dark and stout, with more flab than muscle. Like Diego Torres, they weren't much older than kids. Neither would be the archeologist, David Hansen.

They looked up as Jack approached and were startled to see him.

Jack introduced himself. "I'm looking for David Hansen."

The male blinked a few times, then swallowed and pointed to a spot further along the trail. "He—he's up there. In the rock shelter just around the corner. If you head that way," he said. "You'll see it."

Jack found Hansen below the entrance to the shelter, at the base of a 10-foot ladder tied to brush growing in what looked like solid rock. A makeshift pulley system of blue nylon ropes hung beside it. Jack glanced up at the deep overhang, curious about what was happening inside.

Hansen was bent over, brushing at something in the bottom of a shallow trench with gloved hands. He was small and wiry, wore cargo shorts, a faded blue t-shirt, and a baseball cap turned backward. Wire-rimmed glasses sat on the end of a long, pointed nose. He was a far cry from Harrison Ford's character in *Raiders of the Lost Ark*, and Jack was disappointed.

He glanced up as Jack approached. "You lost?" Without waiting for an answer, he started brushing the ground again.

"I'm looking for David Hansen."

"You found him," he replied, still brushing. "What can I do for you?"

Jack wondered what it was that held the man's attention. He peered into the trench and saw only a slab of rock. Nothing that looked the least bit interesting.

"My name's Jack Martin. I'm a friend of the Rose family. I'd like to ask you a few questions about Diego Torres."

Hansen finally stopped working and looked up. "I heard what happened." He shook his head and frowned. "I couldn't believe it. Diego was a good kid."

It was the second time Jack had heard it. Roy had said the same thing.

"I understand he worked for you a while."

"He did." Hansen pulled off his glasses and rubbed them with a dirty handkerchief. "For almost a year."

"But he stayed on the ranch you were working on before. Can you tell me why?"

Hansen hesitated before answering. "I can't say exactly. All I know is that he had befriended the old guy who owns the place."

"Roy Rose."

"That's him. Anyway, the excavation site was a bust, and we needed to move on. But, for whatever reason, Diego decided to stay. So, he quit."

"How did he come to work for you in the first place?"

"The kids met him soon after we got to town. He was curious about what we were doing. Came out to the excavation site a few times, ended up volunteering for a while. But when I saw how hard he worked and how much he could get done, I put him on the payroll."

"He liked the work?"

"Seemed to."

"But you don't know why he quit?"

Hansen shook his head. "No clue." He stuck his glasses

back on and reached for a small metal canteen and drank from it. "Water?" he asked, holding it out to Jack.

"No, thank you."

Hansen screwed the top back on. "I was disappointed to lose the help. Diego was a hard worker. Better than the two I've got down there."

Jack glanced down at the kids and noticed them watching. For some reason, they still seemed nervous.

Hansen set the canteen down and shook his head. "It's almost impossible to get good help out here in this Godforsaken country. Sometimes I wonder why I'm out here myself."

"Why do it?"

"It pays the bills. And I don't have to sit behind a desk all day. Although on days like today, a desk job sounds fine." He dragged the back of his hand across his forehead, mixing dirt with sweat, smearing a mud streak just above his eyes.

Jack felt the heat through the soles of his boots and had to agree with him. He wasn't a desk man either. He turned and looked across the gulch to Roy's. "Do you guys ever stay out here overnight?"

"Never. Why?"

"I was wondering if you had heard anything the night Diego was shot."

Hansen shook his head, brushing again. "We're always back in town before sundown. You don't want to be stuck out here after dark if you can help it."

Jack agreed with him again. But according to Roy, something on his property had Diego Torres interested enough to spend the night there regularly.

"What was Diego looking for?"

"I have no idea."

Jack sighed. The conversation wasn't going anywhere. "I understand you uncovered human bones."

Hansen blew out air. "Eleven months and that's about

all we found over there. We documented a few faded pictographs," he said. "But nothing as significant as the White Shaman or what they've found over in Panther Cave. If only I could get so lucky." He was shaking his head.

Jack didn't know what he was talking about but was more interested in the skeleton. "The bones weren't old enough?"

"Not hardly. They were mid-nineteenth century. Not nearly old enough. We found some military regalia with them—a belt buckle and some old brass buttons. Mexican. Not much interest in those either. A museum in Austin took the whole lot for a song." He shook his head, disgusted.

"So, the bones weren't Native American?"

Hansen shrugged. "Could have been. But more likely, it was some poor old soldier *scalped* by an Indian. That happened all the time around here back then."

Jack was growing frustrated. None of the information explained why Diego Torres had been working on Roy's land.

He glanced at Hansen's canteen. It was sitting propped against a worn canvas bag.

"What would Diego have had with him while he was working?" Jack asked.

Hansen frowned. "What do you mean?"

"Like supplies, personal effects."

Hansen nodded. "Probably the same stuff he had while he working for me, I guess. A couple spiral notebooks. Pens and pencils to make sketches and take notes. He always had the same water bottle—a green one, I think. He also had a phone he used to take photographs with." Hansen thought for a moment. "We all carry a few snacks with us. He probably would have had some. That's about it."

"A wallet?"

Hansen nodded. "He drove a car, so I assume he'd have a driver's license on him. Maybe some cash."

Yet it had taken the sheriff's office at least a day to identify the body. When Jordan first called Jack, they still believed the dead man was probably an illegal.

It was something else to ask the sheriff.

Jack glanced at Hansen's bag. "Did he have a bag like yours that he kept it all in?"

"He carried a backpack. An old black one. I never saw him without it." Hansen laid the brush he had been using next to the canteen and pulled a smaller brush from his bag. He began working but stopped and looked up. " Is that all, Mister...ah."

"Martin. Jack Martin."

Jack could take a hint. He was getting the brush off—literally. "One last question," he said.

Hansen let out an impatient exhale.

"Did Diego ever say anything, or did you ever see or hear anything that might explain why he was killed?"

Hansen didn't hesitate. He shook his head and began working again. "Nothing."

"Nothing about any past grievances? Maybe something he'd been involved in?"

"Again," Hansen said. "Nothing. I'm sorry I can't be of more help."

On the walk back to the truck, Jack went over everything they'd discussed. David Hansen had valued Diego Torres as an employee. They had spent months together in the middle of nowhere, taking photographs of old Indian paintings and brushing at rocks. Yet Hansen had no idea why Diego quit to continue working on Roy's land. Or what could have gotten Diego murdered.

Jack wasn't buying it.

# CHAPTER 14

*Wednesday, May 25*

THE NEXT MORNING, Jack rose later than usual. He had spent the night before at the small table in his room over the bar researching archeology along the Pecos River, a subject he expected to put him to sleep but had done the opposite. He had stayed awake for hours.

He read countless articles on the area's history and the indigenous tribes that had inhabited the Lower Pecos Valley two thousand years ago. There were reports detailing the findings of early explorers who had first discovered the pictographs the tribes had left behind and articles about ongoing excavations. Jack found it interesting that there was no mention of David Hansen in any of them.

Jack was still groggy but pulled on a pair of jeans and made a trip to the shared kitchen for coffee. Except for the gurgling sound of the Keurig machine, the B&B was quiet. Back in the hallway, he stood a moment, listening to the silence. He suspected he'd been the only renter the previous night and was grateful to be alone.

Back in his room, he sat the coffee next to his laptop and started the computer. It took only a few minutes to find the address where Diego Torres had lived. He pulled up the county property records next, then took a small notepad from his duffle bag and jotted down the names he found: Miguel and Sabina Torres. They must be Diego's parents.

Twenty minutes later, he had showered and dressed, and was parked in front of the Torres's modest wood-framed home on the south side of Del Rio. It had been a quick drive from downtown, but when he crossed a bridge spanning a shallow river, he felt like he'd entered another country.

Most of the houses were small and set close together, many with front yards fenced with chain link. Most were white or gray, but others were painted a shade of pastel—blue or yellow, even pink.

He passed a community square paved with bricks and scattered with park benches. In the center was an elevated pavilion. He imagined the square on weekends brimming with people, friends and families spilling into the streets listening to the sound of mariachi music as a band played in the gazebo.

Across the street, bright-colored murals adorned many of the stucco buildings. Giant images of flamenco dancers and local sports heroes, butterflies and fish, were painted on the walls. It wasn't the same as the graffiti he'd seen in Houston or Baton Rouge. This was art painted with a spirit indicative of a vibrant community.

The Torres's home was only a few blocks from the square. Jack parked at the curb. He double-checked the address on his notepad then got out.

It was a small, wood-framed house painted white. A narrow sidewalk led to a tiny front porch. White pickets bordered the yard that, except for a few sprigs of errant grass, was brown and baked dry.

As Jack opened the gate, the front door to the house opened. A stylish woman in her early 30s was saying something in Spanish to someone inside. Jack stood just inside the gate and watched as she shut the door and turned in his direction, digging through her purse.

She looked up and was startled to see him. "Who are you?" she asked, pulling up short.

Jack hesitated, captivated by her eyes. They were darker than black coffee and framed by thick lashes the same ebony color as her hair. She wasn't just beautiful. She was stunning.

And she looked angry.

"I'm Jack Martin," he said, holding up a hand, trying to assuage her anger. "I'm looking for Miguel or Sabina Torres."

She eyed him suspiciously. But there was something else. Jack thought he detected a hint of fear.

He continued. "I'm a friend of the Rose family who owns the ranch where their son died."

The woman brushed past him on the sidewalk and grabbed the gate, then turned back and held it open.

"I'm Elena," she finally said. "Diego's sister."

"I'd like to ask you a few questions about your brother."

She frowned. "Why? Who are you?"

"I'm Jack Mar—"

"You told me already. I mean, who *are* you, and why are you here?" she demanded. "At my house?"

Jack took a moment. She wasn't going to be easy. "I've been asked to look into what happened."

"Are you the police?"

"No."

She still held the gate and gestured for him to leave the yard. Jack obliged, and she closed the gate behind him. He noticed her hands shaking slightly.

On the sidewalk, he tried again. "Elena, can I ask you a few questions about your brother?"

She shook her head and unlocked a small white car parked behind Jack's truck. "Not now. I'm late for work."

"Is Miguel or Sabina home?"

The question stopped her short, and her eyes narrowed. "My parents are in mourning. Do not disturb them, or I will call the police."

Without saying anything more, she got into the car and

pulled away from the curb, leaving Jack on the sidewalk watching her go.

The encounter with Diego Torres's sister had been bewildering. She was beautiful but also angry and afraid.

Afraid of what?

# CHAPTER 15

THE BUILDING THAT housed the Val Verde County Sheriff's Office looked anything but hospitable. Set on a greasewood flat on the east side of town, it was surrounded by a sea of dirt and cactus. Its low-slung facade was flat and utilitarian, clad in a nondescript concrete block that was standard issue for prisons. A lone palm tree grew to the left of the canopied entrance as if daring someone to question its existence so far from a beach.

Jack hoped Sheriff Odell Gardner would be more welcoming. He wanted insights into their investigation—answers only law enforcement could give him.

He pulled open the glass door and entered a lobby chilled by air conditioning. A woman around fifty sat behind a counter and looked up when he walked in. She set down papers she was holding and studied him over the top of her reading glasses.

"Can I help you?" Her tone wasn't unpleasant but impatient.

Jack knew that, with the current border situation, law enforcement at every level would be stretched as thin as a spider silk. The last thing he wanted to do was waste their time. But he needed answers.

"I'd like to speak to Sheriff Gardner."

The woman scoffed. "You and a hundred other people." She returned to shuffling the papers on her desk, looking for something. "Is this an emergency? Cause if it isn't, you'll need to call and make an appointment."

"It's about the murder of Diego Torres."

Jack's answer had the effect he was hoping for. The woman stopped what she was doing and looked at him again.

She held up a finger. "Hold on a minute." She punched a few numbers into the phone on her desk. "What did you say your name was?"

"I didn't say, but it's Jack Martin." He was growing impatient, as well. "I'm a friend of the Rose family. They own the ranch where Diego Torres was found murdered."

The woman swiveled in her chair until her back was to him, then whispered something into the phone. A second later, she stole a glance at him from over her shoulder.

Her voice had risen a bit, and Jack heard her say. "I think it's him." When she turned back around, she gave Jack nod. "Have a seat. The sheriff will be right with you."

Jack stepped away from the counter but remained standing. A minute or two later, a door that led to a long hallway opened, and a bear of a man stood at the threshold. He wore a tan suit and dark tie and had on the largest Stetson Jack had ever seen.

"Jack Martin?" His voice was deep and gruff.

"That's me." Jack stepped forward and reached out his hand. The man shook it.

"Sheriff Odell Gardner," he said, then turned and started down the long hallway. "Come on back. You a friend of Jordan's, is that right?"

Jack followed him, their cowboy boots clomping in step on the tile floor. "I am. We played football together at A&M."

Gardner stopped at an office near the end of the hall. "Well, I played with him in high school." He ushered Jack into the office and gestured to an empty chair. "Those were the days," he said, taking a seat behind the desk.

"Let me guess," Jack said, wanting to continue the casual conversation. "Offensive line."

The sheriff beamed again, leaning back in his chair and exposing an ample second chin. "Left tackle," he replied, sticking his thumbs into his waistband. "Blocked Jordan's blind side. He never had to leave the pocket unless he wanted to. I would have played longer if I hadn't busted up my leg the spring of our senior year. Car crash." There was a wistful look in his eyes. "I had a full-ride to Angelo State. Went to Sam Houston over in Huntsville instead and got a degree in criminal justice."

Jack noticed a large blue pennant hanging on the wall behind the desk. *Del Rio Rams* was emblazoned in white. Beside it hung a framed team photo, rows of players in pads and royal blue uniforms. A football in a plexiglass box sat on the credenza below.

Jack knew the type. He could imagine the sheriff still wearing his letterman's jacket, maybe trying it on now and then to relive his glory days. He glanced around the office, half expecting to see it hanging somewhere with the other mementos, but it wasn't. Some dreams die hard. Jack knew from experience.

Gardner came forward in his chair and rested his forearms on the desk. "You're here about Diego Torres," he said, the wistful look gone and his tone signaling the small talk was over. "Why?"

Jack told him about the call from Jordan. And that, with everything that had happened on the ranch, Jordan was concerned about Kate and Henry. Jack was careful to leave out that Jordan was also worried law enforcement was overworked and would dismiss the murder too quickly. Jack wasn't about to insult the sheriff. He needed his help.

When Jack finished talking, he held his breath, wondering how Gardner would respond.

The sheriff studied him with a perfect poker face, about

to answer Jack's questions or about to kick him out of his office. Jack couldn't tell which.

Gardner took a deep breath, expanding his already sizable chest and belly, then let the air out slowly.

"Alright," he said, drumming his meaty fingers on the desk. "I'll help you. But I think you're wasting your time. The Torres murder was drug-related. The killer—or killers— are probably back in Mexico. But since you're a friend of Jordan's, and used to be law enforcement yourself, I'll answer your questions."

Jack nodded his appreciation. "What can you tell me about the victim?"

"Torres?" Gardner leaned back in his chair again. "He was into drugs for years. The guys at City have a rap sheet on him a mile long."

"The city police?"

"Yes."

"But he was working outside the city limits when he died. With an archeologist."

"Only the last year or so. Before that, he worked for Rooster Borden at a restaurant in town."

Jack felt the urge to pull out his notepad and jot the name down, but he wanted to keep the conversation casual.

"Who's Rooster Borden?" he asked, filing the name away in his head.

"Owns the Broken Arrow, a restaurant and bar on the outskirts of town. It's on the way to the lake. You passed it coming in."

"I've seen it."

"That's Rooster's supposedly *legitimate* business." Gardner frowned, smashing his bushy brows together. "We've been trying to catch him at his *il-*legitimate business for a long time. Too long."

"Drugs?"

Gardner nodded. "We haven't been able to pin anything

on him—yet." He raised a finger from the desk when he said it. "But we've got the guy's number on speed dial."

"And Diego Torres worked for him?"

"For a couple of years."

"But then he quit," Jack replied, thinking aloud. "And went to work for the archeologist."

Gardner shrugged. "It's hard to say why. Maybe he got tired of dodging the law. Or got tired of the association. Who knows? But it's likely what got him killed. Someone thought the kid knew too much."

It was a possibility, but Jack wasn't convinced. "But he quit working for Borden months ago. Why wait a year to kill him?"

"Maybe he hadn't *completely* quit. Who knows? But Rooster wouldn't have killed him himself. He wouldn't want to get his hands dirty. He'd have had one of his minions do it for him."

"You said the killer is likely back in Mexico."

Gardner took a moment to answer, probably debating how much to say. "I've got friends in Border Patrol," he said, dropping his voice. "Rooster's got strong ties to the cartels."

"Is he under federal investigation?"

Gardner stared at Jack without answering the question. "I've said too much already. You didn't hear any of that from me."

Jack knew better than to press too hard for insider information, so he changed the subject. "What personal effects were found with Torres's body?"

"Nothing. That's why it took us a day to I.D. him."

"No money? Cell phone?"

Gardner shook his head.

"What about a backpack?" Jack remembered David Hansen mentioning Diego's black one.

"Nope. Nothing."

Someone didn't want Diego identified. And it wasn't customary for killers in a drug hit to care about keeping the identity of their victims a secret. Especially the Mexican cartels, who liked to brag about their killings. The information pointed away from it being an organized hit. But for now, Jack would keep his theories to himself.

"Was about evidence found in his car?" Jack asked. "I heard he kept it in Roy Rose's barn."

"We went through it with a fine-tooth comb. Found nothing. It's in our impound lot but will be released to the deceased's family any day now."

Another question nagged at Jack. "What about Thomas Rose's accident?"

Gardner seemed surprised by the question. "What about it?"

"Did you guys look into it?"

The sheriff pursed his lips and shook his head. "No reason to. Nothing to suggest that it was anything other than a tragic accident."

Jack wasn't so sure. Something told him there was more to the story.

# CHAPTER 16

ROY SAW THE dust long before he could tell who was coming. He stood at the front window, looking past the porch and watching the swirling mass of dirt as a vehicle drew closer. Whoever was coming was just over the horizon and headed in his direction.

He left the window and went to the hall tree in the foyer. It was an enormous Victorian thing passed down in the family for generations. Made of oak, it had a mirrored back panel and several hooks. It was where Roy kept his assortment of cowboy hats—straw and felt for the different seasons; his work hat, torn and greased with sweat; and the Stetson he wore solely for company.

But Roy wasn't interested in choosing a hat. He took the double-barrel shotgun he kept propped against the cabinet and broke open the action. He checked the chambers and saw that both were loaded, then jerked the gun closed and carried it with him back to the window.

The truck had crested the rise and was headed toward the house. Roy squinted, but the truck was a shadow obscured by the morning sun. It was several seconds before he realized it was Carter and relaxed.

Carter McConnell was Roy's nephew by marriage. No matter how often it was, each time he saw Carter, Roy was reminded of his late wife, Evelyn. Evelyn's younger sister, Alice, was Carter's mother. She died of esophagus cancer his junior year in high school. That's when Roy and Evelyn had taken him in. Now, both women were dead, and Roy was the only family Carter had. Although Roy appreciated the boy's company, sometimes it grated on him.

Roy carried the gun back to the foyer and laid the stock gently on the floor, then propped the barrel against the hall tree. He silently cursed himself for getting so anxious in his old age, but Diego's murder had him rattled.

It was hard enough getting over Thomas's death—except for Evelyn, the only real confidant Roy had ever had.

And now the kid was dead.

He thought about Diego as he watched Carter's truck approach the house, still kicking up dust. Diego had lived a dangerous past, and Roy knew firsthand the devastating consequences of previous mistakes.

Carter parked the truck just beyond the yard, and Roy went out to greet him.

"They didn't have your medicine ready, Uncle Roy, but I brought you some groceries," Carter said, opening the passenger side door of his truck and reaching inside.

"Don't worry about the medicine. That quack doctor is trying to kill me with all the pills." Roy took bags from his nephew's outstretched hands. "Thank you for the groceries. But shouldn't you be working? It's mid-morning already?"

"I had an early appointment," Carter said, pulling the last of the groceries from the truck and shutting the door. "I don't have another one until after lunch. So here I am."

Roy felt a pang of guilt that his nephew regularly kept him stocked with groceries. Roy had told him many times that it wasn't necessary, that he was capable of driving into Comstock and shopping at the convenience store himself. But Carter's attention had intensified following Evelyn's death. And Roy suspected he used the trips to the ranch as an excuse to get out of town.

The two men walked through the house and into the kitchen.

Roy watched him take the groceries from the bag and set them on the counter. Carter had his mother's fair skin and small hands. Back in the day, Alice McConnell had been quite the town beauty but also a soiled dove. No one knew with any certainty who Carter's father was. *And just as well*, Roy thought, remembering Alice's taste in men.

Thinking of Alice reminded him of Evelyn, who couldn't have been more different than her wayward sister. Remembering his late wife caused a lump to form in his throat.

"I had an interesting visitor yesterday morning," he said, needing a distraction.

"Oh yeah, who?" Carter asked, sticking a gallon of milk into the refrigerator.

"Jordan's friend Jack Martin."

Carter pulled a carton of eggs from the bag but stopped short of the refrigerator. "Jack Martin," Carter repeated. "Now there's a blast from the past."

"I'd never met him. Seems like a nice enough fellow. Thomas always liked him."

"What's he doing in Del Rio? I thought Jordan was in D.C."

"He is. That's why he had him come. To check on things." Roy hesitated. The recent incidents still felt raw. "After…" His voice trailed off.

"After Diego Torres's murder?"

Roy nodded.

"What can Jack Martin do about it? Does Jordan want him to find the drug dealers or rustlers who did it?"

Roy thought of how Diego had been shot. He had seen photos of the carnage. "No thieves stealing sheep killed that boy," he said, twisting one side of his mustache.

"Then it was the drugs that did him in. Probably the cartels, like Odell says."

Roy let his nephew talk.

Finished with the groceries, Carter sat down at the table across from him. "Uncle Roy, I know you don't like to talk about it, but—"

"I'm not moving to town, and that's that."

"But living out here all alone. And with everything that's happened. The rustlers. You said it yourself—"

Roy raised his hands from the table. "You can stop right there, Carter. I appreciate the concern, but you know I'm not leaving. I don't get around like I used to, but I can still get around good enough."

Carter sat studying his uncle. Then, to Roy's relief, he let the subject drop. But it would be only a matter of time before he brought it up again.

They talked a while longer.

Then Carter stood to go. "What about coming into town for church on Sunday? You haven't gone since Aunt Evelyn—"

"I'll think about it," Roy lied. "I'll let you know."

Carter watched him, then nodded once. "I'll be back in a few days," he said. "But let me know if you need something before then."

"I'll be fine," Roy assured him. "Thank you, though."

Roy stood on the porch and watched Carter's truck disappear over the rise, a swirling mass of dust trailing behind it. He scanned the horizon, listening to the sounds of the land—the breeze through the mesquite and the buzz of cicadas. He thought he could hear the distant bleating of sheep, then chalked it up to the wind.

Life was lonely on the ranch, especially now that Thomas was gone. But it was the only life Roy knew. And it was one he loved. As much as it would please his nephew if he would move to town, Roy wasn't going anywhere.

He thought of Evelyn buried beside her sister, Alice, in the cemetery in Del Rio and knew that, like them, he wouldn't live forever. Deep down, he knew Carter was probably right. He wasn't getting any younger, and moving closer to civilization would have its conveniences. For one thing, he could buy his own damn groceries.

He thought about it a moment longer, then turned on his heels and went into the house.

To hell with town. It was too crowded, and he didn't like the traffic. The only way he would leave the ranch was in a pine box.

# CHAPTER 17

BY THE TIME Jack got to the ranch, Henry was gone. Except for a handful of corralled sheep, the barn and pens were a ghost town.

He took the sidewalk to the house.

Kate opened the door as he stepped onto the porch. "Howdy, Jack."

"Good morning. I guess I missed Henry."

"You have to get here a lot earlier than this to catch him. They were saddled up and out of here before daylight. You're welcome to wait. He'll be back for lunch in a couple of hours."

"Thank you," Jack said. "But I'd like to talk to you if you have time."

"I'd love the company," Kate replied, pulling the door open wider. "Come on in."

They settled into the large family room. It had always been Jack's favorite room in the house. Furnished in an easy Spanish style, with heavy, dark furniture upholstered in thick fabrics that reminded him of expensive saddle blankets. The floor was a sea of handmade Mexican Saltillo tiles. A beamed ceiling soared twenty feet overhead. The sun filtered into the room through a row of square windows set high in the thick plaster walls.

Outside, the heat was stifling. But inside, the hacienda was cool.

Kate sat in one of the room's many chairs, and Jack sat facing her.

"Have you been to see Gretchen yet?" she asked, referring to Jordan's wife. "I know she'd love to see you. The boys are growing up so fast."

Jack's heart momentarily clenched at the mention of Gretchen's name. "I haven't been by yet, but I was planning to." It wasn't the complete truth. He had been debating whether or not to see her and hadn't yet made up his mind. Theirs was a complicated history.

"I met Roy yesterday morning," he said, changing the subject.

"I'm surprised it took this long," Kate said, raising her brows. "What did you think?"

"He's interesting."

"You could say that," she said and chuckled.

"How long has he lived alone?"

Kate thought for a moment, doing the math. "Going on thirty-two years. Ever since Evelyn died."

"Henry said he took her death hard."

Kate nodded slowly. "I can count on two hands the number of times I've seen him outside of his own yard since she died. On one, how many times I've seen him off the ranch unless he was in Comstock for supplies. I might be exaggerating a bit, but not much. He closed himself off from the world after she died."

"How does he do it? What about doctor's appointments? Or—"

She chuckled again. "Doesn't believe in them."

"Doctors?"

"Them, and several other professions."

"But what about food? He's got to eat."

"He still makes the occasional trip to Comstock. Almost never to Del Rio. Too far, I guess. Too many people. Or too many memories. Thomas had mentioned Carter was going out to see him more, which is probably good for the both of them."

Jack had forgotten about Jordan and Henry's cousin. He'd met Carter McConnell years earlier but didn't know him well since he was a decade younger.

Kate was still talking. "It's a shame Carter lost interest in the ranch. He lived with Roy and Evelyn a while after his mother passed and seemed to love it. But then he went off to college, then law school, and has lived in town ever since. It would be nice if he'd move back out there. Roy could use the company." She twisted the diamond ring on her left hand. "Especially now that Thomas is gone."

A comfortable silence fell between them. Jack suspected Kate was lost in memories.

"I hate to bring it up," he said, breaking the silence. "Henry told me some of what happened, but can you tell me more about Thomas's accident?"

Kate took a moment to answer, visibly pained by the question. "It just didn't make sense. Thomas was born on this ranch. He knew it like the back of his hand. But it was so hot that morning. I keep telling myself that maybe it caught him off guard. Maybe he got dehydrated or disoriented. Got too close to the edge and stumbled. It's the only thing I can think of."

Jack caught a glimmer of doubt in her eyes and realized she was struggling for an answer. He thought of the remote location where Thomas fell. "Do you know why he was out there?"

Kate shook her head. "That's just it," she said. "It was a Saturday morning. The men weren't working that day, and there was no reason for him to be out where he was. He was going to have coffee with Roy like he did every Saturday morning. But Roy said he never made it."

Jack wondered what could have happened after Thomas left the hacienda that morning. Could he have seen something?

Jack thought of the sheep that had crossed the road while he and Henry sat on the tailgate two days before. Had Thomas seen something suspicious that lured him to that remote part of the ranch? It wouldn't have been on his route to Roy's.

Could he have seen the rustlers? Kate had just said that the men weren't working that morning. It wasn't a compelling theory, but it was the only one Jack had.

They talked a while longer. Then Jack got up to go. Kate invited him back for lunch, and he accepted. But in the meantime, there was someone he wanted to talk to.

Earlier, when Jack left the sheriff's office, he had called Rooster Borden, Diego Torres's former employer. Jack wanted to know what Diego had done for him. According to Gardner, Borden was a known drug dealer. It would be a touchy conversation, but Jack needed to know if Diego was still involved in the drug trade when he died.

But Borden had been cagey. Although Jack offered to drive out to his ranch, Borden had refused, suggesting a meeting at his restaurant instead.

On the highway, headed back toward town, Jack's thoughts returned to his conversation with Roy, and he thought of Thomas.

Roy Rose was an eccentric loner who, according to both Henry and Kate, had withdrawn from the world. Jack wondered how much a man with such little regard for society valued his own family.

# CHAPTER 18

As Jack approached the outskirts of town, the Broken Arrow Restaurant and Bar came into view. He waited for a semi coming in the opposite direction to pass, then turned left into the parking lot.

He checked the time on his dash. It was ten-thirty. The restaurant wouldn't open for an hour, but two cars were already there—an early model Honda desperate for a paint job and a beat-up Chevy truck. A quick scan of the building revealed a second truck parked around the side. A black Ford Raptor. Although covered in dust, it looked new. Probably Rooster Borden's.

If it wasn't for the sign set just off the highway identifying the restaurant, the building could have been mistaken for a large house. It was long and low and sheathed in brown brick. There were several dormers on the shingled roof, barely visible through the oak and ash trees that shaded the building's front facade. In its desert surroundings, the restaurant was a mini oasis.

Jack parked next to the Honda and shut off the engine, then scanned the car's interior. The inside was in no better shape than the exterior. The felt seats had been worn from decades of use, exposing a foam core that had aged a dingy yellow. Trash and cigarette butts littered the floorboard and back seat. Amidst the filth was an aftermarket stereo system worth as much as the car.

He got out of the truck and walked past the Chevy. Except for a bolt cutter and a crowbar lying on the front seat and a layer of dust covering the door panels and dash, the truck was empty.

Although the restaurant was closed, the front door was unlocked. Jack pulled it open and stepped inside, letting his eyes adjust to the sudden drop in light.

The Broken Arrow looked like a dining hall in an Old West hotel or saloon. It was a large room with a low, wood-planked ceiling supported by rough-hewn columns resting on a brick floor. Several ceiling fans turned lazily overhead. The chairs and tables were dark and almost camouflaged by their wood surroundings.

A mirrored bar ran along the back wall, with a dozen empty stools on three sides. Except for Johnny Cash singing through a hidden stereo system, the restaurant was quiet.

Three men sat at a corner table watching him. Two Hispanics and one Caucasian. They were young, mid to late twenties. The same age as Diego Torres. They had phones and half-empty glasses of water on the table in front of them.

"Howdy," Jack said. He got a single nod from one of the men in return. "I'm looking for Rooster Borden."

"You found him." The voice came from the back of the restaurant. Jack turned and saw a man drop a box onto the bar. The sleeves of his starched western shirt were rolled up, exposing a massive gold Rolex on his left wrist. "You must be Jack Martin," the man said, pulling a bottle of Wild Turkey from the box.

"I am." Jack stepped toward him, but Borden continued to unload bottles of liquor from the box, giving no indication he intended to shake Jack's hand.

Rooster Borden was mid-40s, with close-cropped gray hair and a gray goatee. Jack couldn't tell the color of his eyes because the man wouldn't look at him. He finished unloading the box and then tossed it aside.

"I want to ask you a few questions about Diego Torres."

"What about him?" Borden asked, rearranging the bottles on the shelves behind the bar. His shirt was stretched tight across the muscles of his back.

"I understand he worked for you."

"He did."

"When did he quit?"

"Almost a year ago."

"When was the last time you saw him?"

"It's been months," Borden said, pulling a nearly empty bottle of tequila from the top shelf.

Jack turned to the three men at the corner table and found them still watching him.

"What about those fellas?" he asked, still talking to Borden's back. "When was the last time one of them saw him?"

"You'll have to ask them."

"They work for you?"

"Sometimes."

"What do they do?"

"Whatever I need them to."

The conversation was going from bad to worse.

Jack turned to the trio again. One was punching something into his phone, but the other two were still watching. "Doesn't look like they do much of anything."

"Sometimes they don't."

"Is that what Diego did for you? Sat around drinking and playing on his phone? Looks like a pretty easy job to me. Where can I sign up?"

Borden finally turned around. "Look, I open in less than an hour. I don't have time for—"

"A few questions about a former employee who was murdered?" Jack laid both hands on the bar. "Most terms of employment—*legitimate* terms of employment—aren't secret."

The muscles in Borden's neck tensed. "Listen, I know that you're some hotshot detective from Colorado. But what I don't know is why you're harassing me."

Borden must have Googled him as soon as they got off the phone. It's what Jack would have done.

"I've been asked to find out what happened to Diego."

"Why? You're not the law."

"The law's busy." Jack let that sink in. "You tell me the truth about what Diego Torres did for you, if he was involved in anything that could have gotten him killed, and I'll get out of your hair."

Borden came out from behind the bar and started toward the front door. He was shorter than Jack but solid muscle, with jeans stretched tight around muscular thighs. His boots had recently been shined. Black alligator. Flashy.

Jack followed him, knowing he was running out of time. He glanced at Borden's left hand. No wedding ring. A man without family often had nothing to lose.

"What about the cartels?" Jack asked.

Borden started to open the door but stopped. His eyes had turned to gray steel. "What about them?"

"Diego ever have any business with them?"

"Why ask me?"

"I was just thinking," Jack said. "A man with your reputation might know."

Borden balled his hands into fists, causing his knuckles to go white. "I run a legitimate business here," he said slow and deliberate. "Torres was a greasy kid with a greasy record. I can't say that I was sorry to see him go. Or cared much when I found out he was dead."

"I guess he wasn't an upstanding citizen like one of those guys over there?" Jack asked, jerking a chin toward the three goons. "I want to know if something you had Diego involved in got him murdered."

"You get the hell out of here," Borden said, yanking open

the front door. "What Torres did or didn't do for me is none of your damn business."

Jack took the door from him. "You just made it my business," he said, then stepped outside and let the door fall shut behind him.

# CHAPTER 19

AFTER HIS CONVERSATION with Rooster Borden, Jack was glad to be back with friendly company. He pulled up to the hacienda just as Henry walked up from the barn.

"You here for lunch?" Henry asked, slapping dust off his jeans.

"I am."

"Who invited you?"

"Your mother."

"Then you can stay." Henry was grinning. He pulled off his hat, revealing a ring of white skin around the top of his forehead, shiny with sweat. "What day is it?"

"Wednesday. Why?"

"Wednesday." Henry's smile grew larger. "Then you're in for a treat." He slapped Jack on the arm, and the two headed for the house.

"Ah, hell," Henry said. "Here comes Lynch."

Jack turned to see a white truck headed in their direction. It was the deputy he had met two days earlier. "Maybe he's got news about Diego Torres."

"Nah. He's just fishing for a free lunch." Henry started toward the truck. "Stay here. I'll get rid of him."

The deputy rolled to a stop, then waited for the dust to settle and wound down his window. He took a toothpick from his mouth and flicked it to the ground near Henry's feet.

Jack watched as two men talked. The deputy glanced at

Jack and nodded once without smiling, and the two talked some more.

"What was that all about?" Jack asked after Lynch left.

"Claims he's doing rounds, checking if anybody lost sheep last night." Henry shook his head. "Then he asked about lunch."

There was history there, and Jack wanted to know what it was. "You don't like him?"

Henry started for the house again. "Nah, I don't like him," he said over his shoulder in a tone that indicated the subject was dropped.

As soon as they stepped inside, Jack smelled it. An aroma so rich and spicy it made his stomach growl. Immediately, he knew what it was. A Mexican stew with chunks of tender beef in a thick tomato and pepper gravy.

"Carne guisada," he said aloud. Until that moment, he hadn't realized he was hungry.

"Mom cooked it. Lucky for you, it's Ado's day off, or it'd taste like boiled mule." He yanked off his boots with the bootjack.

Jack's boots weren't dirty, but he did the same.

They found Kate in the kitchen pulling a stack of tortillas from the oven. "Just in time, boys. Twelve o'clock, straight up. I was about to start without you."

Jack had forgotten the rigidity of life on the ranch, where the workday was ruled by the sun. Where things were expected to be done at certain times, and there was little tolerance for being late. Sitting down for lunch precisely at noon was one of them. Jack didn't doubt Kate would have started without them.

They served themselves from the stove. Beef stew, beans, and Spanish rice. And a stack of homemade flour tortillas. There wasn't a green vegetable in sight, and Jack was in heaven.

When they were seated at the table, Kate was the first to speak. "How was your visit with Rooster?"

"Rooster Borden?" Henry spat. He had a fork of beans headed toward his mouth but stopped. "What in the world would you want to talk to him about?"

"Diego Torres used to work for him, and I was curious if he still did. The sheriff insinuated Borden was into something illegal."

Henry scoffed. "Rooster's been tangling with the law his whole life."

"You know him well?" Jack hoped Henry could give him some backstory.

"Do I ever."

"Take it easy," Kate said, admonishing her son. "You, of all people, should know that everyone deserves a second chance."

"Yeah, but not a third." Henry shoveled beans into his mouth. "Or a fourth or a fifth," he said after he swallowed.

Kate turned to Jack. "I didn't mention it this morning, but Rooster used to work for us."

"Here?" Jack was surprised. He couldn't imagine the slimy likes of Rooster Borden working for the Roses.

Kate continued. "Thomas hired him years ago."

Henry shook his head. "Rooster was a hard luck case. Dad felt sorry for him and made the mistake of giving the sorry SOB a job."

"Henry." Kate held his stare a moment, then turned back to Jack. "Rooster's father was an alcoholic. His mother left both of them when Rooster was young. Thomas heard his story from a friend at the wool house and gave him a chance. He did odd jobs around the ranch for almost two years."

"Then Dad fired him," Henry said, butting in. "Caught him stealing tools from the barn. The idiot tried selling them to Marco Santillan, a local pawn broker and one of Dad's old classmates."

"So, Thomas fired him," Jack said. He was glad he hadn't mentioned the Roses when he talked to Borden. "What about the drugs? The sheriff mentioned that, too."

Kate answered before Henry could. "Thomas found out later that Rooster had been using them while he worked for us. The rumor is, sometime after we let him go, is when he started dealing them."

"He was still young?"

Kate nodded. "High school. Thomas never forgave himself for not giving him another chance. He thought maybe he could have turned him around."

Jack thought of the flashy gold Rolex and alligator boots. "Seems he ended up doing alright."

Henry blew out air. "Thanks to his connections with the cartels."

"Henry, that's just another rumor."

"It's the truth." Henry pointed his fork at Jack as he spoke. "Rooster didn't get rich selling steaks and whiskey. He's in thick with the Zetas."

During his tenure with the FBI, Jack had worked on several cases involving the Mexican cartels, mainly their associates in the Houston and south Texas areas. He'd seen their brutality firsthand and knew their colleagues stateside could be just as violent. If the rumors were true, Rooster Borden would be a very dangerous man.

"Do you think someone who worked for Borden would have direct involvement with the cartels?"

"While working for Rooster?" Henry asked. "You can count on it. And once they got you sucked into their business, there's no getting out. They'll do whatever it takes to keep you on the inside. Or to keep you quiet. Permanently."

"Like murder?"

Henry wiped his mouth with his napkin. "Especially murder."

# CHAPTER 20

ON HIS WAY back to Del Rio, Jack tried calling Elena Torres several times at the number Sheriff Gardner had given to him. Each time, the phone rang on the other end, then nothing. The calls were received but rejected. For some reason, Elena Torres was avoiding him.

Jack wanted to talk to her to find out more about Diego. One thing he had learned from years spent as an investigator was that the victim was usually the best clue to the crime.

When Diego Torres wasn't staying the night on Roy's ranch, he had lived at home with his parents and Elena. If Diego had confided in anyone, it probably would have been his sister, not his parents.

Jack thought about Miguel and Sabina Torres. Like any parent, they would be devastated by the loss of their son. As much as Jack wanted to let them mourn in peace, if Elena continued to avoid him, he would have no choice but to talk to them.

He tried Elena's number again, but like the other times, the call was rejected and went to voicemail.

"Elena, this is Jack Martin. Please call me back. I'm just trying to find out what happened to Diego, and I have a couple of questions I'd like to ask you."

He hung up, then tossed the phone on the passenger seat. He tightened his grip on the steering wheel and checked the speedometer. He hadn't realized he was speeding and eased up on the accelerator.

Jack wondered about Diego's friends. Although told twice that Diego had been a *good* kid, Jack had known plenty of *good* kids sucked into a life of crime through their association with bad ones. Aside from stalking the funeral and taking names, talking to the family could be the only way to find out. Too many years had passed since Diego graduated from high school. His former teachers and coaches would likely be of no use.

Jack thought of the three hoodlums he'd seen at the Broken Arrow. Had they been Diego's friends? Cohorts in Borden's criminal activities?

Jack flexed his fingers, thinking about it. There was no way around it—he needed to talk to Diego's family.

Several minutes later, when the highway turned south toward town, the Broken Arrow came into view. There were several cars still in the parking lot, holdovers from the lunch crowd. The Honda was still there, but the beat-up Chevy was gone.

Jack thought of the hoodlums and their boss and suspected the whole lot of them was up to no good.

As he passed the restaurant, he saw Borden unload a box from his truck and carry it inside.

More liquor?

Maybe. Maybe not.

Jack resisted the urge to turn around and confront Borden again face to face. What were his conditions of employment? Had Diego broken one and paid the ultimate price? What about Thomas Rose? Did Borden still harbor a grudge after being fired so many years earlier?

As much as he wanted to confront him, Jack knew it would be futile. Or worse, it could be dangerous.

A red sedan passed him and honked, its driver flipping him the bird. The gesture brought Jack around. He had been preoccupied and hadn't realized he'd slowed down as much as he had.

The case had gotten under his skin. But was it his case? He hadn't known Diego Torres. And Torres's sister was avoiding him. No one was paying Jack to care.

Did he care? Jack wondered. He thought about it for a moment and decided that he did.

He wanted to know more about Borden. Were the rumors about Borden's connection to the cartels true? Had it somehow gotten Diego murdered on Rose land? And were Kate and Henry now in danger?

The case would be tricky. Jack needed help from law enforcement but knew pressing for answers about Borden was out of the question. Prying into an ongoing investigation was the surest way to get run out of town.

Jack sped up and overtook the red sedan.

One way or another, he would talk to Elena.

# CHAPTER 21

CARTER MCCONNELL APPROACHED the home of Jordan and Gretchen Rose on Griner Street. The house wasn't large, but the classic Spanish architecture was tasteful. White stucco with arched windows and a red, barrel-tile roof. He wished he owned one just like it. Instead, he lived in the ramshackle home his mother left him when she died, a tiny thing that begged for a remodel. One day, Carter promised himself.

He took the sidewalk to the front door and admired the deep green lawn, shaded by oaks as old as the city and always meticulously maintained, convinced an army of landscapers must tend to it regularly.

The house had been in the Rose family for generations and was one of his favorite houses in town. He wasn't surprised that Jordan, the Roses' son who could do no wrong, had inherited it and now lived there with his beautiful bride and young family.

Carter was glad Jordan got the house. He couldn't imagine what it would look like had it gone to his cousin Henry instead. As he approached the front door, he imagined empty beer cans littering the lawn and Mexican yard art cut from metal in the shapes of giant frogs in sombreros playing in a mariachi band placed front and center.

Carter lifted the bronze knocker and rapped twice on the door, then held his breath when he heard someone unlock it from the inside.

"Carter, what a nice surprise," Gretchen said. "Come in." She pulled the door open further, and he stepped into the foyer.

"Is Jordan home? I tried calling him earlier but couldn't reach him."

"He's not. He's still in D.C."

Gretchen led him past a narrow staircase to the small study at the back of the house, where they sat in facing club chairs.

"I'm sorry to bother you then," Carter said. "I thought he was going to be back by now."

She sighed. "He would have been, but the hearing he's supposed to testify at was postponed. Now, he won't be back until next week."

"Is that why he had Jack Martin come to Del Rio?"

Gretchen looked surprised. "Is Jack in town?"

Carter nodded.

"Jordan told me he was thinking of asking him to come," she said. "He was worried about leaving after everything that's happened. But I had no idea Jack was already here. I hope he'll come by. I haven't seen him in years. Have you seen him?"

"Not me," Carter said. "But he went to see Uncle Roy."

"Roy?" Gretchen frowned, and then her face relaxed. "Jack must be looking into the murder."

"Huh," Carter said. "I didn't think of that. I figured he was trying to find whoever's been stealing sheep. But you're probably right." Carter shifted in his seat, then crossed one leg over the other.

Gretchen was still thinking. "I assumed he just wanted Jack to check on Kate and Henry. Make sure everything was alright. But he must have wanted him to do more than that. Jordan is such a worrier."

Gretchen was naive. It was apparent Jordan hadn't told her the truth about why he asked his old friend to come. But, then again, Jordan wouldn't want to scare her. With the issues at the border and thieves roaming the countryside, then the Torres murder, living on the ranch had never been as dangerous as it was now.

Carter thought of Roy out there all alone.

"How's Uncle Roy doing?" Gretchen asked. "I need to get out to see him one of these weekends."

Carter sighed. "I worry about him. I keep telling him it's not safe to be out there alone. But you know how he is."

Gretchen smiled. "I do. Jordan has tried talking to him about it, too. He even offered our guest house behind the garage until he found something he liked better."

"He won't budge," Carter said. "I'd feel better if they'd catch the rustlers. If Roy ever caught them out there himself…" Carter shook his head, thinking about what Roy might do. Or what could happen to him.

They talked a while longer.

When he left, Carter realized he hadn't learned anything new from his visit.

He checked the sky and saw that the sun had dropped below the horizon. Daylight was fading but wasn't yet taking the heat with it. He got into the truck and started the ignition, then set the air conditioning on high.

As he swung out from the curb and started for home, his thoughts turned again to his uncle. It was a dangerous time to be living on the ranch alone. He thought of the rustlers, and desperately hoped that Odell would find them before they made the tragic mistake of running into Roy.

# CHAPTER 22

IT WAS ONE of those nights. Jack laid down, knowing sleep wouldn't come. Visions of blood-soaked ground and old bones swirled in his head. And he was trying desperately to make sense of it all.

His thoughts drifted to Thomas Rose. Jack folded his arms, tucked them under the pillow, and stared at the ceiling. Thomas's death was puzzling. He sensed it didn't sit right with Kate or Henry either. For a family who lived on a ranch their ancestors had owned for over a century, the spate of recent events so close to home was unsettling.

Jack threw off the covers and got out of bed. He went to the window and pulled back the curtain, then peered down into the alley. He listened to the soft muffle of music and laughter from the bar below and realized he needed a drink.

He checked the time on his phone and guessed that Mesquite Creek would likely close soon. So, he dressed quickly and headed downstairs.

Although the hours on the door indicated the bar was closed, Jack saw through the glass that the place was still hopping. So, he opened the door and stepped inside.

No one noticed.

The conversations and laughter continued.

Jack felt comfortable there. Lost in the crowd of locals, part of the festive commotion, yet anonymous. Just the way he liked it.

He threaded his way through the crowd and went to the bar at the back of the room.

"What can I get ya?" It was the girl with blue-tipped hair.

Jack ordered a beer, then turned around and scanned the room. That's when he saw them. The two kids from Hansen's excavation. They were seated alone at a table for four. The girl's blond ponytail swung as she talked, gesturing with her hands. She looked angry. Her companion was sprawled in his chair, sipping the beer in his glass. His swollen eyes and posture indicated it wasn't his first.

Jack paid for his beer and strolled over to their table. The girl noticed him first and was startled. Her body went stiff. Something about seeing him had made her nervous again.

"Mind if I join you?" Jack asked, pulling out a chair. The two were silent as he sat down. "We met early today. On the Moran ranch."

The girl's flabby companion came forward in his chair. "Sure, we remember. You're that detective, Jack Martin. You came to see David."

Jack nodded. "What are your names?"

The two exchanged a quick glance.

"I'm Sherry," the girl said. "And this is Bryan."

"Nice to meet you, Sherry and Bryan." Jack tipped his glass at them, then took a drink.

"We know all about you," Bryan said, his voice slurring. "Sherry reads *The National Tattler*. She told me you were that detective from Colorado."

Jack winced, thinking about being in the tabloid. He would never get used to the notoriety the handful of high-profile cases in Colorado had brought him. First in Aspen, then Vail, then Telluride. He preferred being anonymous and hoped people would soon forget about the investigations.

*There was no use in being coy with these two*, he thought. They would know why he was in Del Rio asking questions.

"I'm looking into Diego's murder."

Sherry blanched. She brought her hand to her throat. "I can't believe he's dead."

"Your boss mentioned that Diego worked with you guys for almost a year."

"He did," she said. "He was nice."

*Nice.* At least she hadn't called him a *good kid* like everyone else had when describing him. But Jack knew that being nice wasn't what got Diego killed. He needed to know more.

"Did Diego ever talk to you about his friends?"

They both pondered the question, and Bryan answered first. "I can't say that he ever did. He would talk about his family some. Sounded like he was close to them. But I don't recall him ever mentioning any friends in particular."

Sherry remembered something. "Diego never would work on Sundays because his family would go to mass. Does that help?"

"It might," Jack answered. "What about a previous job? Did Diego ever mention what he did before working with you guys?"

The two looked at each other. Bryan was about to speak but was interrupted.

"Jack Martin."

The voice came from behind him. Jack turned and saw Deputy Bert Lynch staring down at him, chewing on a toothpick. He was out of uniform, probably off duty, and standing too close for comfort.

Jack stood and stuck out his hand. "Deputy."

Lynch shook it. His hand was clammy. "You staying downtown?"

Jack wanted to wipe his hand on his jeans but didn't. "I am," he said.

"I figured you'd be shacking up out at the Roses'."

For some reason, Jack was reluctant to tell the deputy where he was staying, so he didn't. "I like my own space," he replied.

For a few awkward seconds, Lynch stared at him, then pursed his lips and looked away. "I hear ya. I'm a solitary kind of man myself."

Jack wondered where the conversation was going. "Is there something I can do for you, Deputy?"

"Nope." Lynch's eyes locked on him again. "Just making sure you're being treated right in this fine city of ours. I see Sapphire's taken care of you." Lynch threw a nod where Jack's beer was sitting on the table.

Jack turned around and noticed the kids were gone. How in the hell had they snuck out without him noticing? He was disappointed. He had more questions for them. He was confident they knew more about Diego Torres than what they were admitting.

Jack turned back to Lynch and let out a frustrated breath. "Sapphire?"

The deputy threw a nod toward the bar, and Jack understood.

"The bartender," he said, remembering the blue hair.

"How much longer are you planning on staying in town?"

Even if Jack knew, he wouldn't tell the deputy that either. "I'm not sure. As long as it takes, I guess."

Lynch stared at him a while longer.

Jack felt like an outlaw being scrutinized by the marshal in a half-wit Western. The deputy was wearing his patience thin.

"If that's all, Bert, I think I'll finish my drink."

Lynch's eyes narrowed, shifted left, then back to center again. Calling the lawman by his first name had gotten the intended reaction. He chewed hard on the toothpick between his lips. "I'll be seeing you, Martin," he said. "You stay out of trouble."

Jack sat back down at the table, frustrated by the weird encounter with the deputy, and because the archeology kids had given him the slip before he finished questioning them.

He sat a few more minutes, finishing his beer and enjoying an Alan Jackson song. The beer had had the desired effect. Jack felt relaxed and thought maybe he would finally be able to sleep.

He left the empty glass on the table with a tip and went to the front. Although the crowd had thinned, a few stragglers remained.

He stepped outside, then turned to the door that led up to the B&B. He stuck his key in the deadbolt and unlocked it. But before he went in, he noticed a man standing in the shadows at the corner of the building. He couldn't see the man's face. But the man immediately turned away, and Jack caught a glimpse of his profile.

Although Jack only saw the man's silhouette, he could see that he held a hand to his mouth and was chewing a toothpick.

# CHAPTER 23

*Thursday, May 26*

IT WAS NINE in the morning and already a hundred degrees. Jack swung off Highway 90 onto Frank Moran's ranch and found David Hansen's truck parked in the same spot it had been the day before.

Although the kids who worked for Hansen had given Jack the slip, he wasn't done questioning them.

Jack hiked to the top of the trail and looked down. The gulch that divided the Moran and Rose ranches was still in the shadows from the morning sun.

He found the kids working the spot they had been working before. Sherry was bent over something in the ground, brushing at it, and Bryan was standing over her, holding a shovel.

They both looked up as he approached. Bryan's bloodshot eyes grew wide, and Sherry's mouth fell open. Jack wondered again what had them spooked.

"Hey guys," he said as he strolled past. "Remember me?"

"H-hey," Bryan mumbled.

They were hiding something. Jack was sure of it. He wanted to talk to them again, but he hadn't come to see the kids. He would speak to them later.

David Hansen was bent over, examining something resembling a slab of rock lying on the ground. When he noticed Jack, he threw a blanket over it and stepped in front, blocking it from Jack's view.

"We're extremely busy, Mr. ahh…"

"Martin. Jack Martin."

"That's right," Hansen said. "Is there something I can help you with, Mr. Martin? But you've got to make it quick. Like I said, we're busy."

"I have a few more questions about Diego Torres."

"I told you everything I know. I don't know how else I can help."

"Was there ever any indication that Diego was involved in something illegal?"

Hansen's face twitched. "Like what?"

"Drugs? Theft?"

Hansen cleared his throat. "No. Not that I know of." He pushed his glasses higher on the bridge of his nose.

"Did he ever mention friends or bring someone out while ya'll were working?"

"Never."

"Did he ever mention his previous employer?"

"No."

"You hired him without a reference?"

Hansen shrugged. "I didn't feel the need for a reference. Like I already told you, he started out volunteering—working for free. When I saw how efficient he was, I started paying him to keep him coming back."

Jack wasn't getting anywhere.

Hansen picked up the canteen, twisted the top off it, and took a drink. He wiped his mouth with the back of his hand. "I'd offer you some," he said, screwing the top back on. "But I've only got so much."

Jack turned and caught Sherry and Bryan watching. When they saw him look, they immediately went back to work, trying to look busy.

Jack turned back to Hansen, who returned his stare.

"If that's all, Mr. Martin. We have a lot to do today."

Hansen was hiding something. They all were.

Jack suspected all three knew more about Diego Torres than what they were admitting. And he was determined to find a way to get them to talk.

# CHAPTER 24

When Jack drove up, he saw Roy Rose step out of the house and onto the porch. He had gone years without meeting the eccentric uncle and was now about to see him for a second time in as many days. Jack hoped the old guy wouldn't resent more questions.

"Back already," Roy said, taking the steps off the porch and extending his hand.

His voice was gruff, but there wasn't any animosity in the tone. Or anything resembling curiosity either, Jack noted. It had been merely a statement.

"I'd like to ask you a few more questions if I can?"

Roy pulled at one side of his mustache, studying him. Jack thought he was about to refuse, but he nodded.

"Come on in," Roy said, turning for the house. "I've done had my coffee. But I can make us another pot if you like."

"I had some in town this morning," Jack said, following him inside. "But thank you."

Roy walked, favoring his right leg. Jack wanted to ask about the injury but didn't. It wasn't the time.

"Let's sit in here," Roy said, entering the study. "Have a seat." He pointed to a couple of armchairs set in a corner, then opened a wood box on the desk and pulled out a cigar. He lifted it in Jack's direction, offering him one.

"No, thank you." It was early. Surely, he wasn't about to smoke it.

Jack took a seat and glanced around the book-filled room. "I hear you're a historian."

"By hobby. Not by trade." Roy stuck the cigar into his mouth without lighting it, took the empty chair, and crossed an ankle over the opposite knee.

Jack read the titles on several of the spines. *The Trail Drivers of Texas*, *We Pointed Them North*, and *Lone Star Rising*. "All Texas history?" he asked.

"Mostly. But not all."

There were so many. Jack had no idea so much had been written on the subject. Roy had books written about the Texas Revolution and memoirs written by early settlers and Texas Rangers. There were books on Mexico and different Indian tribes who had inhabited the area.

"Frank Hamer?" Jack asked, rising from his chair and pulling the book from the shelf. He'd heard about the famous lawman who had put an end to Bonnie and Clyde's reign of terror, gunning them down somewhere near the Texas border with Louisiana.

"My grandfather knew him," Roy said.

Jack glanced up from the book.

"Early in his career, Hamer spent time here in Del Rio. It was uncivilized back then—outlaws, Mexican bandits, even the occasional Indians. There were two or three Rangers stationed here full-time, and all the ranchers knew them. For a while, one was Frank Hamer."

Jack flipped through the book, looking at the old black-and-white photographs.

"Take it with you," Roy said.

Jack closed the book and studied the cover. "No, I couldn't—"

"Take it," Roy insisted. "I've read it several times."

Jack placed the book on a small table between the two chairs and sat down again. "Thank you. I'll get it back—"

Roy waved his hand. "Don't bother. I've probably got an

extra lying around here somewhere anyway. I bought a load of books off Larry McMurtry when he shut down his store in Archer City. Some were duplicates of books I already had." He chewed on the unlit cigar as he talked.

"I've heard of Larry McMurtry," Jack said.

"Heard of him?" Roy took the cigar from his mouth. "Son, you mean to tell me you haven't read *Lonesome Dove*?"

"No, sir. I haven't."

"Well, you should," Roy said. "There're a lot of Texans that claim to love the land, but I don't believe them unless they read its history. You read it," he said, pulling a copy of *Lonesome Dove* from a shelf and tapping its cover with the cigar. He set the book down on the table between them, then stuck the cigar back in his mouth.

"Thank you." Jack didn't mention that, although he felt like a Texan, he was born in Louisiana.

"I hear they don't teach history in school anymore." Roy said it like he couldn't believe it was true. "They're too busy teaching things that don't matter." He leaned back in the chair. "But enough about that. What'd you need to talk to me about?"

"I wanted to know if you ever got the sense that Diego was involved in anything illegal?"

"You're referring to his history with drugs." Roy shook his head. "I'd heard the rumors, and we talked about it some, but as far as I could tell, he'd left that life behind."

"That's what he told you?"

"He did."

"And you believed him?"

"I did."

There was no equivocation in Roy's answers. Jack decided to change the direction of the conversation. "Did he ever mention anyone threatening him? Maybe someone from his past?"

Roy thought about it, then shook his head. "No."

"And you never saw any signs that he was still using drugs?"

"No. None."

Jack let the subject of drugs drop. Roy was defensive. It was clear he had grown fond of Diego.

"When was the last time you saw him?" Jack asked.

"The morning before he was killed," Roy answered. "He parked his car in the barn, and I came out to see him before he headed off on his bicycle."

"Did he seem upset by anything? Maybe worried or preoccupied?"

Roy shook his head. "No."

The conversation wasn't revealing, and Jack was growing frustrated. "What can you tell me about David Hansen?"

Roy pulled at his mustache with his free hand. "Not much. I let him dig around for a year, and then he was gone."

"What did you think about him?"

Roy shrugged. "I never thought much about him. Seemed a bit full of himself for my taste but never did me or my property any harm."

The front door opened.

"Uncle Roy?" It was a male voice.

"We're in the study," Roy hollered back.

"I brought your medicine." The man pulled up when he saw Jack in the study. "Oh. Hello, Jack."

It had been nearly a decade since Jack had seen Carter McConnell. He wouldn't have recognized him if he hadn't referred to Roy as uncle. Carter had always been a skinny kid but had filled out with age. He wore khaki pants and a starched white shirt. The polished loafers on his feet were in stark contrast with Roy's old boots. His complexion was fair yet ruddy like he'd recently been in the sun. Carter looked out of place on the ranch. Then Jack remembered Henry mentioning he was an attorney and lived in town.

Jack stood up and shook his hand. "Good to see you again, Carter."

Roy was on his feet and took the bag from his nephew. "Thank you, Carter. But I told you it wasn't necessary to drive all the way out here and bring pills I probably won't take."

"I have an appointment in Comstock with Artie Brazelton."

"Who?"

"He bought the Townsend ranch outside of Juno, but he owns one of the *maquiladoras* across the river." Roy nodded in recognition, and Carter continued. "So, I was headed out anyway. Oh, and I brought the information on those houses I told you about. I printed it all out for you. It's in the bag with the medicine."

Roy pulled the cigar from his mouth. "I told you; I'm not interested in moving."

"Just take a look at them, Uncle Roy." Carter turned to Jack, obviously wanting to change the subject. "How long are you in town for?"

"I'm not sure yet," Jack replied.

Roy set the bag on the table along with his cigar. "Jack's been asking about Diego's past."

"Oh?"

Carter turned to him, but Jack didn't want to explain. The fewer people that knew what he was doing in town, the better.

"Your uncle's been kind enough to answer a few questions," Jack said.

"Did he mention that the Torres kid was involved in illegal narcotics?" Carter asked. "And that's more than likely what got him killed."

Roy scoffed. "Only thing illegal around here is sheep rustling." He paused a moment, then added. "Or whatever Frank Moran is up to these days."

The statement caught Jack off guard. Why bring up the

man who owned the ranch where David Hansen was now working?

Carter sighed. "Don't drag Frank Moran into this, Uncle Roy. Just because the two of you never got along doesn't mean he's the source of all evil."

"That's debatable."

Carter shook his head and looked at Jack apologetically. "I've got to get going," he said. "I'm going to be late."

Jack grabbed the books Roy had given him from the table, and the three men walked toward the door.

Outside, Carter said his goodbyes and started for his truck. It was a shiny new Chevrolet in metallic black but covered in dust.

Jack stood in the yard with Roy. He had a couple more questions.

"That kid should be wearing a hat," Roy said as Carter waved, then backed away from the house. "Spends most days in an office and still burns. I never could get him to wear a hat." Roy shook his head. "City kid."

Jack watched him turn for the highway and felt a pang of empathy for Carter McConnell. Growing up among the Roses, men brimming with machismo and virility, life wouldn't have been easy.

But Jack was glad Carter had come. His visit had raised a few more questions. "What's a *maquiladora*?"

"*Maquiladoras*." Roy repeated. "They're manufacturing plants that straddle the border. Usually, with the administration offices on our side, and the manufacturing done in Mexico. You'll sometimes hear them called 'twin plants.'"

"What do they make?"

"All sorts of stuff. Why?"

Jack shook his head. "Just curious."

Roy chuckled, pulling at his mustache again. "I guess questions are your business."

"I've got another one for you," Jack said.

Roy nodded. "Alright."

"What can you tell me about Frank Moran?"

"What do you want to know?"

"David Hansen is digging on his ranch."

"I heard."

Hansen was working across a dry gulch from where Diego Torres was murdered. It was too close for comfort, and Jack wanted to know if it was a coincidence.

"You mentioned Frank Moran was involved in something illegal."

"I was just running my mouth."

"You two don't get along?"

Roy pulled at his mustache, thinking about the question. His answer came slowly. "Son, this is hard country. And it takes hard people to live here. Sometimes we just don't get along."

Jack didn't believe it was that simple and decided to throw a Hail Mary. "Do you think Moran, or something going on his ranch, had anything to do with Diego's murder?"

Roy held Jack's stare. It was a poker face as good as any Jack had ever seen.

"No," he finally answered.

And Jack knew immediately.

Roy was lying.

# CHAPTER 25

AT THE HIGHWAY, Jack turned toward town, discouraged. Although he had spent the morning talking to David Hansen and then Roy, both for the second time, he felt like the investigation was going nowhere. The few answers he received had only raised more questions. And the only thing Jack knew for certain was that both men were hiding something.

At a rise in the highway, a gate in the distance came into view, the same gate Henry had taken when he showed Jack where he found Diego Torres.

Jack slowed the truck, for some reason feeling compelled to see it again. He turned off the highway at the gate and took the road that split the two Rose ranches. Twenty minutes later, he parked in the same spot Henry had parked three days earlier.

Jack climbed the trail, then began the slow descent to the rock shelter where Henry found Diego murdered.

Jack took his time, carefully picking his way among the rock and cactus while the midday sun scorched his body. Rivulets of sweat ran down his back, again soaking his shirt.

After several minutes, he stopped to catch his breath and took in the vastness of the landscape around him. The country was wild and rugged but beautiful. He scanned the western horizon, then squinted, focusing on a mountain range in Mexico shrouded in a haze. It resembled the profile of a reclining woman. Locals referred to them as the Sleeping

Lady Mountains. But Jack wondered if, instead of sleeping, she was lying on her death bed.

He continued down the slope until he reached the shelf below the overhang where someone shot Diego. Everywhere, rock and cactus and scrubby mesquite reached out with thorns that threatened to tear clothes and flesh. A scorpion crawled close to the tip of Jack's boot, and he kick it away. It was a brutal place to die.

Jack twisted left then right, searching the dark crevices on the side of the mountain behind him. The complete isolation was startling. Jack couldn't imagine anyone camping there alone overnight. But for some reason, Diego Torres had done it regularly.

Jack shielded his eyes from the sun, glanced up at the stone overhang, and felt heat radiating from the rock. He searched the area around him again, looking for any clue that would tell him what Diego had been looking for.

Something about the ground was different than it had been three days earlier. And Jack knew immediately that someone had been there. Old footprints in the dirt were covered with new ones. The old shovel was in a different location and the hole Jack had seen before now seemed larger. Had someone been digging?

Jack stood still, his eyes scouring the scene, looking for anything to explain why someone had been there. But there was nothing.

Jack wondered if Henry had come back without him. Could it have been Roy? Jack thought of his limp and couldn't imagine Roy making it over the mountain and down to the shelter.

But someone had been there.

Maybe the sheriff. Had one of Odell Gardner's deputies come back to the scene? Jack would make a point to ask the next time he ran into one.

The wind suddenly kicked up, throwing dust at him. Jack

turned his head and felt the grit sting the back of his neck. He had seen enough and turned to go.

The land was harsh and the conditions savage, yet something had drawn Diego Torres there for days at a time. And Jack was beginning to believe that whatever it was had gotten him killed.

# CHAPTER 26

JACK DIDN'T REGAIN cell service until he was almost to the highway. He drove through the gate but stopped and put the truck in park on the side of the road. Then scrolled through his contacts.

"Jack, where are you?" Henry answered.

Jack got straight to the point. "Did you go back to the scene of the murder?"

"Diego Torres's?"

Jack wondered how many other murders there had been. "Yes, Diego's."

"No. Why?"

"I was just out there," Jack said. "I wanted to see it again. Someone's been out there."

"Since Tuesday?"

"Yes."

Henry was silent a moment. "Maybe it was one of Odell's men."

Jack would ask and find out.

"You coming by for dinner?" Henry asked, changing the subject. "You caught me in the pasture, but we're about to head back in. I have to warn you, though. Mother said Ado's been smoking a brisket. And like everything else she cooks, it'll taste like mule."

Jack laughed. "Thank you. I'm tempted. But there are a

couple of people in town I want to talk to. That's another reason I'm calling. What can you tell me about Frank Moran?"

"Moran?" Henry practically spat the name back at him. "What do you want to know about that SOB."

"That bad?"

"That bad."

"I got the impression Roy doesn't like him either."

Henry blew air into the phone. "There isn't a Rose out there that does."

"What do you mean?"

"How much time do you have?"

Jack watched a semi-truck blow past on the highway and felt his truck shake. "Give me the Cliffs Notes version."

Henry took in a deep breath and then let it out slowly. "The Rose family used to own close to a hundred thousand acres in Mexico."

"Roy and your dad?"

"No, the generation before them. There were four sons— my grandfather and Roy's father, along with their two brothers. Anyway, Frank Moran's father comes along and bribes the *federales* and ends up with the ranch."

"They just took it?" Jack asked. "How can they do that?"

"It's Mexico. If you've got the right connections and enough pesos, you can get the government to do just about anything. Oh, they dressed it up, tried to make the take-back look legit. But it wasn't. Foreigners have to set up trust accounts at a Mexican bank in order to purchase property. The *federales* claimed the Roses hadn't stuck to the conditions of their trust and took the land back. Then sold it to Moran. It was bullshit."

"Where is Frank's father now?"

"Dead."

"Does Frank still own the ranch?"

"He does. Probably hasn't stepped foot on it in decades, but it keeps him relevant over there."

Jack was beginning to understand. "And there's been bad blood between the Roses and Morans ever since."

"That's an understatement," Henry replied. "Hell, he swindled the ranch he's got now from another one of Dad's cousins before I was born. It was part of the old Rose Ranch. Should have stayed in the family, but Frank wrangled it from him on his deathbed. But that wasn't enough. He bugged Dad till his dying day to sell him our portion of the old ranch. He'd bug Uncle Roy regularly, too, if Roy didn't consistently tell him to go to hell. Imagine the nerve. He fancies himself as some sort of empire builder, but he's nothing but a common thief. Frank Moran can burn in hell."

Jack wondered if the vitriol flowed both ways. He suddenly had the urge to talk to Moran. "You mentioned he lived in town."

"He does. His house is directly across the street from Jordan and Gretchen's. But you'd be better off catching him at Benny's Cafe. He has coffee there every morning."

"Why not go to his house?"

"Because he can't shoot you if you meet him in public."

Jack had seen the sign for Benny's Cafe down the street from where he was staying. "What time does he usually have coffee?"

"Probably when they open. Seven-thirty, I think."

Jack watched as a white truck sped toward him, then abruptly slowed as it approached the gate. He noticed *Val Verde County Sheriff* painted in green on the side. The sun's glare on the windshield obscured the driver, but Jack had a hunch he knew who it would be.

"I gotta let you go," he told Henry. "I'll call you later."

The driver pulled alongside Jack's truck and stopped, then stared at him through the windows.

Jack's hunch had been correct. And he wasn't happy about it.

# CHAPTER 27

Deputy Bert Lynch chewed on a toothpick. He wound down his window and indicated for Jack to do the same.

Jack didn't like it. Both men sitting behind the wheel only feet apart. They were too close. If something went down, Jack couldn't open his driver's side door. And he wasn't sure how much he trusted Deputy Lynch.

He hesitated, then wound down the window.

Lynch took the toothpick from his mouth and dropped it to the ground between them. "You having car trouble?"

"I stopped to make a phone call. My reception out here is spotty."

Lynch eyed him a moment, then looked past him at the ranch road Jack was just on. "Interesting place to stop," he said. "You go back out there?"

Jack played dumb. "Out where?" He didn't like Lynch. Why make it easy?

"Where we found the Torres kid."

Jack wasn't sure how much he wanted the deputy to know. He remembered Lynch's silhouette in the shadows the night before and suspected the deputy had been following him.

"I thought I'd have another look," Jack finally answered.

"Why? Not much to see."

"Have you guys been back out there?"

Lynch looked surprised by the question, then quickly looked away. "Why would we?"

It was then Jack fully understood Jordan's hesitation to leave Torres's murder to law enforcement. The sheriff seemed competent enough, but his deputy was another story.

"Why would we?" Lynch repeated. For some reason, the question agitated him.

"It's not uncommon for investigators to revisit the scene of a murder," Jack said. He let it sink in. "And this murder was committed in *your* jurisdiction."

Lynch pursed his lips together hard, flaring his nostrils. Jack's barb had hit its target. And although he didn't make a habit of insulting the law, poking Lynch seemed justified.

It took a moment for the deputy to regain his composure. "We thoroughly investigated the scene the first time," he said. "Going back out there would be a waste of our time. But I can tell you, if something changes and we feel the need to take another look, we will."

"I'm sure you would." Jack noticed a pair of binoculars set on the deputy's dash. "It's none of my business, but how's the investigation into the rustling going?"

"You're right," Lynch said. "It's none of your business."

Jack ignored the remark. "There are folks who think the rustlers could be responsible for the Torres murder."

"That theory is ridiculous."

"Why?"

"The rustlers are probably a bunch of harmless kids. Killing someone is a far cry from stealing a few head of sheep."

Jack had to agree with him.

"Nah," Lynch continued. "The Torres hit was drug-related."

"The cartels?"

"Without a doubt, the cartels are involved somehow. Torres was no stranger to our friends at the police department. From what I've heard, they picked him up regularly."

He pulled a fresh toothpick from his shirt pocket. "Drug hit. I'd put money on it."

"What about Rooster Borden?"

Lynch was lifting the toothpick to his mouth but stopped. "What about him?"

"My understanding is that Diego used to work for Borden. Maybe he still did."

Lynch shook his head, not looking at Jack. "Nah. Rooster had nothing to do with the murder. It was the cartels."

It was exactly as Jordan said. Pointing to the cartels was the easy way out for overworked law enforcement. Case closed.

Jack wasn't buying it, but he let the subject drop. "What do you know about Diego's family?"

"The Torreses? What about them?"

"Do you know his sister?"

"He had four of them."

"Elena."

Lynch whistled through his teeth. "Yeah, I know Elena. Quite the looker."

Jack ignored the comment. "She's hard to get a hold of."

"Tell me about it. You got to catch her at work. She's a waitress at The Brown Bag Deli on Veterans Avenue. Home is off-limits. Unless it's official business, of course. But even then, we'd have to track her down sometimes at her church. She's there all the time."

"What church does she attend?"

"Something rosary," Lynch said with a dismissive wave. "It's on the south side of town. On Garza Street."

It gave Jack an idea. "I need to get going," he said.

Lynch stuck the toothpick between his teeth. "You stay out of trouble. You hear?"

Jack watched as Lynch swung his truck onto the highway and sped away. It had been another awkward encounter. He didn't know what to make of the deputy but knew enough to know that he wasn't about to trust him.

On the way back to Del Rio, Jack thought again of the crime scene. Someone had been there. If it wasn't Henry or law enforcement, who had it been?

And why were they there?

# CHAPTER 28

JACK SEARCHED FOR Del Rio churches on his phone as he drove toward town. He found one on Garza Street and put the address into GPS.

Jack first drove past the Torreses' house and decided to check the church when he didn't see Elena's car. He followed the directions to Our Lady of the Holy Rosary. Less than a minute later, the church came into view.

Set on a large corner lot, it was an impressive structure bordered by tall palms lining the streets on two sides. A tall, octagonal spire, topped by a simple cross, soared overhead.

Jack parked at the curb and got out, then took the steps to a set of wooden doors but found them locked. He stood on the stoop for a moment, thinking, and watched as a handful of cars passed on the street. He wasn't catholic but knew from catholic friends, some who regularly lit candles at all hours, that somewhere a door would be open.

He walked around the side of the building and saw a small parking lot in the back, where two cars sat alone. Neither was Elena's. He knew catching her there would be a long shot, but she could have walked. When he pulled on the handle of a side door, it opened into a small anteroom.

Jack stepped inside, and the door closed behind him with an echoing click. Then, there was only silence.

After letting his eyes adjust to the darkness, he crossed the room, his boots clomping on the tile floor with each step.

He entered the sanctuary, passing a carved table with tiers of votive candles in red glass jars. Several were lit, their flames dancing gently.

He stood near the altar and scanned the enormous room and realized he was alone.

He took a moment, enjoying the solitude.

The church was beautiful—and peaceful. The waning daylight filtered through dozens of stained-glass windows, casting prisms of color across the wood pews. The floor was a sea of patterned Mexican tiles polished to a high sheen.

Behind the altar, a giant crucifix hung high on the wall. Christ's face reflected his agony as he looked toward heaven.

"He died for your sins, my son." The voice had a rich Hispanic accent.

Jack whirled around and was startled to find a man standing there. He wore a black cassock and white clerical collar. Stocky, probably late 60s, with gray hair and dark, probing eyes. It was as if he had materialized from nowhere.

"Are you here to confess them?"

"Confess what?" Jack asked, still startled by the man's sudden appearance.

"Your sins."

"No. Uh. I'm looking for someone."

The priest crossed his arms, tucking his hands in his sleeves. "I am Father Andres Manuel Nieto. How may I be of assistance?"

"My name is Jack Martin. I'm looking for Elena Torres."

The priest stood silent. The look on his face was stern. Jack felt the weight of his stare and resisted the urge to step back. It was then it dawned on him. He had asked about the sister of the victim recently murdered. Of course the priest would be suspicious of his intentions.

"I'm a private detective," Jack said. "And I've been asked to look into her brother Diego's murder."

The priest stood silent, watching him. "The Torres family

are valued members of this congregation. I respect their privacy. But I can pass along a message to them, if you like."

"I was told Elena stops in regularly."

Father Nieto glanced toward the lit candles, then back again. And Jack knew. Elena had already been there.

"We have many faithful parishioners," he said.

"I was told the Torres family attends mass regularly," Jack said. "You must have known Diego."

The priest didn't answer.

"Listen, Father," Jack said. "I'm just trying to find out what happened to Diego. It would help if you could answer a few questions.

The priest stood silent.

Jack continued. "Can you tell me if Diego mentioned anything before he died that might explain what happened? Maybe that he was involved in something he shouldn't have been. Or he had made someone angry."

The priest's dark eyes narrowed. He re-crossed his arms over his chest, once again tucking his hands into his sleeves. "Are you asking me to reveal what a parishioner said in the holy sacrament of confession?"

Jack sighed. The conversation was going from bad to worse. Then again, it was understandable that a man who regularly hears men's sins would be suspicious or cynical.

Jack knew when to throw in the towel. "No, Father. I don't want you to do that," he said. "But thank you for speaking with me."

The priest bowed solemnly.

Jack nodded and started for the side door, his footsteps echoing on the tile floor once more, making him wonder again how the priest had appeared from nowhere. The encounter with him had been somewhat surreal, and Jack wasn't sure what to make of it.

Jack had struck out finding Elena and probably just

missed her. He had also failed to get information out of the Torres family's priest.

But there was one thing Jack was sure of. Like everyone else Jack had questioned, Father Andres Manuel Nieto knew more than he was willing to say.

# CHAPTER 29

THE TRIP TO Our Lady of the Holy Rosary had been a bust, but Jack didn't have time to dwell on it. The sun had dropped in the sky, and he checked the time on his phone. Five-thirty. He knew the library closed at seven o'clock.

He drove over San Felipe Creek and through downtown, then took a right on Spring Street, and the Val Verde County Library came into view. He chose an empty space in the parking lot and shut off the ignition, then grabbed his notebook on the seat beside him and went inside.

Tall ceilings and massive arched windows gave the building an airy feel. There was row after row of books, and Jack wasn't sure where to start.

"Can I help you?" a woman with a kind face asked him. She was sitting behind a reception desk.

Jack told her what he was looking for, and she showed him to a computer on a table tucked in a back corner. With a few keystrokes, she pulled up the archives for the now defunct *Del Rio News Herald*.

"You can access the internet on this terminal, too," she said. "But keep in mind, it's a public computer. I wouldn't log into your bank account or social media."

Jack didn't mention he didn't use social media or that looking into his finances would only depress him. What he *would* be searching for was vastly different.

"My name is Sylvia. If you need anything else, just ask."

Jack thanked her, then spent the next half-hour searching newspaper archives for articles that mentioned Frank Moran. He found surprisingly few. As one of the area's largest landowners, including owning more than a hundred thousand acres across the border in Mexico, there was almost no mention of him in the local press.

From experience, Jack knew there were typically two types of successful men who shunned the media—those who genuinely wanted to keep their legitimate affairs private and those who did so to fly under the radar of the law. From what Henry had told Jack about Frank Moran, he suspected Moran was among the latter.

Jack found an article published when Moran's daughter had wed years earlier that included a family photograph. Jack zoomed in to get a better look at the bride's father and wasn't impressed. Moran was the size of a house; his tux stretched taut across a sizable belly. His hair was thin and plastered to his scalp, making his head look like an egg. His expression was stern. Jack wondered about a man who wouldn't smile for a wedding portrait.

Next, Jack searched the internet for information about Thomas Rose's death but found nothing but an obituary. It was long. Jack jotted down the web address and decided to read it later.

Except for references in official arrest records, his search for Diego Torres resulted in little information. Although Diego was arrested a handful of times for drug possession and once for shoplifting, the incidents had all occured years before. Too long ago to be significant.

Jack zoomed into the photograph accompanying Diego's obituary, noting the snake tattoo that curled around one side of his neck. Despite the ink, the kid had a friendly face. But Jack knew from experience that looks could be deceiving.

He checked the time on his phone and saw that the

library would close in under an hour. Little time left for the most complex topic.

As Jack had feared, his search for Lower Pecos River archeology resulted in thousands of hits. He clicked on a few of the articles, hoping something in them would hint at what Diego had been doing when someone killed him.

Jack read articles on pictographs, the archeological term for the rock paintings. He read others on the indigenous tribes responsible for creating them thousands of years earlier. Jack read about Panther Cave and the White Shaman and studied photographs of artifacts, including articles of clothing, ancient tools, and crumbling nets used for snares and fishing.

The articles quoted archeologists and other experts on the subject and the area. Several were associated with the Juno Archeological Center, an education facility and museum north of Comstock. Jack wrote down the name and planned to visit.

At some point, Sylvia came to check on him and announced the library would be closing soon.

Jack dove back into the research, losing track of time until several overhead lights went out, leaving the room only partially lit.

He furiously scanned several more articles and scholarly reports, searching names, before finally giving up.

The articles quoted archeologists associated with the Juno Center, Texas State University, and Texas A&M. There were others connected to several different museums.

Jack had scanned hundreds of names—PhDs, professors, archeologists in the field, and private enthusiasts. Curiously, David Hansen's name wasn't mentioned among any of them.

As he left the library, it had Jack wondering.

If David Hansen wasn't a legitimate archeologist, then who in the hell was he?

# CHAPTER 30

*Friday, May 27*

THE FOLLOWING MORNING, Jack pulled open the front door to Benny's Cafe and stepped inside. When he did, the murmur of conversation hushed. Everyone turned, appraising the stranger in town. But after several seconds, satisfied the newcomer didn't pose a threat, the diners went about their business, resuming conversations.

The restaurant smelled divine. Jack drew in deep breath, redolent of eggs and bacon, as his eyes swept the room.

The cafe was long and narrow, a throwback to the '50s. A lunch counter ran the length of the building on the right. In front of it, a dozen empty stools were bolted to the floor. Two women bustled behind the counter, preparing food.

Diners sat at tables arranged in a single row down the middle of the cafe and in booths lining the wall on the left. Jack scanned the faces he could see, and spotted Frank Moran seated alone at a booth in the back corner, bent over a plate of food.

Even from a distance, Moran looked massive, taking up most of the bench on the table's far side. He read a newspaper while he ate.

Although groups of older men occupied many of the tables, Moran sat alone and seemed to prefer it that way.

Jack crossed the room toward him. Moran wore a starched shirt and silk suspenders and looked even larger up

close. His graying hair was thin and coated with an old-fash-
ioned pomade, exposing strips of pasty scalp.

"Frank Moran?"

Moran didn't look up. "Who wants to know?" he asked
before shoveling egg and salsa into his mouth and continuing
to read. His bulbous nose was webbed with broken capillaries
and bobbed with each chew.

"My name's Jack Martin."

"Don't know you." Moran scooped up more eggs, still
reading the paper.

His nails looked manicured, and his hands were pudgy
and soft like they hadn't seen an honest day's work in decades.
He looked more like a Houston oilman from the '50s than a
West Texas rancher.

"I'm a friend of Jordan and Henry Rose," Jack said,
growing disgusted.

Moran glanced up briefly, then turned his attention back
to the paper. "Are those boys ready to sell?"

"I wouldn't know anything about that."

"Then I don't got much to say to you."

Jack's jaw clenched, but he held his temper. "I'd like to
ask you a few questions."

Moran set down his fork with great deliberation, then
folded the newspaper in half and laid it beside his plate. It
was the *San Angelo Standard-Times*. He pointed to the headline.
"Says here a man died in Ozona from a snakebite. Rattler got
the poor old fool. Hell of a way to die."

Jack wasn't sure what the point was and remained silent.

Moran picked up the fork and began stabbing at his eggs.
"Worse way to go would be to have an accident on your own
land. Any reasonably heart-broke kinfolk would be inclined
to sell and be rid of the ghost, don't you think?"

Jack's body tensed. He resisted the urge to shove the son-
of-a-bitch's face in his plate. Maybe he would later. But he
needed answers from him first.

He slid into the opposite side of the booth, and Moran startled at the bold move. It was the reaction Jack had hoped for. He now had the fat man's full attention.

"What can you tell me about David Hansen?"

Moran's eyes narrowed to slits. "Not much."

"He's working on your ranch."

"So he is."

"Tell me why he's there," Jack said, then leaned back, getting more comfortable. "I'm not leaving until you do."

Moran glared at him, then set his fork down and used his napkin to wipe grease from his chin. "All I know is the guy's some shovel bum the state pays me to let dig on my ranch. I don't know what he's doing, and I don't care as long as I get my check every month."

"What's he looking for?"

"Like I said, I don't know, and I don't care. He worked on Roy Rose's place first. You can go ask him."

"I did."

"What'd he tell you?"

"About as much as you have."

Moran sawed at a slab of ham with his knife. "That old coot needs to be committed." He stuck a bite of ham in his mouth and swallowed without chewing. "Lost his marbles after his wife died. Now, nobody can drag him off that ranch. Too bad, too. I'd be happy to take it off his hands."

"Roy seems plenty lucid to me."

Moran pointed the knife at him. "Sanity is relative," he said. "You must have crazies in your family, too. Either that or you've been hanging around the Roses too long."

Jack had had enough. "Why do you hate them?"

"Who?"

"The Roses." Jack had his attention again.

"They're sore losers."

"I heard about the swindle in Mexico. Seems like any reasonable person would be sore about that."

Moran's face twisted. "There was no swindle to it," he said. Jack had hit a nerve. "They let the terms of their agreement with the Mexican government lapse. My father just took advantage of it. He was a smart businessman."

"That's not what I heard."

Moran's eyes narrowed again. "And just what do you know about my father?"

"I heard, *like you*, he was a cheat."

# CHAPTER 31

ALTHOUGH THEIR CONVERSATION lasted less than five minutes, Jack knew he'd burned a bridge with Frank Moran. But he didn't care. He couldn't stand the man.

His next visit was to see Sheriff Odell Gardner, which he hoped would go better.

When Jack walked into his office, Gardner was talking to one of his deputies. They were standing together before a large map tacked to the wall. The deputy was pointing at something. The men fell silent when Jack entered the room, making him wonder what they had been discussing.

"Sheriff," Jack said. "Thank you for seeing me again."

"I almost didn't." Gardner exhaled sharply. He wasn't happy. "Get back with me later, Danny."

The deputy nodded at his boss, then crossed the room on his way out. It was a determined stride, and the deputy's face was all business. He glanced at Jack on his way out but said nothing. The name on his badge read *Ochoa*. Jack committed it to memory.

Sheriff Gardner dropped into the chair behind his desk. "Make it quick, Martin. I've had a bad morning."

"Anything I can help you with?" It was an absurd offer, but Jack threw it out, fishing.

Gardner placed his hands palm-down on the desk and stared at him. Jack was afraid he had crossed the line, then saw the sheriff's face relax.

"I'm up to my eyeballs in theft. A ranch outside of Langtry was hit by a band of illegals yesterday afternoon. They ransacked the bunkhouse while the men were out working. Wiped the place out of food and guns." He dragged a hand down his face before he continued. "And if that weren't enough, sheep were stolen off the Chisholm ranch last night. It's the third time they've been hit in two months. There's not much I can do about the illegals. Most of them are just passing through. And the way I see it, they're mainly a Border Patrol problem. But I'm catching hell with the ranchers that we haven't arrested the rustlers yet. And with good reason. So, ask what you need to. I don't have time for small talk today."

"What can you tell me about Frank Moran?"

Gardener looked surprised by the question. "What do you want to know?"

"I hear there's bad blood between him and the Roses."

"You heard right. The feud goes back decades." He leaned back in his chair. "It's not like the Hatfields and the McCoys. There's been no bloodshed. They just don't get a long."

Jack thought of Thomas Rose and wasn't convinced the sheriff was right about no bloodshed. But he wouldn't go there with the conversation. Not yet.

"What do you know about Moran swindling land from the Roses in Mexico?"

"Probably no more than you do. The Roses owned a large ranch across the border, then they didn't. Mexicans took it from them and gave it to George Moran, Frank's father. The Roses have always blamed the Morans for it. Then Frank pulled some shenanigans, got Hobart Rose to sign over his part of the old Rose ranch to him, and the feud only got worse."

"Was everything legal?" Jack asked.

"The purchase from Hobart?" Jack nodded. "As far as I know." Gardner paused. "Legal, but maybe not *ethical*." He came forward in his chair. "But you didn't hear that from me. Is Jordan back in town?"

"Not yet."

"So, you're getting most of your information from Henry." Gardner laced his meaty fingers together and laid them on the desk. "Look, Henry is a friend of mine, but he was no stranger to law enforcement back in the day. Nothing serious. Skipping school, drinking, speeding on his motorcycle before he had a license, stuff like that. But he drove my predecessor nuts. He's known around here as a bit of a hothead. If you want more info about the Rose-Moran feud, I'd ask Carter McConnell."

"Carter?"

Gardner nodded. "He's family, but not a Rose by blood. And he's an attorney. You might get a more unbiased account of events from him than from Henry. Although he's Roy's nephew by marriage, so you still want to take what he says with a grain of salt. Family is sacred around here."

It was all Jack would get out of the sheriff about Frank Moran. He took a deep breath, steeling himself for what he would ask next.

"Tell me about Thomas Rose."

The sheriff frowned. "What about him?"

"Are you sure his death was an accident?"

# CHAPTER 32

JACK HAD PUSHED his luck too far. The last question he asked Sheriff Gardner had crossed the line. Thomas Rose died outside the city limits, in the jurisdiction of the sheriff's office. And they had ruled the death an accident. Asking Gardner if it could have been something other than an unfortunate mishap was the same as questioning his competence.

As far as Jack knew, Odell Gardner was a competent lawman. But the murder of Diego Torres on the same ranch where Thomas died only a few weeks earlier would've had any competent lawman questioning their previous findings.

But the momentary flicker in Gardner's eyes had spoken volumes. Like Jack, the sheriff was no longer sure that Thomas's death had been an accident.

Jack drove through town. Just before the highway turned toward the lake, the Broken Arrow came into view. Jack checked the time on the truck's dash and saw it was eight-thirty. The restaurant wouldn't open for hours. The parking lot was empty. But as Jack passed, he checked for Rooster Borden's truck around the back but saw it wasn't there.

He drove on, eventually passing both Rose ranches. As he neared Frank Moran's place, he thought of the man he'd met that morning. Jack couldn't put a finger on it but knew there was more to Moran's story than unethically accumulating ranch land.

Jack found the Juno Archeology Center a few miles north

of Comstock, near what was left of the small ghost town of Juno that the center was named after. It was a single-story white metal building with a gray shingled roof. The building was small but well-maintained. Jack pulled off the highway and killed the engine. He glanced over the handful of cars already in the parking lot and hoped one belonged to the woman he'd come to see.

Inside, the building was spacious. There were display cases scattered around an open room, and the hum of a wall-mounted air conditioning unit droned from somewhere in the back. A handful of tourists milled about.

Jack noticed a young woman not much older than a teenager behind a counter. She was smacking chewing gum and engrossed in something on her phone. He read the name patch on her khaki shirt as he approached the counter and cleared his throat.

"Good morning, Lexi. I'm looking for Dr. Catherine Michaels."

The girl looked up at Jack and grinned, still smacking her gum. "Well, howdy, stranger." She smoothed her hair with a hand. "Who might you be?"

Jack didn't want to give the inquisitive girl more information than she needed, but he needed her attention. "I'm a private investigator looking into a recent murder. I'd like to ask your boss a few questions."

The girl's mouth hung open a moment, giving Jack a clear view of the wad of gum resting on her tongue.

"She—she's down at the excavation site with a class." The girl pointed to a door at the back wall. An exit sign hung overhead. "It's out that way. Follow the trail a hundred yards or so. You'll see her."

Jack let out a sigh. Another archeological dig. More sun and dirt. He thanked her and left the building.

It was nine-fifteen. Although it was already hot, he figured he had another hour before it would be blazing. A coachwhip snake slithered across the trail ahead of him, and he gave it a moment to clear out of the way.

Jack never imagined he would miss investigating in the city, but he was beginning to think West Texas was less forgiving than even the mean streets of Houston. He had walked nearly as many miles in the last few days as on one of his hikes in Colorado. The difference was, here, he had done it caked in dust and in scorching heat. And without his favorite four-legged hiking buddy.

The trail dropped to one side, weaving through boulders and mesquites. When it cleared a slight rise after a dry creek bed, the excavation site came into view. A dozen or so college-aged kids were milling about, several standing in a long, open trench that ran the far side. Next to it were three rectangular folding tables laden with spiral notebooks and rocks of various sizes. A woman was bent over one of the tables, holding a pencil and studying something with a magnifying glass. She was in her mid-60s and wore a white linen shirt with green cargo pants. On her head was a straw hat the size of a flying saucer. The woman didn't exude Indiana Jones but looked more the part than David Hansen. And since she was the only one not in their twenties, Jack assumed she was Dr. Michaels.

As he got closer, he noticed bits of straw and twine spread on the table she worked at. More notebooks sat piled to one side. But one was laid open in front of her, and she was sketching in it.

The woman heard him approach and straightened up from the table, laying her magnifying glass aside.

"Are you Dr. Catherine Michaels?"

She pushed tortoiseshell glasses higher on her nose. "I am," she said. "How can I help you?"

Her voice had an air of authority that Jack found reassuring. He hoped he had found someone who could answer his questions on archeology. He introduced himself and explained why he had come, mentioning Diego Torres's murder.

"I heard what happened," she said. "I never met the young man, but I was sorry to learn of his demise. Especially in such a violent manner." She frowned. "I don't know how I could possibly be of any help."

"Do you know David Hansen?"

There was a slight rise of her brows, and she took a moment to answer. "Only by reputation. I do not know him personally." It was a cool reaction.

"I thought maybe all the archeologists in the area would be affiliated with your center."

"Quite the contrary. We're different than a typical excavation. We're a research and education facility that's largely privately funded. Our goals at the Juno Center are long-term. We're interested in discovery and study like other archeologists, but we also strive for shared education and the sustainable preservation of our archeological sites."

"You said you know Hansen *by reputation*," he said. "What can you tell me about him."

She pinched her lips together before she answered. "I can only speak factually about what has been reported in the state record, which he has contributed surprisingly little to."

Jack got the impression she didn't think much of David Hansen. "What do you mean by 'reported in the state record'?"

"We are required to report any artifacts we excavate to the Texas Archeological Society. The artifacts are then transferred to repositories, where they are cataloged, stored, and made available to other researchers or institutions. Here at the Juno Center, we track everything added to the state record. And Mr. Hansen and his associates have contributed surprisingly little over the years. And nothing recently that I know of."

"Hansen mentioned to me that the work 'pays well.' Those were his exact words."

Dr. Michaels laughed quietly. "Even the most successful of us would hardly say we were in archeology for the money."

"Do you know about the bones they found on the Rose Ranch?"

"I heard about them. We all did. The discovery caused a bit of excitement in our circles. Until they were carbon dated, that is."

"Not old enough?"

"Mid-nineteenth century." She shook her head. "Not nearly old enough."

Jack thought a moment, glancing over the cluttered work-tables. "You said the center is privately funded. Is that how archeologists are usually paid?"

"No. As far as I know, we're the only ones in the area." She took off her glasses and rubbed them with a handker-chief. "Excavations are typically funded through state insti-tutions—either the state archeological society or a university. It's hardly lucrative work. Securing private funding, by which I mean securing private donations, is *very* difficult. We are suc-cessful at it because we're also an education center."

What David Hansen had told him now didn't make sense. How was Hansen motivated by money if he was being funded by the state?

Jack pointed to the scraps of twine spread on the table. "Is there a market for this stuff?"

"This *stuff,* as you call it, are remnants of ancient snares and fishing nets used by indigenous tribes that inhabited the area over a thousand years ago."

Jack was sorry he had come across as crass. He cleared his throat. "Would any of the artifacts you find be valuable?" She was confused by the question, so he elaborated. "Meaning, would any of these things, or maybe old tools or arrowheads you might find during an excavation, be worth anything on the private market? Would anyone be interested in buying it?"

"Ah, now I see what you mean." She thought a moment. "Yes. Ancient artifacts find their way into private auctions from time to time. Heritage Auctions in Dallas, for instance, will hold a natural history and antiquities auction now and then. However, I can't say that any Lower Pecos artifacts have ever been included in one. What we excavate out here mainly appeals to institutions of higher education and research. They're not quite as…aesthetic, I guess you would say. At least when compared to antiquities found elsewhere."

Jack considered the information. David Hansen would hardly be able to supplement his income by selling scraps of fishing nets and arrowheads.

Then Jack remembered the cave paintings. "What about the rock art?"

She thought about the question. "You mean, is there a market for the pictographs?"

Jack nodded.

She immediately shook her head. "Never. We document and study pictographs, but they remain where they're found. The pictographs of the Lower Pecos are world-class," she continued. "There's nothing else quite like them anywhere. They provide a window through time, a peek into the lives of the hunter-gatherer tribes that inhabited this area millennia ago. We have dated several pictographs as far back as four thousand years ago."

Dr. Michaels talked about the art with a reverence that intrigued him. "Would the paintings be more valuable than the other artifacts you find?"

"Infinitely more," she replied. "But your question is moot. Again, we never disturb them."

Jack had an idea. "Say someone did, though—theoretically speaking. If one was somehow removed, would you be able to sell it?"

She frowned, considering the question. "Probably not. Although there is a robust private market for ancient Egyptian and Asian artwork, as far as I know, there has never been a demand for Lower Pecos pictographs in the United States."

Jack looked south and squinted toward the southern horizon, studying the distant mountain range that resembled the sleeping woman.

He turned back to Dr. Michaels. "You say there's no market for it in the United States, but what about Mexico?"

"Well, I don't know." She stuck her glasses back on and blinked a few times. "Mexico could be a whole other story."

# CHAPTER 33

AFTER JACK LEFT the Juno Center, he dialed the number Dr. Catherine Michaels gave him for the Texas Archeological Society. After several rings, the call went straight to voicemail. Jack left his name, telephone number, and the reason for his call then hung up. But it was midday on Friday, and there was a good chance he wouldn't hear back until the following week.

Jack clicked the phone off and tossed it onto the passenger seat. At the intersection in Comstock, he turned east. David Hansen was up to no good, and Jack wasn't about to sit around waiting for a call back from a state bureaucrat.

According to Catherine Michaels, Hansen's excavations were unsuccessful, and Jack wondered why the state would continue to fund him. But the bigger question was, how could Hansen pay for two assistants? And pay for three while Diego Torres was alive?

Jack turned off the highway at the Moran ranch and drove through the gate. Twenty minutes later, he was on the highest part of the trail and began the descent.

Sherry and Bryan were wrapping something square with a blanket. It looked heavy. Sherry struggled to tuck the blanket under a corner as Bryan held the object steady. There were various tools and shovels scattered around them. A few feet away, the wheelbarrow was again laying on its side.

Sherry was the first to notice Jack and froze. When she

did, Bryan looked up and laid the object on the ground, carefully ensuring it was covered.

Jack wondered what it was they were hiding. "Can I give you a hand with that?"

"No," Bryan answered quickly. "We've got it."

Sherry stole a glance at the rock shelter where Jack suspected David Hansen was working.

"Is he up there?" Jack asked.

She nodded but remained silent. Something had the kids spooked.

As Jack hiked toward the cave, Hansen appeared at its entrance and saw him, then climbed down the ladder. When he turned around, he was frowning.

"You again," he said, pulling off work gloves.

"I've got a few more questions."

Hansen held up a hand. "I don't have time, Mr. ahh…"

"Martin," Jack said. "Jack Martin." It was the third time he had told Hansen his name, and his patience was wearing thin.

"Well, as I said, Mr. Martin, I don't have time."

"I need you to make time."

His glasses were caked with grime, but Jack could see his glare.

Hansen stepped away from the ladder. "I've been very patient with you, Mr. Martin," he said, rubbing his glasses with an equally dirty handkerchief. "It might not look like it to you, but I'm running a business here."

"That's what I wanted to ask you about."

Hansen stuck the handkerchief in his pocket. "What is it that you want to know?"

Jack turned and looked up at the rock shelter. "What exactly is it that you're looking for out here?"

Hansen hesitated before he answered. "What every archeologist is looking for—art, artifacts." His tone suggested Jack was an idiot for asking.

"So, what have you found so far?"

"Well…" Hansen cleared his throat. "What we all find in this area—old stuff left by the Indians that lived here thousands of years ago."

"Like what?" Jack watched him nervously shift his weight from one foot to the other.

Hansen struggled for a reply.

Jack didn't wait. "What's under the blanket?" he asked, jutting his chin down the mountain where Sherry and Bryan were watching.

Despite the heat, Hansen's face went white.

A half-hour later, Jack swung the truck back out onto the highway. He had spent decades in law enforcement and been involved in more than his share of unusual situations. He had conducted investigations in numerous unsavory locations. And he was no stranger to threats from hardened criminals. But a suspect kicking him off an archeological dig had been a first.

Hansen had pretended to call the sheriff. It had been a bluff, but Jack knew the conversation was over, so he left.

But the trip had been a success. Jack was now confident Hansen was a fraud.

Even after his research, Jack didn't know much about archeology. Still, he had learned enough to know that no legitimate archeologist would refer to the tribes that had inhabited the area thousands of years earlier as *Indians*.

# CHAPTER 34

JACK ROUNDED THE corner onto the street where Diego Torres had lived and hoped he wasn't too late. When he saw the house, he was relieved that Elena's white sedan wasn't there. He wanted to talk to Sabina and Miguel Torres alone, without interference from their over-protective daughter. Hopefully, he would get in and out before she got home.

Jack had learned that, before Diego's murder, he had worked for two disreputable employers. First Rooster Borden, then David Hansen. Both men were hiding something. And Jack suspected that one of them was somehow involved in Diego's murder.

Jack knocked on the door, and a woman answered. She was in her mid to late 60s, short and thin. She wore a flimsy cotton housedress and slippers. But her face was kind and radiated hints of the beauty she must have been in her youth.

She smiled up at him, and Jack introduced himself. "Are you Sabina Torres?"

"I am."

"I would like to ask you a few questions about your son, Diego."

The woman's smile faded.

"I'm trying to find out what happened to him," Jack assured her.

There was pain in her eyes. It took a moment, but she

reluctantly smiled again, then pulled the door open and invited Jack in.

The house was small but neat. Somewhere, a window unit hummed, keeping it cool. Jack could feel the vibration on the floorboards through his boots.

He had stepped directly into a tiny living room. The only furniture was a couch, a tattered recliner, and a hospital bed. There was a man in the bed, sleeping. Beyond him was a window where several hummingbirds were darting back and forth around a red plastic and glass feeder outside.

"This is my husband," Sabina said, moving to the bed. She bent toward the man and spoke softly. "Miguel, we have a visitor."

He stirred, then opened his eyes and smiled at his wife. Jack saw that there wasn't much left of the man, but the love in his eyes for his wife was still there.

Sabina took her husband's hand in her own. "We have a visitor, Miguel," she repeated.

It took a moment for it to register, and then the man turned and saw Jack. He grinned, exposing a mouth of nearly toothless gums. He nodded once, slowly. Despite his condition, Jack realized there was still dignity and kindness in the man.

"He wants to help us find out what happened to Diego," Sabina told him. There was hope in her voice.

The man gestured at the recliner with his hand.

"He would like for you to sit," Sabina said. She waited for Jack to move to the chair, then sat on the couch, facing them.

They spent the next several minutes talking about Diego. Sabina told Jack that he had been a good student and played the trumpet in the band. Her eyes lit up as she recalled the excitement of seeing him play halftime performances at the high school football games.

"And he was so handsome when he marched in the Fiesta

de Amistad Parade," she said, her eyes misting. "You should have seen him."

Miguel nodded constantly, agreeing with everything she said and likely reliving the fond memories.

Sabina talked of Diego's childhood, saying he had been an easy baby. "*Mi precioso bebé,*" she whispered, remembering. "He was always smiling."

Jack let her talk a while longer but knew there was more to Diego Torres's story. At some point, Diego had taken a wrong turn and chosen a darker path. And that was the side of the woman's son that Jack wanted to know more about.

Jack hated to interrupt Sabina's reminiscing, but he was almost out of time. Elena could be there any minute. Jack hoped she would stop by the church on her way home, giving him more time.

Jack asked about Rooster Borden. "I understand Diego worked for him after high school."

When he mentioned Borden's name, a shadow fell over the room. Miguel got agitated, twisting in his bed and trying to speak. Sabina went to him and laid a hand on his arm, and he settled back onto his pillows.

She turned her attention to Jack as she sat on the couch again. "We did not approve of Diego working for Mr. Borden," she said. "He is not a good man."

"Do you know what work Diego did for him? What was his job?"

"We do not know, and we do not care." There was an edge in her tone that hadn't been there before. "Diego stopped working for him and worked on a ranch instead."

"With the archeologist," Jack said.

Her face relaxed. "Yes. My Diego was so happy there."

Jack knew to tread lightly. He needed answers fast but didn't want to spook them. "What did he like about it?" he asked.

Sabina was animated as she talked. "Diego was hunting

for treasure. He would come home and tell us of the stories of Maximiliano."

"Maximiliano?"

"The emperor of Mexico. Diego was finding his treasure."

Jack sat erect, now on the edge of the recliner. "What treasure?"

"*El oro,*" Sabina said. Her eyes were dancing. "The gold!"

In her excitement, she slipped from English to Spanish, then back again. Jack sat still, letting her talk.

Tears welled in her eyes as she told him how Diego would come home brimming with excitement after days spent on the ranch. "He was going to buy us a house big enough for *Papi* to have his own room," she said. "He bought us the new TV."

Sabina pointed at the enormous flatscreen resting on an old dresser. So, someone was paying him. But Jack doubted the money came from David Hansen. There was only one other conclusion. Diego Torres had been on someone's payroll when he died. But whose?

Jack checked the time on his phone and knew he was risking the wrath of sister Elena. He thanked Sabina and Miguel for their time and assured them he would do his best to find out what had happened to their son.

As he was leaving, he noticed a small table against the front wall. A framed photograph of Diego in a tuxedo, probably a high school portrait, was surrounded by a handful of candles. Several were in tall, frosted vases bearing images of Catholic saints and the Virgin Mary.

In the few minutes Jack was there, he had developed a deep compassion and respect for Sabina and Miguel and was sorry so much tragedy had afflicted them.

In their suffering, they had shown a stranger kindness and hospitality. And now Jack was more determined than ever to find out what had happened to their son.

# CHAPTER 35

JACK'S NEXT STOP was to see Carter McConnell. He hoped Sheriff Gardner was right when he said Carter could give a more unbiased account of the long-running feud between the Roses and the Morans.

Carter's office was in an old two-story building across the street from the B&B. A dime store occupied the first floor. Above it, CARTER MCCONNELL, ATTORNEY-AT-LAW was painted in black letters on one of four large windows.

Upstairs, Jack found the door to Carter's office and stepped inside. The office was small and furnished with cheap furniture made to look expensive, factory-pressed wood masquerading as Victorian antiques. A desk and credenza faced the entrance. A fake palm set in a gold basket was shoved into a corner. Everything was trying too hard to give the illusion of success. Jack had seen the same tacky stuff in attorneys' offices many times before.

But it wasn't the furniture that surprised him. It was the giant elk mount hung on the far wall, staring down at him with lifeless glass eyes. He experienced a momentary flashback of being inside Alice Fremont's mansion outside Telluride months earlier. He hadn't liked all the dead animals staring at him then, and he didn't like this one doing it now.

No one was sitting at the reception desk, but Jack could hear Carter speaking Spanish in another room. The brief pauses between his statements indicated he was talking on the phone.

Jack sat in one of two matching chairs covered in polyester masquerading as silk positioned in front of the window.

A few minutes later, the door to the interior office swung open.

"Jack, this is a nice surprise. I thought I heard someone come in."

"I don't have an appointment."

Carter laughed, waving his hand dismissively. He checked the time on his watch. "I was about to call it a day, anyway. What brings you in?"

"I'd like to ask you a few questions about Frank Moran."

"And here I thought you might need some legal advice," he teased, gesturing with his arm. "Come on in."

Jack followed Carter into his private office, relieved he'd caught him in a talkative mood.

"Have a seat." He pointed to an empty chair in front of his desk. "Can I offer you some coffee?"

Jack sat down and rested a boot on his knee. "No, but thank you."

Carter walked to a counter at the back of the room. "It's a bad habit of mine," he said, filling a mug. He then reached into a small refrigerator and pulled out a carton of milk. "I drink it practically all day long."

Jack knew lots of Texans who drank their coffee by the gallon. But most of them took it black.

Carter sat down behind the desk, stirring the coffee with a spoon. The milk had turned it a light brown color. "So, what do you want to know about Frank Moran?"

"I've heard he's not well-liked by the Roses."

Carter whistled through his teeth. "That's an understatement," he said. "You've been talking to Uncle Roy."

"Him and Henry."

Carter tapped the spoon on the mug and rested it on a

coaster. "It's true Frank isn't a nice man, but he's not the devil my uncle makes him out to be."

"Henry doesn't like him either."

"That's because Thomas didn't."

"Henry told me about the ranch in Mexico. I wanted to hear your side of the story."

Carter spent the next several minutes talking about what had happened in Mexico, filling in a few details but leaving out the vitriol Jack had gotten from Henry and Roy. Clearly, Carter didn't feel the same animosity toward Moran. But then again, he wasn't a Rose, Jack reminded himself. Roy was his uncle by marriage.

When Carter finished talking, Jack took the opportunity to change the subject.

"What is your take on Thomas's death?"

Carter frowned, then took a sip of coffee and set the cup down on the desk. "It was a horrible accident. Why do you ask?"

"I'm trying to get a better idea about what happened."

"It's terrible. So senseless." He shook his head. "I felt so bad for Kate."

"I suppose Roy took it hard, too."

"He did. Uncle Roy and Thomas were very close. They have been since they were kids. They had coffee every Saturday morning like clockwork." Carter dropped his gaze to his hands and fell silent.

Jack gave him a moment. "How is he now?"

"As well as can be expected, I guess. Uncle Roy has always been a loner, but I worry about how Thomas being gone will affect him long-term. He needs to be around people." Carter paused a minute. "And he's getting older. I worry about him living way out there alone. I've tried every argument I can think of to get him to move into town, but he won't budge."

Jack agreed with him. A million things could go wrong

living on the ranch alone. He mentioned the rustlers. "Deputy Lynch thinks it's kids who are stealing the sheep."

Carter scoffed. "Bert doesn't know what he's talking about. From what I hear, they're hitting a different ranch every few nights." He shook his head. "That's not kids. It's too sophisticated an operation."

Carter leaned forward in his chair and laced his fingers together, then laid his hands on the desk. "Whoever's behind the theft has access to a black market somewhere. They're selling the sheep to *somebody*. And then there's the transportation issue. They're hauling them out of the county, at least. Probably out of the state."

"Mexico?"

Carter shook his head. "Smuggling livestock across the border is too difficult. And there's not enough money in sheep to justify the risk of getting caught."

Jack brought up Diego Torres next. "It seems Roy had gotten close to him."

"I think he had," Carter replied. "I only met him once. I gave him a ride to town when his car wouldn't start. But he seemed friendly enough. I can see why Uncle Roy enjoyed his company."

"The sheriff seems to think his murder was drug-related. Maybe even a cartel hit."

"It definitely was. Torres associated with the wrong people for years. I heard he was a drug dealer as well as a user."

Jack didn't share Carter's confidence that Diego's murder was connected to the cartels, but he let the subject drop.

"One last question," he said.

Carter lifted his hands from the table. "Of course."

"Have you ever heard of Maximiliano's treasure?"

Carter seemed surprised by the question. "Maximilian? The Emperor of Mexico?"

Jack nodded.

"It's a myth," Carter said, shaking his head dismissively. "Why?"

Jack wanted to know more. "What do you know about the story of his treasure?"

"Not much. Just that Maximilian was the Emperor of Mexico for a time, then fell out of power and was executed. There are several versions of the story, but the most popular one is that, before he died, he had the treasure smuggled out of the country and it disappeared somewhere in Texas. But it's just a myth. A local legend."

"Some people believe it?"

Carter shrugged. "I'm sure some do. There're crazies everywhere."

Jack thought of the Torreses' new television and Diego's promises to Sabina and Miguel. Was Diego expecting to earn enough money from running drugs to buy his parents a new house? Or was he on some ridiculous hunt for mythical treasure?

Jack sighed.

The case had just gotten more complicated.

# CHAPTER 36

ELENA TORRES ARRIVED home several minutes later than usual. She parked her car at the curb, grabbed the food from the deli where she worked off the passenger seat, and started up the sidewalk. The front door swung open as she fumbled through her purse for her keys.

"*Mija*, you missed him."

Her mother was beaming. Elena couldn't imagine what had her so excited.

"Missed who?"

Sabina was motioning for her to hurry inside.

"Missed who, *Mami*?" Elena asked again.

Sabina pulled her inside and shut the door, then grabbed her daughter's arm and dragged her close to her father's bed.

"We had a visitor, didn't we, Miguel?"

Miguel nodded complacently, obviously not as interested. He smiled at his youngest daughter, then turned his attention back to the hummingbirds feeding just outside the window.

"*Who was it, Mami?*" Elena asked again, setting the bags of food on the foot of the bed and growing impatient.

Sabina clasped her hands together at her chest. "A detective."

A detective? Had they found out who murdered Diego? But even if they had, why would her mother be so delighted by the news?

"The detective from the sheriff's office?" Elena asked.

"No," Sabina said, shaking her head. "A different one."

"Did he have news about Diego?"

"No."

Like her father, Elena was beginning to lose interest. She picked the bags up from the bed and started for the kitchen. "I brought dinner. I'll put it on plates, and you can tell me all about it."

"*Mija*, listen to me." Sabina followed her into the kitchen. "The detective," she said, touching Elena's arm. "I couldn't remember where but I knew I had seen him before. He is the detective from Colorado. The one we saw on the TV."

Elena drew in a breath and set the bags down on the counter. "Was he tall…with dark hair?" She brought her hand up to her shoulder, indicating the length of his hair. *And handsome?* she wanted to ask but didn't.

Sabina nodded. She had stars in her eyes and grinned even larger than before. "Yes. You remember. The same as the one on the TV."

"And in the magazine," Elena said quietly to herself. She had read the lengthy article about him in *Texas Monthly*. It was the man on the sidewalk, the one who had confronted her as she was leaving for work. Something about him had seemed familiar, but she never would have guessed the detective from the stories in the news would be in Del Rio.

Her skin suddenly felt clammy. What was he doing here? And why had he come to talk to her parents?

She tried remembering their brief conversation. He was friends with the people who owned the ranch where Diego died and wanted to find out what had happened. But why? Why did a detective from Colorado care about what had happened to her brother?

She suddenly felt her heart in her throat. "*Mami*, what did you tell him?"

Sabina took plates from the cabinet. "He was so nice, *Mija. Y muy guapo*," she said. Very handsome.

Elena took the dishes from her and set them down on the counter. "*Mami*, tell me everything you told him."

Sabina frowned, confused by her daughter's reaction. Under normal circumstances, Elena would have felt guilty about squelching her mother's joy. But there was no time for remorse.

Although Sabina was thrilled with the detective's visit, she had no idea how much devastation it could bring the family.

# CHAPTER 37

WHEN HE LEFT Carter's office, Jack drove straight to Jordan and Gretchen's on Griner Street. He had put off seeing her as long as he could. If he waited any longer, it would seem suspicious.

He parked the truck at the curb and looked up the long walk to the house, admiring the quaint Spanish-style home. He had stayed there several times through the years. But coming to see Gretchen while Jordan was out of town had butterflies swimming in his stomach.

He drew in a breath and got out of the truck. A glance at the house across the street reminded him that Henry said it belonged to Frank Moran.

Jack studied the large home closely. It was also a Spanish style, but on a grander scale and set closer to the street than Jordan and Gretchen's. Jack scanned the windows on both floors, but the curtains were all closed, shutting out the late-day sun—and the prying eyes of curious onlookers.

Jack was on the sidewalk when Gretchen opened the front door. "I was wondering when you would come by to see us." She smiled at him, causing Jack's heart to lurch.

Nothing had changed in the ten years since he had last seen her. Not her fiery auburn hair that fell just past her shoulders. Or her hazel eyes that danced when she was happy. Jack couldn't help remembering.

"How are you, Gretchen?" he asked, stepping onto the porch.

"I'm great." She hugged him. "It's so good to see you."

The feel of her arms around him took him back to college, but he pulled himself back to the present as he withdrew from her embrace and pushed the memories aside.

"Jordan told me you might be coming to town," she said. "I was hoping you'd stop by. Come in."

Jack followed her down the narrow hallway to the study that looked out over the backyard dotted with mature oak trees. The sun was going down, but it was still light. Two boys were rollerblading on the concrete patio.

"Is that Will and Patrick?" Jack asked, watching them race around outdoor furniture.

"It is."

Jack couldn't believe it. "They were babies the last time I saw them."

"They're twelve now," she said. "They grow up so fast." There was love and more than a hint of regret in her voice. She started for the back door. "I'll call them in to say hello."

"Leave them," Jack told her. "They're having too much fun."

Gretchen hesitated. "For now. But I want you to meet them before you leave."

"I'd like to."

A painting of a lone horseman hung on a side wall above Jordan's pine desk. The cowboy rode a fence line that separated two vast, dry pastures. Jack had never seen it before.

"It's by Peter Hurd," Gretchen said when she saw him looking. "Jordan says something about the cowboy reminds him of you."

Jack couldn't imagine why.

"He has your build," Gretchen said. "And he resembles you in the face."

Jack leaned in for a closer look. He could feel her presence behind him, studying the painting over his shoulder.

"But I think it's because he's alone," she said. "And looks like he wants to be."

Jack turned to look at her.

Gretchen was standing close and took a step back. "You can only see the side of his face," she said, pointing at the rider. "But you can tell he's happy."

Jack stared at her a moment. It would have been easy to start down the trail of "what ifs" and "if onlys."

He picked up a framed photograph from the desk. Two young men, not much older than boys, in maroon football uniforms and holding helmets, stood beside each other. One was resting his arm on the other's shoulder. They were smiling at the camera—two friends with the world by the tail. Jack remembered the day the photograph was taken. Media Day their senior season. He also remembered what happened in the weeks that followed. But he wouldn't let himself go there.

Jack set the photograph back down on the desk. "Henry said Frank Moran lives across the street."

"Unfortunately, he does."

"I've learned that the Roses don't like him."

"That's an understatement." She sat down in one of two club chairs, then gestured at the other for Jack to sit. "Let's just put it this way. Jordan canceled his subscription to the San Angelo paper because Frank was stealing it every morning. He reads it on his iPad now."

"You're kidding?" Jack remembered the newspaper Moran was reading at Benny's.

Gretchen laughed and shook her head. "I wish I was. Before daylight, he would sneak across the street in his robe and bare feet. Take it right off our sidewalk. He's probably stealing it from someone else now. That's the kind of man he is."

"A thief."

She nodded. "A thief indeed. You heard about the ranch in Mexico?"

"Henry told me. I'm surprised Jordan never did."

"Jordan doesn't like to talk about it."

Jack remembered how his old friend hated confrontation, except on the football field, where he could flip an internal switch and play with a fury that baffled their teammates.

Although Jack and Jordan had been roommates in the athletic dorm all five years, their arguments were mostly petty, and had never escalated to anything physical. Except once.

Jack pushed the memory from his mind.

"We've followed you in the news," Gretchen said, changing the subject. "You've had quite the adventures in Colorado."

"It's been an unusual couple of years," Jack admitted.

"And now you're here in Del Rio. And it's not for vacation, is it?"

There was a look of concern in her eyes that made him uncomfortable. Jack didn't know how much Jordan had told her.

They visited for several more minutes, and the boys came in from outside, laughing and sweating.

Gretchen introduced them to Jack, and they were immediately excited. They took turns finishing each other's sentences and laughing uproariously, repeating old stories Jordan had told them. Jack listened and laughed as the two recounted story after story of their days in college. Including a few that Jack would have preferred Jordan leave out.

On his way out, Jack vowed it wouldn't be another decade before he saw the boys again. He had thoroughly enjoyed the visit and hadn't realized how much he missed his old friend. He hoped Jordan would be home before it was time to head back to Colorado.

It was dark by the time he left. As Jack swung the truck from the curb, he saw Will and Patrick waving from the front porch and waved back. Their mother was smiling beside them.

Jack forced his attention to the road. But as he drove away, he couldn't help thinking of Gretchen and the boys and wondering what might have been. She had been Jack's before she was Jordan's. Then, his girlfriend and roommate met, and fate took over.

The clues had been subtle at first: unreturned phone calls and missing chunks of time. When it became painfully obvious what was happening, the sparks flew. When the dust settled, Jack realized what upset him more than losing his girl was the prospect of losing his best friend. Thankfully, time eventually healed their wounds.

Although Jack could still feel the scar tissue on his heart, seeing Gretchen so happy, he knew it had all turned out for the best. He had lived with regret for decades but now pushed it from his mind forever.

# CHAPTER 38

ROY SAT ALONE on the recliner in the living room, rolling a large gold coin between his fingers. The television was tuned into a national news program, but he wasn't watching. He was staring at the coin. And thinking.

The sun had gone down, and the rocky desert was slowly casting off the day's heat, a brief respite before the earth boiled again the next day.

Roy did the same thing every night. After dinner, he would retire to his chair and watch the evening news. His latest favorite was a weekly show on Coastal News Network hosted by a pretty blonde from Colorado named Georgia Glass.

But tonight, Roy was distracted. He switched off the television, stuck the coin in his pocket, then walked outside onto the porch and stared at a sky strewn with a million stars. Drawing in a deep breath that smelled of warm rock and sage, he searched the constellations he'd known since childhood. He had stared at the same sky thousands of times before and considered it an old friend.

Inside the house, the phone rang, shattering the peace. But Roy didn't move. He wasn't interested in talking to anyone. The people he cared about most were dead.

As he searched the depths of the Milky Way, he thought first of Evelyn and then Thomas. He stood with his hands in his pockets, staring into the heavens, remembering.

Life had never been easy, and Roy had never been one to complain, but the last month had dealt him more than his fair share of blows.

He squinted into the night, now looking and listening. His thoughts turned to the kid, and he felt remorse.

Roy had enjoyed the kid's company. He remembered the hours Diego sat with him on the porch, listening with rapt attention as Roy told his old stories. Remembering made Roy smile. He found the old coin in his pocket and pressed it to his palm with his fingers.

He thought of Diego's family. He had heard the kid's father was an invalid confined to a hospital bed. Life had to have been hard on the kid and his mother. After Diego's murder, it would have been harder on his mother still.

The goats appeared, and Roy gave them a few pats. "You girls stay here," he told them. He entered the house and came out holding an old tin coffee can. He continued to scan the darkness and listen to the night as he fed them handfuls of dry dog food he kept as a treat.

After a few minutes, he put the lid back on, set the can on the ground beside him, and stared out into the darkness again. He was able to make out the inky horizon miles away.

He thought about the land. It was empty and vast, and its stark beauty didn't appeal to everyone. But Roy loved it. He had never wanted to live anywhere else. He knew people called him a recluse or even a hermit, but he didn't care.

He spoke aloud softly. "There are none happy in the world but beings who enjoy freely a vast horizon," he said, quoting Henry David Thoreau.

After a lifetime on the ranch, he knew living in West Texas was tough and often unfair. Theirs was a harsh land settled by hard people, and it took a certain kind of person to live there.

He thought again of Diego.

Diego had been a tough kid who had overcome a dark

past. He should have had his whole life ahead of him and not died so young.

But Roy knew all too well how evil deeds often hurt the innocent.

# CHAPTER 39

It was Friday night. On a hunch, Jack stepped into Mesquite Creek Outfitters instead of heading to his room over the bar. His instincts paid off. Bryan and Sherry, covered in grit and dust, were having a drink at a back table.

Jack strolled over. "Hey guys."

The two looked up, surprised to see him, and Sherry nodded.

"I'm going to grab a drink. Mind if I join you?" He jerked a thumb at the bar.

They hesitated. Then Sherry said, "Sure."

If their glass weren't full and there wasn't a tray of food in front of them, Jack would have worried they'd run. But he was gambling they didn't make enough money to ditch beer and dinner untouched.

Jack ordered a beer from the girl with blue hair behind the register. Sapphire. He remembered.

He glanced around the bar, scanning faces. It was a lively crowd again, conversation and laughter drowning out the music. He liked the place.

With his beer in one hand, he pulled out an empty chair with the other and sat. "How's it going?" he asked. "Just get off work?"

Sherry tucked a loose strand of hair behind her ear. "We got off about an hour ago," she said.

"You regularly work till sundown?"

"Practically every day."

"Your boss seems tough."

Bryan blew air. "You can say that again. The guy's a jerk."

Jack took a swig of beer. "Then why work for him?"

"It pays," Bryan answered.

The same answer David Hansen had given him. But Jack knew the trio wasn't known for excavating much of anything. He was curious to learn where the money was coming from.

"How do you get a job in archeology?"

Bryan frowned. "You looking?"

Jack took a moment, then shrugged. "Maybe. But I don't have any training in it. Not like you guys."

They both laughed.

"We haven't had squat for training," Bryan said, wiping beer foam from his mouth with the back of his hand.

"Then how'd you get the job?"

"Only job qualifications are you have to be desperate enough and idiot enough to take it."

"What do you mean?" Jack asked.

"You gotta be able to put up with David."

"And the dirt and the heat," Sherry added.

"I figured you needed a degree in archeology. Or history, maybe."

Sherry laughed.

"Nah," Bryan said. "You don't need nothing like that."

So, there are no educational requirements and no training. Jack couldn't imagine the two being hired by a legitimate group like the Juno Center.

"What about your boss?" he asked. "He's probably got a degree from somewhere."

The kids shrugged.

Bryan pulled a pickle from the tray and stuck it in his mouth.

Jack was ready to steer the conversation to Diego Torres but didn't want to spook them. He had to be careful.

"What about the Torres kid? How'd he get hired?"

Sherry pulled a slice of cheese from the tray. "We met Diego here," she said.

"At Mesquite Creek?"

She nodded. "He was working as a busboy, and we got to know him. He was nice. He asked us a lot of questions about what we did and stuff. Then one night, he asked if he could go out there with us the next day. David didn't like the idea at first, but then said okay."

Bryan spoke next. "Believe it or not, Diego liked the work and started coming out a few days a week. He worked for free for a while, if you can imagine it. But then David started paying him."

"Did he and David get along?"

"Yeah, David loved him," Sherry said. "Told me and Bryan all the time what a better worker he was."

"Was he angry when Diego quit?"

"More like disappointed," Bryan said. "But he got over it."

"Why didn't Diego go with you when you moved to the Moran ranch?"

"Diego was delusional," Sherry said, shaking her head. "He started talking about looking for lost treasure. But the only things we pulled out of there were a couple of old tools and a few painted rocks." Bryan kicked her under the table, and she shrugged. "Whatever."

Jack thought he was finally getting somewhere with the conversation. "What happens to the stuff after you find it?"

Bryan and Sherry exchanged a nervous glance that seemed suspicious.

"We don't know," Sherry replied.

Bryan added, "That's none of our business."

Jack let the subject drop. The mention of treasure had him curious. "Did Diego ever mention Maximilian? He was emperor of Mexico a long time ago."

Sherry frowned as she swallowed a swig of beer. "Not that I remember."

Jack looked at Bryan, who was stuffing a slice of salami in his mouth.

Bryan shook his head. "I would have remembered it," he said. "That's a funny name."

"It's terrible Diego got murdered." Sherry looked genuinely sad. "But he shouldn't have stayed out there alone. It's dangerous. Sometimes there's people walking through who have crossed the border."

"And snakes," Bryan added.

Sherry shot him a look, annoyed by the interruption. "It's bad enough when we're all out there together. With the heat and the dirt and all. I don't know why anyone would do it alone."

Bryan set his empty beer glass down on the table. "Or do it at all." He burped. "I'm getting sick of it."

It was the opening Jack wanted. "At least tomorrow is Saturday," he said, fishing. "I'm sure you don't work weekends."

"Sometimes we do," Bryan answered. "But not if we can help it."

"We work some Saturdays," Sherry added. "But not tomorrow. We've worked the last two weeks straight."

The conversation had Jack wondering. David Hansen was a crook and involved in something dubious. But had he been involved in Diego Torres's murder?

"Sounds like a great boss," Jack said.

Bryan sneered. "Yeah, he's a real peach."

# CHAPTER 40

*Saturday, May 28*

THE MORNING SUN had broken the horizon, painting the land-scape a brooding shade of red.

Roy stood on the porch, watching a plume of dust come closer. Then Carter's truck came into view.

What did he want now? It was like having a babysitter. Much to Roy's chagrin, the kid had willingly slipped into the role after Evelyn died.

Roy would rather pay someone to bring him supplies from town instead of Carter fawning over him like he was some sort of geriatric patient with one foot already in the grave.

Roy was still plenty capable of taking care of himself. And although he avoided town like the plague, not wanting to be forced into small talk with some good-intentioned relic of his past, he could very well drive himself into Del Rio if he needed to.

The last time he'd had to was just over a year earlier when a rattler caught hold of his ankle on the porch. The dang thing had been sunning, pushed itself into the narrow crevice where the floor met the wall, and caught Roy as he stepped outside in his stocking feet after a nap.

Roy had lived on the ranch long enough to know better than to set foot outside without boots on. But a Border Patrol helicopter had been doing circles not far from the house, meaning there were illegals somewhere nearby on the ranch. Roy had gotten out of bed and gone outside to see how far away the commotion was when the rattler got him.

Although Carter had shown Roy how to call his doctors from his computer during the COVID pandemic, a snakebite wasn't an ailment to consult over Zoom. So he'd driven himself to the ER. And he could drive himself to town again if he had to.

But Carter refused to leave him alone and insisted on regularly checking in on him like Roy was a child. *Funny thing*, Roy thought, *how some folks had to be babied in their old age like they had been when they were toddlers.* But he'd be damned if he was going to be one of them. One way or another, he would get the kid off his back.

Roy fiddled with the coin in his pocket, watching Carter get out of the truck.

"It's the weekend, boy. Don't you have something better to do than to come all the way out here?"

Carter brushed his uncle's concern aside. "I came out for a cup of coffee," he said.

Roy realized it was Saturday morning. He thought of Thomas and the countless hours catching up during their weekly visits. He felt a stab of regret, remembering.

"Come inside then," Roy said, opening the screen door. "It's already too damn hot out here."

Carter led the way to the kitchen, poured a cup of coffee for himself, and then topped off the mug sitting half empty on the counter. He poured milk into his but left his uncle's black. "Let's sit in your study," he suggested.

It was where Thomas and Roy had their coffee every Saturday morning. It wasn't enough the kid played nursemaid. Now, he felt obligated to fill Thomas's shoes.

Roy hesitated.

"I need to talk to you," Carter said.

Roy relented, and they settled into the study. Carter took

one of the armchairs, and Roy sat in the other, setting a boot on the opposite knee. They set their coffees on the table between them.

"Now, what's all this about?" Roy asked. "I hope it's not about me moving into town again."

"Jack Martin came to see me."

"Did he?" Roy picked at the sole of his boot, pretending not to care. But Carter had his full attention.

"He asked me about Maximilian's treasure."

For several seconds, the room fell silent.

"What did you tell him?" Roy asked.

"I told him the truth. I told him it was a ridiculous story."

Roy said nothing, only nodded.

Carter leaned forward, placing his feet on the floor and resting his elbows on his thighs. "Uncle Roy, I've told you before. You can't go telling people about Maximilian. Especially not the stories of his lost treasure. Crazy talk like that will get you committed to the looney bin or attract wacko treasure hunters. Or both."

"I didn't say anything to Jack Martin about Maximilian's treasure." Carter eyed him skeptically, making Roy angry. "If Jack's asking about the gold, somebody else must have told him about it. But it sure as hell wasn't me."

"You told the kid the story."

"Who, Diego?" Roy asked. "How would you know that?"

"The time I gave him a ride back to town when his car broke down. He mentioned to me that you told him the ridiculous story about the treasure."

"What else did he say?"

Carter shook his head. "Nothing. But please, Uncle Roy, don't go telling anyone else. People are going to think you're crazy."

*They already do*, Roy thought. *What damn difference did it make?*

Roy was losing patience with his nephew, but Carter had

sense enough to change the subject. The two drank their coffee and discussed politics and the weather. Roy asked about the latest news on the border crises, and Carter filled him in on what his contacts in Border Patrol had told him.

Roy was relieved when his nephew finally left. Grudgingly, he appreciated Carter's concern, but it was starting to bug the hell out of him.

# CHAPTER 41

JACK WAS ON the road early and tired. He hadn't slept well the night before. A kaleidoscope of disturbing images had haunted his dreams. There were bloody snake tattoos, cactus, and rocks. Lots of rocks. Sabina and Miguel Torres had made a brief appearance, pleading for Jack to find out what had happened to their son. There were silhouettes of men chewing toothpicks. Roy was in the dream, too. He stood on his porch, pointing deep into the landscape without speaking, as if trying to communicate something telepathically. Did Roy know more than he was saying? Was there something out there that he wanted Jack to see? Or to find? The encounter had felt strangely like a warning.

The dream's meaning was elusive, frustrating him as he drove west out of town, his back to the rising sun.

Something Bryan or Sherry had said the night before was still rolling around in his mind. *"The only things we pulled out of there were old tools and a few painted rocks."*

Jack wanted to know more about the painted rocks. David Hansen was somehow making enough money to keep the trio in business. And Jack had a sneaking feeling he knew what that was.

Thirty minutes later, he turned off the highway onto Frank Moran's ranch and took the gravel spur to where Hansen's truck was parked the day before. But today, except for several dozen sheep grazing, Jack was alone.

He took the trail to the excavation site and found it much as it was before. The tools were all there, but the wheelbarrow was upright. But whatever the kids had been wrapping in a blanket was gone. He checked the trenches but didn't see anything but dirt. Then again, he didn't know what he was looking for.

He looked up the hill at the ladder propped against the cliff face and went closer. The ladder was old and rusted and missing the lowest rung. It might not hold, but he wanted to see the inside of the shelter. David Hansen had been working in it the day before and immediately descended the ladder and turned Jack away from it as they spoke. There was something up there Hansen didn't want him to see. And that's precisely why Jack was going up there.

He grabbed ahold of one side of the ladder and shook it. There was a lot of give—too much—but he stuck a boot on the first available rung and pulled his weight up anyway. He was a couple of feet off the ground and bounced several times, checking if it was sturdy. *Sturdy enough*, he thought and started climbing.

At the top, he hoisted himself onto the rocky ledge and came to his knees. He stood up, took several steps into the shelter, and couldn't believe what he saw.

Inside, the shelter was dark, still shadowed from the morning sun. But there was enough light to see that the walls were hideously scarred. Large chunks of them were missing. It looked as if someone had chiseled away several large sections of solid rock.

Jack used the flashlight on his phone and stepped further into the cave for a closer look. Deep grooves ran out vertically and horizontally from where the rock was missing, as if the section was scored before it was removed.

Next, Jack shined the light on the undisturbed parts of the shelter and saw the faint outline of a complex web of images. He leaned closer, and with his face only inches from the wall's surface, stepped sideways several feet, following the tangle of painted designs.

The art was primitive. There were crude depictions of animals and misshaped humans intertwined with a mishmash of lines and geometric shapes. It was like a strange ancient language that spoke from the past. But none of it made any sense to him.

Jack swept the light over the surrounding area, looking at the tools and equipment scattered about. There was a portable generator and two pneumatic hammers, along with an assortment of drills and chisels of various sizes. Gas cans were sitting next to the generator, and several others lay to the side. The smell of fuel was overwhelming.

These were demolition tools. And by the looks of the scarred rock, it was clear Hansen was defacing the shelter, stealing the ancient art.

Jack laid a hand on a jagged edge where the rock had been chiseled away and thought of Catherine Michaels at the Juno Center. He wondered what she would think of what David Hansen had done and suspected the destruction was akin to archeological blasphemy.

Jack thought of Diego Torres and his connection with Hansen. Had Diego known what was going on? Had he been a part of it? And when he didn't move to the Moran ranch with Hansen and the others, had it cost him his life?

# CHAPTER 42

"WHAT IN THE hell do you mean by *removed?*" Roy asked, frowning. "Like cut from the wall?"

Jack held up his hands. "I don't know that he did," he said, referring to David Hansen. "I'm just asking if you know anything about it."

Roy was upset by the question, but Jack suspected Roy knew more about what Hansen was up to than what he was admitting. And about why Diego Torres had stayed to work on his ranch instead of moving on like the others.

Roy pushed off the armchair and pulled a cigar from the humidor on his desk. "I've never heard of such a thing." He stuck the cigar in his mouth, gave it a couple of chews, then pulled it back out. "Those pictographs are thousands of years old."

"So he didn't ask you about removing them?"

"He didn't. And if he had've, I'd've said no."

Jack had twice been to the excavation site on Roy's land and hadn't noticed destruction like what he'd discovered on the Moran place. But the couple pictographs he had seen on Roy's were faded almost to obscurity and was probably one reason Hansen had moved on.

But something had kept Diego Torres there. Jack wondered what had held his interest. If it wasn't for the art or artifacts, why had he stayed?

Jack searched a moment for the answer. "Was Diego

interested in the old bones they found?" he asked and saw Roy flinch.

"Don't know why he would've been. Old bones aren't anything special out here. There are unmarked graves all over the place. Indians, Mexicans, drifters. Those bones could have belonged to any of them." He spoke through clenched teeth, the cigar back in his mouth. Something had him tense.

Jack thought of Catherine Michaels at the Juno Center. "I keep hearing they were from the mid-1800s."

"That's what I was told."

"What was the country like then?"

"Here on the ranch?"

Jack nodded. "And the area in general."

Roy spent the next fifteen minutes talking at length about the history of West Texas. From what Jack gathered, the Lower Pecos area of Texas was still wild when the bones were buried. There was no Val Verde County. And Del Rio was only a tiny settlement near the Rio Grande River. The town wasn't incorporated until 1911.

It was more information than Jack needed. None of it explained why Diego had continued working there. But Jack was sure Roy knew.

"Tell me more about Diego."

Roy frowned. "I already told you he was a good—"

"Kid," Jack finished for him impatiently. "You told me. I mean, what was he *doing* out there? What was he looking for? You had befriended him. Surely, he mentioned something about what he was doing."

Roy chewed the unlit cigar. He was stalling. After a few seconds, he pulled the cigar from his mouth and sighed. "He never said exactly. But I figured he was looking for the same stuff as before when Hansen was out there with him."

The conversation was going in circles. Roy Rose was a tough one to crack.

Jack shifted the conversation. "Did he ever mention being involved in anything illegal?"

"Drugs?" Roy was quick to shake his head. "He was no longer into that stuff."

"That's not what I meant. But since you brought it up, do you know if he was still in contact with his old boss, Rooster Borden?"

"He said he wasn't."

"And you believed him?"

"I sure as hell did, or I wouldn't have let him back on my place. Borden's a crook. Always has been."

From what Jack had learned of Borden, he had to agree.

He adjusted himself in the chair. It was time to get to the point of his visit. "Did Diego ever mention anything about selling artifacts?"

"Artifacts?"

"The stuff Hansen found on the ranch– the old tools and such. Did you ever hear about them selling any of it to private buyers instead of sending it to a museum?"

Roy thought a moment, then pointed to a framed assortment of arrowheads hanging on the wall of his study. Two dozen or so flint tips of various sizes were arranged in concentric circles against green felt. "I got these from an auction of Charles Goodnight's estate, the old trail driver. They're mostly Comanche and in near-mint condition. But there still weren't many of us bidding on them. I can't think of anyone but a museum being interested in the old stuff they dig up around here."

"What about the rock art?" Jack said. "That would be more valuable."

"The pictographs?"

Jack nodded.

"Selling them would likely be illegal."

"Selling a lot of stuff is illegal, but people do it all the time. Hansen could be selling the pictographs on the black market. Or maybe smuggling them into Mexico. My guess is that they'd be a lot more valuable than arrowheads."

Roy frowned, thinking. Then something registered in his eyes. He was about to say something but stopped.

"What is it?" Jack pressed.

"Nothing." Roy chomped on the cigar. Bits of wet tobacco had come to rest on his lower lip, and his face went flush.

Jack grew concerned. "Are you alright?"

"I'm fine." Roy waved a dismissive hand.

But he didn't look fine.

"Can I get you a glass of water?"

Roy shook his head. "Now you sound like my nephew," he said dismissively.

"Carter seems concerned about you."

"He needs to concern himself with his own business and keep his nose out of mine."

Jack hadn't come to talk about Carter. Roy was hiding something. He knew more than he was saying about Diego Torres and probably David Hansen. But there was something else Jack wanted to know.

"I heard you had coffee with Thomas every Saturday."

"I did."

"Do you have any idea what happened the morning he died?"

"I know as much as everyone else does. He fell into a crevice."

Jack watched him closely and went in for the kill. "Were you with Thomas when he died?"

Roy's face twitched once, then grew stone cold with anger.

# CHAPTER 43

HENRY'S NECK FELT like he laid on a frying pan. Except for a sliver of skin between the top of the gloves and the bottom of his shirt sleeves, his neck was the only part of his body exposed while he worked.

He bent over a section of pipe. It was a water line that ran from a windmill to a stock tank a quarter of a mile away.

It was Saturday, and most of his friends were probably sleeping in. But there were no holidays on the ranch. Every day was a workday. It didn't matter if it was a weekend or Christmas; if something needed fixing, it got done. And no repair was more critical than a busted water line in the scorching heat of summer.

The black polyethylene pipe that ran between the windmill and the tank could last a hundred years. You could drive a semi over it or have a herd of cattle stomp it, and the pipe would survive. But it couldn't withstand the stab of a knife.

The afternoon before, one of the men had noticed the dry tank. So, at first light, Henry had come out to investigate. He had thrown tools and a few spare parts into a backpack and hopped on the Honda motorcycle, then kicked the bike to life and set out across the ranch.

He began the search at the tank and followed the water line up the gentle slope toward the windmill until he found the problem. Someone had cut it open. It was what he had expected to find. It happened every year.

Water ran from the gouge in the pipe, soaking the ground around it before evaporating in the dry heat.

Henry turned toward the windmill and saw it was only a hundred yards away. He sighed. Running out of water was a common—and often deadly—problem for immigrants traversing the country unprepared. But if they had followed the line a little further, they could have drunk from the source and saved Henry the trouble of fixing it.

He cut the pipe on both sides of the break, laid the scrap aside, and then pushed a joining piece into both ends of the remaining sections. It was tedious work.

After a while, he stood up and stretched the kinks from his back, then pushed the hat off his forehead and wiped the sweat from his brow with the forearm of his shirt. He wore long sleeves despite the heat. Any rancher worth their salt knew not to wear short sleeves in summer. They'd had a ranch hand once who, despite the warnings, had tried. The guy didn't last a week. High-tailed it back to town, his forearms like lobster pincers.

But it was a lesson learned for the Roses. The guy had been the last inexperienced hand they'd hired.

Henry dug a couple of clamps out of the backpack and finished the patch, then got on the motorcycle and followed the water line the rest of the way to the windmill. The tall, spindly tower standing resolute in its harsh environs. A dozen of them were scattered across the ranch. One was over a century old. Each was a tiny miracle, a lifeline in a parched environment that would otherwise be uninhabitable.

But a single broken component and the whole system failed.

Henry shielded his eyes from the sun and watched the slender blades turning lazily in the hot breeze. His gaze slid to the tail and where, years ago, the factory had painted *Aermotor* on the side.

Next, he checked the pump rod, followed the discharge

pipeline, and looked into the storage tank, where there were clumps of green algae clinging to the sides and floating on the water's surface.

Everything looked fine.

Relieved, he killed the bike's engine, then strolled to the valve on the pump rod and opened it. He pulled off his hat and stuck his head under the rush of water, letting it cool his scalp.

After a few seconds, he shook his head, stuck his hat back on, and noticed a dust cloud in the distance. He squinted, watching the truck churn up dirt as it headed in the direction of the hacienda.

It was Jack.

Henry checked his phone but hadn't missed any calls. He wondered what Jack was doing. Maybe Kate had invited him to lunch. Henry hoped she had and that he would still be there when he got back to the house. Jack had been in town nearly a week, and Henry wanted answers. His hand drifted instinctively to the revolver holstered at his hip and rested there.

As he watched the truck travel the gravel road, he remembered the time Jordan had lobbied for hiring another inexperienced hand. They had been short of help on the ranch then, and Jack was out of a job. Henry knew Jack had been working in Houston for the FBI when he resigned because of something to do with a shooting.

Jordan wanted to help his old friend, saying Jack had gotten in a *bad way*. Henry wasn't sure what that meant but knew better than to push for an explanation. Despite Jordan's insistence that his old teammate was capable of the work, Henry had argued against it, citing the inexperienced hand with lobster pincer forearms. Ranch work is a different kind of job that takes a different kind of tough. And Henry knew damn well that most men couldn't handle it.

Jordan had been quick to point out past shortcomings

in Henry's character, citing several less-than-stellar moments from his past. Henry had argued it was ancient history and not relevant. But Jordan had prevailed. And Thomas was on the verge of offering Jack the job when they learned he was hired by a police department in Colorado.

A hawk screeched overhead, breaking Henry from his thoughts. He leaned over and spat dust from his mouth, then walked back to the bike.

He stood and watched the truck until it disappeared into the watery mirage on the horizon, then swung a leg over the bike and kicked it to life, shattering the peace with its mechanical screams.

Seeing Jack had dug up old feelings he had hoped to keep buried.

# CHAPTER 44

THE HACIENDA SAT basking in the sun, and something about it was mesmerizing. Jack studied the enormous house as he drove closer. It was beautiful. Like it had somehow emerged from the land instead being imposed upon it. The adobe walls were the same color as its desert surroundings. Everything was cast in a glorious shade of gold in the morning sun.

Jack saw Henry's truck at the barn, but the barn looked empty. He went to the house instead and used the massive bronze knocker on the front door.

"*Buenos dias, Señor Jack. Entra.*"

"Good morning, Ado," Jack said, stepping inside. "Is Henry here?"

"*No, perro Señora Kate es aquí.*"

Jack was disappointed. He wanted to ask Henry a few questions but thought maybe Kate could help.

"*Ella esta en la cocina.*" She is in the kitchen.

Kate was facing him when he entered the room. She stood behind a long counter with her hands deep in a giant bowl. She wore an apron, and her arms were red up to the elbows like they were covered in blood. Jack pulled up when he saw her and stared at them.

She laughed and waved him closer, her hand dripping with something crimson. "It's not what you think," she said, grinning. "I'm making prickly pear jelly."

"From the cactus?"

She nodded.

Jack breathed a sigh of relief and stepped closer. He stared down into the bowl and watched her push red fruit pulp through a sieve. There were dozens of whole fruits in a pot of water next to her and several more sitting dry on the counter. Their skins looked soft, like a red-purple velvet. Several empty Mason jars sat in neat rows to one side.

"The fruits are called tunas," she said. "I always thought that was a funny name for them."

"Where are the thorns?"

She thrust her chin toward the pot of water. "I wash them first, then scrub them clean. The thorns come right off." She pushed at the sieve, watching him. "But you didn't come here to talk about jelly, did you? I can see something is bothering you."

Kate was a wise woman. She reminded Jack of Judith Hadley back in Telluride. It would be futile trying to keep a secret from either of them.

"I was hoping to talk to Henry," he said.

"He's out checking a water line. But he should be back in time for lunch. How's the investigation going? Any idea who murdered that poor boy?"

Jack didn't want to admit that he was still baffled by it all. He took a moment to answer. "I'm still looking into it."

She was quiet, watching him, then set the sieve aside and picked up a wooden spoon lying next to the bowl.

Jack watched her stir the jelly. "Can I ask you something?"

"Of course you can."

He took a moment, unsure how to ask the questions he needed answered, and decided to work them in slowly. "Is it hard living out here?"

Kate set the spoon down and seemed lost in thought for a moment. There was a faraway look in her eyes. She washed and dried her hands, then turned back to him and sighed.

"I was a very young bride when I married Thomas and

came to Del Rio. I was a debutant from San Antonio. That sounds silly to me now, but that's what I was." She smiled, remembering. "And I had no idea what I was getting myself into."

Jack was quiet and let her talk, listening as her voice grew slow and gentle.

"Living out here did take some getting used to. But I grew to love it—both the land and the people. And now I can't imagine living anywhere else. It's my home. You don't have to be born somewhere for it to be home. It is a state of mind—a state of the heart." She was silent for a moment. "So, I guess the short answer to your question is *no*. It's not hard living out here. Don't get me wrong, it hasn't been easy, but I wouldn't be anywhere else. I wasn't born here, but I'll be buried here."

Jack shifted on his feet. Something about what she said affected him in a way he didn't understand.

"You'll have to excuse the ramblings of an old woman," she said with an easy laugh.

"What about now that Thomas…" Jack's voice trailed off.

She smiled despite her sadness. "It's difficult without Thomas. I loved him to pieces. Still do. He was my best friend for fifty years." The distant look was back. "But I have the boys. And life goes on, doesn't it?"

Jack wasn't sure how to answer. He steered the conversation closer to the reason for the visit. "You told me the other day that you thought Thomas might have been dehydrated or disoriented when he fell."

Kate stared at him a second. "Yes, that's what I said."

She was having doubts. Jack could see it in her eyes.

"Do you really believe that's what happened?" he asked.

She stood quiet. He watched her apron rise and fall with each breath and saw the thumb of her left hand move to her fourth finger, where her wedding ring would have been if it wasn't resting safely in a small dish next to the sink.

"Kate," Jack said gently, "Do you still think that's what happened to Thomas?"

He watched her face slowly harden, revealing the steel behind the velvet veneer.

Tears welled in her eyes, and she looked at him and said, "I don't know what to think anymore."

# CHAPTER 45

JACK WAS A mile outside Del Rio when an early model black truck with oversized tires and a grill guard sped past him, headed in the opposite direction. He recognized the driver immediately. Bert Lynch. He watched the truck grow smaller in the rearview mirror, then brought his attention back to the road. Jack had known a handful of crooked lawmen in his day and suspected Lynch was another.

It wasn't anything Jack could point to in particular, but several things bothered him. The crass manner in which Lynch had referred to Thomas's death. The way he spoke with shifty eyes and an exaggerated overconfidence that was particularly grating. But what bugged Jack the most was how often he showed up. Val Verde County was one of the largest counties in Texas, yet everywhere Jack turned, Lynch was there.

Jack had reached the outskirts of town and slowed the truck when he approached the Broken Arrow. The parking lot was full, but he was hungry and pulled in. If Rooster Borden was there, it would be a good excuse to question him again.

Jack stepped out of the truck and the heat from the gravel lot immediately radiated up his legs. His boots kicked up clouds of dust as he walked toward the entrance. Although the weather report on the radio had mentioned the possibility of a thunderstorm in the next several days, Jack looked up, shielding his eyes from the sun, and saw there wasn't a cloud in the sky.

He pulled open the door to the restaurant and felt a rush of cold air. When he stepped inside, conversations fell silent, and diners turned to stare. A group of cowboys sitting at the bar stared the longest. But after a few seconds, the talking started up again. It was the same reception as when he'd gone to Benny's to see Frank Moran. The local joints weren't used to seeing strangers.

He scanned the crowd and recognized one of the Hispanic kids he'd seen there before. The kid was shoveling food into his mouth, oblivious to his surroundings. There was a snake tattoo on his neck similar to the one Jack had seen in the photograph of Diego. Coincidence? He didn't think so.

Jack wondered where the kid's two companions were and scanned the room again. He saw Rooster Borden push open the kitchen door and drop a box of liquor on the bar, then exchange a few words with the cowboys, making them laugh. He disappeared into the kitchen again, and the cowboys resumed their conversation.

Everything appeared to be business as usual. But Jack was careful. He knew looks could be deceiving.

He started toward the kid with the tattoo when he noticed a man sitting alone at a corner table behind him. The man had his back to the wall, watching the room. Although he wore civilian clothes, Jack recognized him instantly and went over.

"Ochoa, isn't it?" Jack asked.

The man nodded once.

"I'm Jack—"

"Martin," Deputy Ochoa finished for him. "Yes, I remember." His poker face showed no emotion, and his tone was flat.

Jack took a chance. "Mind if I sit?"

Ochoa held his stare a moment, then gestured to the empty chair across the table.

Jack didn't like putting his back to the room. He glanced around at the kid with the tattoo and saw he was still eating, so he pulled out the chair and sat.

The deputy didn't look happy to see him.

A waitress appeared and asked if Jack wanted to order food.

"Just a glass of water."

She nodded, then looked nervously from him to Ochoa, sensing the tension between them. Jack wondered what had the deputy on edge. He didn't have to wait long for the answer.

When the woman was gone, Ochoa asked, "You're looking into the Torres murder, aren't you?"

"I'm here at the request of the Rose family." There was no sense in pulling the punch. "Some people think your boss was too quick to point his finger at the cartels."

Ochoa fell silent, his dark eyes boring into him. Insulting law enforcement was a risky move, but Jack wanted answers.

The deputy scanned the room again, settling for a moment on each exit before turning his attention back to Jack. He leaned across the table and dropped his voice. "I'm glad you're here."

It was the last response Jack expected. He didn't know what to say next, but Ochoa beat him to it.

"What have you found out?"

They spent the next several minutes talking about the facts of the case. Jack asked him about David Hansen, and Ochoa admitted he thought they had cut their interrogation of him short and that there was more to the archeologist's story than what they knew.

They talked a while longer on various subjects, lawman to lawman. Jack answered questions the deputy asked about his cases in Colorado. Ochoa was young, but he was knowledgeable, and Jack was impressed.

Then Jack asked about the rustling investigation, and Ochoa's demeanor changed. He went rigid and glanced again around the room. He was looking for someone.

Jack watched him carefully. "So the sheriff's got you guys working on a Saturday?"

"It's my day off," Ochoa said, shifting in his seat. Something about the question had bothered him. "But what did you mean by 'you guys'?"

"I passed Bert Lynch on the highway before I stopped in. He was in a hurry to get somewhere."

For a split second, the deputy's face stiffened. It was only a flicker of emotion but enough to reveal something was amiss.

Ochoa checked the time on his watch and stood up. "I need to get going," he said. "Which way did you say Bert was headed?"

"I didn't say, but he was headed west," Jack answered, confused by the change in the deputy's demeanor. "What about your lunch?"

Ochoa glanced down at the plate, then dug a twenty out of his pocket and tossed it onto the table. "You eat it," he said. "I'll catch you later."

Jack watched the deputy hurry from the room, then looked at the untouched food. Ochoa had said he wasn't working, but Jack wasn't buying it. The question was, what was he doing? And why had the mention of Lynch caused a near panic?

The restaurant had mostly cleared, but Jack angled his chair so his back was no longer to the room and noticed the kid with the tattoo was gone.

Jack glanced down at Ochoa's abandoned food. He was hungry. He considered it a moment, then pulled the plate across the table and picked at the food. Barbecue. It would have been better if it wasn't cold. Jack took a couple more bites and then pushed the plate aside.

He started to get up when the door to the kitchen swung open, and Rooster Borden appeared. Jack watched as he said something to the guy working behind the bar, then strolled to an empty table and sat.

A few seconds later, the bartender set a beer bottle on the table in front of him. Borden scooped it up without thanking him, and the man returned to the bar. Borden took a long draw, then glanced lazily around the nearly empty room until his eyes fell on Jack. He left the bottle on the table and came over.

"Food not to your liking?"

"It's not mine." Jack felt vulnerable sitting, but he didn't budge. To his relief, Borden pulled out a chair next to him and sat.

"I know what you're up to." Borden leaned closer. His eyes were slits.

"Well, that makes two of us."

The muscles in Borden's face hardened. "What are you doing here?"

Jack was feeling confident and decided to keep poking the bear. "I came in for lunch, but the guy before me obviously didn't think much of the food. So I'm having second thoughts."

Borden wasn't amused. "What do you want, Martin? I'm busy."

"I want to ask you some questions."

"I already answered your questions."

"I have more."

Borden sat with his jaw clenched, exposing the tendons in his neck.

"What do you know about Diego Torres's murder?"

"I already told you. Nothing."

"I don't believe you."

"That's your problem, not mine."

Jack noticed Borden's grip on the arm of the chair—his knuckles were white.

The bartender had disappeared. Except for a handful of diners and two women cleaning tables, the room had nearly emptied.

Jack squared his feet on the floor, ready for trouble. "Tell me about Thomas Rose."

Borden flinched but recovered quickly. "What about him?"

The two sat silent, staring at each other. Borden was hiding something.

Jack let him stew on the question a moment, then asked, "When was the last time you saw him?"

"A long time ago."

"Where were you the morning Thomas died?"

Borden's nostrils twitched. "Just who the hell do you think you are?" He came forward in his chair. "You come riding into town like John Wayne in *High Noon*, harassing law-abiding citizens. I'm sick and tired of seeing you in here. Consider yourself kicked out."

The conversation was over.

Jack stared a moment, then pushed his chair back and stood up. "I was just leaving."

"Convenient."

Borden followed him to the front, Jack aware of how close he was behind him and listening for any unusual movement. He wasn't about to let Borden jump him from behind.

At the door, Jack turned back. "Let's just get two things straight."

Borden crossed his arms over his chest.

"First, you haven't seen the last of me." Jack gave it time to sink in. "And second, John Wayne wasn't in *High Noon*. It was Gary Cooper."

Jack shoved open the door and let it fall closed behind him.

# CHAPTER 46

ROOSTER BORDEN STOOD at a window and watched through the blinds as Jack Martin got into his truck and pulled onto the highway. He turned away when the truck disappeared in the direction of town. Even then, Rooster worried the detective would pull a fast one and double back to case the Broken Arrow.

He sat down at an empty table with a view of the highway and waved over an employee who had come out from the kitchen. "Hector, get me a Corona."

"Yes, boss." The skinny twenty-something turned and hurried to the bar.

Rooster watched him walk away and caught a glimpse of the snake tattoo the kid had inked on his neck. *Damn idiots*, he thought. Advertising your drug-related gang affiliation for all the world to see.

Diego Torres had flaunted the same tattoo. Rooster shook his head, thinking about it. At least Torres had been smarter than most and probably would've had it removed had he lived long enough. From what Rooster heard, the kid was trying to go straight. But look what it got him. He was now dead.

Rooster leaned over, grabbed the cord to the blinds, and lifted them open. The lunch crowd had thinned considerably, clearing out the parking lot and giving him a view of the highway. If the detective came back, Rooster would see him.

But it wasn't only the detective from Colorado that had him nervous. Why had Ochoa been there? The deputy had worn plain clothes and could have been undercover. But if he thought Rooster hadn't recognized him, he would've been wrong. There wasn't a law enforcement officer in the county that Rooster didn't know by sight. He made sure of it. And each time one of them entered the restaurant, something inside him tensed, wondering how much cash was hidden in the freezer that day.

Hector returned with the bottle of beer. "Anything else, boss?"

Rooster waved him off, then sipped the Corona. He set the bottle on the table and leaned back in the chair, stretching his legs out in front of him. Glancing around the restaurant, he saw that the few remaining diners were finishing up. The staff was scrambling around cleaning the place.

Rooster was grateful for the brief lull in business before the early dinner crowd began showing up. In his wildest dreams, he wouldn't have guessed the place would have turned out to be such a success. Initially opened to launder drug proceeds, the restaurant quickly became a surprise hit with the locals. It made the business of money laundering more difficult.

Rooster knew he could simplify things, let the quality of the food slip, or shrink the waitstaff. But the success of the Broken Arrow was something he had grown proud of. Sometimes he felt it was the only bright light in his whole damn life.

He thought of his father and felt bile rise in his throat. He took a drink of Corona to wash it back down. Cletus Borden had been a notorious town drunk, and adept at only two things—downing whiskey and beating his only son. On his sixteenth birthday, Rooster had put a stop to the latter. He ran a finger over the lip of the bottle, remembering how he had pummeled his old man.

Memories of his mother weren't much better. She was trash with a proclivity for one-night stands. *Good riddance*, Rooster thought. He took a swig of beer and set the bottle down hard on the table.

He no longer let the memory of his parents rile him. What ate at him now were the local ranchers like the Roses, families he knew still looked down on him, even though he was now a successful businessman. Sure, they came in and ate his food and drank at his bar. But Rooster knew that, no matter how many acres he bought, they would never accept him into their circle.

The old ranching families lorded over the county like some landed gentry. Who did they think they were? Although Rooster would talk and laugh with them, gladly taking their money while they ate his food or drank at his bar, he secretly hated them.

He raised his hand and snapped to get Hector's attention. "Yes, boss."

"Bring me another," he said, raising the empty bottle. He then turned and looked out the window again.

*Damn law enforcement*, he thought. Even the good ones— the ones on his payroll—were a pain in the ass.

# CHAPTER 47

*Sunday, May 29*

SUNDAY MORNING, JACK parked across the street from Our Lady of the Holy Rosary Church and waited. He wasn't going inside but had a hunch Elena Torres would attend mass and hoped to catch her in a benevolent mood afterward.

He kept the truck running to keep the air on. The heat was already suffocating, and there wasn't a cloud in the sky. No sign of the impending rain that had the town hopeful.

He fidgeted with the radio, found several local stations, but shut it back off. He was restless, and the noise only made it worse.

His phone rang with a call from Henry, but Jack let it go to voicemail. It had been the same nearly every morning since he had arrived in town. Henry would call for an update, and Jack would have nothing to say. Kate invited him out to the ranch for lunch later, but he declined. He had been in Del Rio for almost a week and was frustrated he hadn't made more progress in his investigation.

After what felt like an eternity, the church doors opened. Two kids in robes propped them open and went back inside. Soon, the parishioners were spilling out.

Jack scanned the faces as dozens of people filed out but didn't see her. When the exodus slowed, he worried he'd struck out. That's when he saw her.

She wore a royal blue dress that fell just past her knees and high-heeled shoes. She looked beautiful.

She was with Sabina and another woman slightly older. Probably a sister. They looked similar and were both taller than their mother. Jack watched them visit with an elderly couple.

When they turned to go, Jack got out of the truck and crossed the street. He fell in behind them on the sidewalk. Mother and daughters were laughing and talking in Spanish.

Jack cleared his throat. "Elena."

The three stopped and turned back in unison. When Elena saw him, her face dropped.

Jack nodded at Sabina. "Señora Torres."

Sabina smiled shyly. "*Buenos días*, Señor Martin." She took the third woman's arm. "This is my daughter, Fernanda. You already know Elena."

Jack said hello to the sister, then turned to Elena. "Can I speak with you for a moment?"

The look on Elena's face revealed she wasn't glad to see him. Considering the request, she pressed her lips together, then turned to her mother and said something in Spanish. It was too fast for Jack to understand, but it sounded like she would see them at home later.

Sabina smiled at him. "*Adios, Señor* Martin. *Fue bueno verlo.*"

Jack nodded. "It was nice to see you, too," he replied.

Mother and daughter left, leaving Elena standing on the sidewalk. She frowned, and her olive skin flushed in anger. "You went to see them."

Jack held up a hand. "I couldn't get you to talk to me."

Her dark Latin eyes bored into him. "What is it that you want from me?"

"A few answers."

She stood staring at him.

Father Nieto stepped outside the sanctuary and lifted the doorstops when he saw them.

"Elena, is everything alright?" he called out to her. He eyed them suspiciously, making Jack uncomfortable.

"*Si, Padre. Todo está bien. Gracias.*" She turned to Jack. "It's hot. You can take me for a soda down the street. I'll give you ten minutes. No more."

They walked a block and a half to a corner grocery store. By the time they got there, Jack's shirt was soaked. Except for a bead of moisture across her lip, Elena hadn't broken a sweat. He didn't know how it was possible.

Inside the small store was a soda bar with a long counter and stools. A short Mexican man in a white coat and striped paper hat loaded ice cream into a glass cooler. The place was old and reminded Jack of the drug store in Baton Rouge he visited regularly with his grandfather as a kid.

Elena took one of the stools and ordered. "*Un* Dr. Pepper, *por favor. El está pagando.*" She turned to Jack. "I told him you're paying."

Jack straddled the stool next to her. "I heard." He caught a whiff of something floral. Her soap or perfume, he wasn't sure which. But it smelled good.

The man handed her the Dr. Pepper. It came in a tall bottle. Condensation clung to the side. Jack wasn't going to have one, but he changed his mind. It was early, but he was hot, and the soda looked good.

He ordered a second, and something about it amused her. He had broken the ice.

The man handed Jack a soda, and he took a drink.

Elena was watching him. "You talked to my parents." Her voice had an edge, but it was no longer anger.

"They're very nice."

"I know they are, but that's beside the point. I told you to leave them alone. They're in mourning."

"I had questions about your brother, and you've been avoiding me."

"You could have tried talking to my sister or one of my brothers and left my parents in peace."

"Diego didn't live with your sister or your brothers."

She took a drink of soda and set the bottle down, then crossed her arms in front of her. "You seem to know a lot about us."

"It's my job."

She hesitated. "I tried to learn more about you, too," she admitted. "I looked for you on Facebook."

Jack didn't say anything, and Elena laughed.

"I'm not surprised a man like you isn't on there. You don't seem the type to have a lot of friends." There was nothing malicious in the way she said it. Her finger circled the rim of the bottle as she spoke.

"Tell me about Diego," Jack said and saw the wind go out of her.

She sighed. "Diego was a good brother. And a good son to my parents. What else do you want to know?"

"Was he upset about anything before he died? Maybe nervous about something?"

She shook her head. "No. It was the opposite. He was happy for the first time in years. He was excited about what he was doing."

"Working on the ranch?"

Elena looked down into the bottle and shrugged. "He loved it out there."

"What was he doing?"

She hesitated long enough to reveal she was hiding something. "I don't know exactly."

"Your mother said he was looking for gold."

Her eyes flashed. "That is crazy talk she never should have mentioned." She took a moment. "Diego put ridiculous ideas in their head. He was a dreamer."

"Sabina mentioned it was Maximilian's gold."

Elena scoffed. "A gringo legend," she said. "They dream

of gold brought from Mexico and think it's hidden somewhere in Texas or New Mexico. It's a myth."

"Did Diego ever mention the legend to you?"

She sighed again. "He did. It was that old man out there who put the ideas into his head. But if it gave Diego joy the last days of his life…" she raised her bottle. "So be it." She took a sip.

"What old man?"

"The one who owns the ranch."

"Roy Rose?" Jack was fitting the pieces together. "Is that why Diego quit working for David Hansen? To hunt for gold?"

"Who?" Then she remembered. "Ah, the archeologist. Yes. The old man convinced him to stay when the archeologist left. He paid Diego to keep looking."

Roy Rose had employed Diego to look for gold. Jack had seen Roy twice, yet he hadn't mentioned it. Why? Jack decided to ask him.

But it didn't explain why Diego was murdered.

Jack worried his next question would upset her. He set his Dr. Pepper on the counter and swiveled the stool to face her. "Elena, was Diego still involved with drugs?"

She set the bottle down hard, causing the man behind the counter to turn and look.

Jack held up his hands at her. "I'm just trying to find out what happened to him."

Elena tensed, and several seconds of uncomfortable silence fell between them. Then her posture relaxed, and she sagged on the stool. "He *did* have a drug problem," she admitted. "But that was in his past."

"The rumor is he sold them for Rooster Borden."

Her eyes narrowed at the mention of Borden's name. "Yes, that's the rumor," she said. "Maybe he did, or maybe he didn't. But he quit that job a long time ago. He was working at a restaurant downtown."

"That's where he met Sherry and Bryan."

It took a moment for the names to register. "Those were the others working with the archeologist?"

Jack nodded.

"Yes. Diego met them and started going out where they worked. He did it for free for a while. It was like a new world had opened up to him. It interested him. He would come home and tell us about what they would find." She smiled, remembering. "He had never been so passionate about anything in his life. You should have seen him after they found a sandal." She laughed. "A sandal. Can you imagine? But he was so excited telling us it was over 2,000 years old."

"But Hansen wasn't paying him?"

"Not at first. He worked the first few weeks for free, then the archeologist started paying him. That's when he quit his job in town."

"But no more drugs?"

"No," Elena said emphatically. "I told you. He wasn't into drugs after he quit working for Mr. Borden. I would have known. Father Nieto would have known, too."

"The priest?"

"Yes," she said. "Father Nieto helped talk sense into Diego. He told him his way of life was against God's will and would destroy him."

"Do you think Diego's past is what got him killed?"

She shook her head. "No. He was done with all that."

"And done with Rooster Borden?"

"Especially done with him."

"What about the archeologist David Hansen. Did Diego get along with him?"

Elena was silent a moment. "For the most part, I think."

"What do you mean?"

"He never said exactly, but I got the feeling Diego didn't trust him."

Jack leaned forward. "Was he worried Hansen wouldn't pay him?"

"No, nothing like that." She thought about it, then chose her words carefully. "Diego didn't say exactly. But I got the feeling he was doing something that wasn't right."

"Something illegal?"

"Maybe."

"Did Diego tell anyone?"

"Like the police?" She laughed. "He would never have told them. Who would believe a kid who'd been a druggie?"

Jack remembered the scarred rock where the pictographs had been. "Did he mention anything about selling things they excavated?"

She frowned and shook her head. "No."

He twisted on the stool, squaring himself with the counter as he worked through the theory in his head.

Diego had already spent time in jail. If he was turning his life around, had he worried Hansen's scheme would send him back to prison?

Jack started to lift the Dr. Pepper but stopped. Had Diego confronted Hansen and gotten himself killed?

# CHAPTER 48

AFTER JACK MARTIN'S visit the day before, Roy spent the rest of the weekend stewing over something Jack said. He had spent hours trying to come up with an alternative theory, but it had been a futile effort. The pieces all fit, and it disturbed him.

The night was dark, a thin layer of clouds shrouding the light of the moon. Roy sat at the desk in the study, spinning the chamber of the pistol he kept loaded, just in case. It was an 1847 Walker Colt revolver once owned by Captain Augustus Jones of the Texas Rangers. Passed down through the family for generations, Roy had bought the pistol from its previous owner, a derelict cousin, when he'd gone broke.

He pulled a polishing cloth from a desk drawer and rubbed the barrel as he chomped on an unlit cigar. After a while, he brought the gun up and aimed it at a spot on the wall across the room. The pistol was old but in near pristine condition and could still kill a man if Roy needed it to.

He set the gun down gently on the desk and stuck the cloth in a drawer. It was dark out, but still too early for bed. Damn Jack Martin for having his mind racing.

Roy settled into one of the armchairs and rifled through the small stack of books he was reading, hoping one would be engaging enough to be a distraction. He chose the memoir of General George Custer. There were a hundred pages left to read, enough to keep him busy for a while. He set the other books aside.

A while later, Roy heard a clanging noise outside and got up and pushed the curtains aside. He searched the yard and saw nothing. But to be safe, he took the Colt from the desk and stepped onto the porch, leaving the lights off.

He squinted into the night, straining to hear over the drone of cicadas, then heard a rustling sound around the side of the house. He pivoted, lifting the revolver, his heart in his throat. The goats clambered onto the porch, and he relaxed, releasing the breath he'd been holding and lowering the gun to his side.

"I oughta shoot you two," Roy said, laying a hand on the goat nearest him and patting it. "Was that you making all that racket, Charlotte, old girl?" The second came closer. "Or you, Cecilia."

He straightened up, and the goats wandered off, bleating as they disappeared around the house.

Despite the darkness, the heat was stifling. It was past ten, but Roy knew sleep wouldn't come anytime soon. He couldn't get the conversation with Jack out of his mind.

There was a clanging sound again, and Roy realized it was the coffee can. He must have left it outside. Damn goats. He listened to them messing with it as he stared into the darkness, thinking.

Then, a name came to him.

Harlan Baker.

He should have thought of Harlan before.

Roy turned and went back into the house, letting the screen door slam shut behind him. In the study, he sat down at the desk and set the pistol aside. He pulled a creased leather-bound address book from the top drawer and rifled through it until he found the name he needed.

Roy reached for the telephone on the desk and dialed the

number. After several rings, someone answered on the other end.

"Harlan, it's Roy. I've got a problem that I want you to take care of for me."

# CHAPTER 49

*Monday, May 30*

"WHAT DO YOU know about Rooster Borden?"

Sheriff Gardner looked up at Jack and frowned. "What about him?"

"Funny, that was Borden's reply when I asked about Thomas Rose." Jack took an empty chair in front of the sheriff's desk and sat.

"You talked to Rooster?"

"I did."

"When?"

"Does it matter?"

Gardner suddenly looked like he could spit nails. "Listen, Jack. Stay away from Rooster. You're barking up the wrong tree. He's not involved with what happened to the Torres kid."

Jack had hit a nerve and wanted to know why. He had also done his research. "Rooster's your wife's cousin, isn't he?"

The sheriff's face went hard. He leaned over the desk. "And you think I'm telling you to stay away from him because of it?"

"Are you?"

"Now you're just pissing me off." Gardner sat back and crossed his forearms over his chest. "Yes. Rooster is my wife's cousin. *Third* cousin. But that doesn't mean crap around here.

Practically everyone in this town is related to each other in some way. It's a very small—and very old—community."

"So why shouldn't I talk to him?"

Gardner took in a deep breath, expanding his sizable chest even further, then let the breath out slowly. "Because he's not your guy. He has an alibi. He was closing up at the restaurant. A couple of his employees were there with him."

Jack thought of the guys Borden had working for him.

"Trust me on this one," Gardner said.

There was something in the way he said it. Jack let the subject drop for now.

"What about Roy Rose's alibi?"

"Home alone."

"And you believe him?"

"No reason not to."

"Did you do ballistics on his guns?"

"There was no need. Torres was shot with a .50 caliber round."

Jack whistled through his teeth. It was a huge bullet.

Gardner continued. "And Roy doesn't own anything that would fire that."

"You're sure?"

"I am. Roy has a small arsenal out there, but everything he's got is practically antique. I don't think he's bought a gun in fifty years."

"You'd know if he had?"

Gardner nodded and dropped his palms on the desk. "All federally licensed firearms dealers must conduct background checks for gun purchases. You know that already. But those applications are also run through my office."

"What about private sales?"

Gardner stared at him without answering. Jack had found a loophole.

"Spent casing?"

The sheriff shook his head. "We didn't find any. But

a round that size could have been shot from a mile in any direction. It would be harder than looking for a needle in a haystack."

Jack thought of the carnage he'd seen at the site of the murder. Although he hadn't seen photos, knowing it was a .50 caliber round, he could imagine the destruction. Probably put a hole in Diego the size of a tennis ball. He remembered the kind faces of Miguel and Sabina Torres, and something inside Jack stirred.

"What about the rustling case?" he asked. "Any progress in your investigation?"

Gardner rebuffed the question. For some reason, the sheriff was in a nasty mood, and Jack knew better than to push his luck.

He was walking out of the building when his cell phone rang. He pulled it from his pocket and checked the Caller ID.

"Mr. Martin, this is Gloria Herrera, lead coordinator with the Texas Archeological Society." Her tone was direct and to the point. "I received your voicemail this morning and have some information for you."

It was the callback Jack had been waiting for. Despite the heat, he stood outside the truck, not wanting to risk a drop in the connection when the call switched to Bluetooth. "Yes, ma'am. Thank you for returning my call."

"Of course." She said it like she was surprised failing to return it was an option. *Unusually diligent for a bureaucrat*, Jack thought.

She continued. "I recently ran the name of David Hansen through our system and saw that he's been working in Val Verde County. Although he hasn't reported any findings to us in almost a year."

"But he gets money from the state?"

"I'm sorry," she said. "I'm not at liberty to say."

"Please, Gloria."

"It's confidential."

Jack wasn't going to take no for an answer. "I need to understand exactly what David Hansen is doing. A former assistant of his was recently murdered." He could hear her draw in a sharp breath.

She cleared her throat. "His assistant?"

"Yes. A young man who'd been working for him was recently murdered where they had been excavating."

She took time to process the information. "Several months ago, the amount of Mr. Hansen's grant was reduced to the minimum. And now, even that is being reevaluated."

"Why?"

"I told you. He hasn't reported any new findings in almost a year," she said. "I double-checked this morning, and it's still the case."

"What about the landowner, Frank Moran?" Jack asked. "He mentioned getting checks from the state."

There was the sound of a computer mouse clicking on the other end of the call.

"Yes," she said. "I see here the state is currently leasing land owned by a Frank Moran. But that is being reevaluated as well."

"Because Hansen hasn't found anything?"

"That's correct." She hesitated.

But Jack knew Hansen *had* found something. Images of the scarred rock shelter came to mind. The web of lies was growing more complex. "How would someone go about selling the stuff they find out here?" he asked.

"The archeologists?"

"Yes."

"They wouldn't. That's not the way it works."

"Humor me, Ms. Herrera. What if one of them *did* want to sell something."

"Well…" she hesitated, thinking. "There's no formal secondary market for artifacts. We see items come up now and again in natural history auctions. And I'm sure things found by private citizens are occasionally sold or traded. But chances are, the volume of those sales is not significant, or we would have heard about them."

Jack wasn't so sure. Hansen was somehow making enough money to keep working and hire assistants. "Who's paying him to dig?" he wondered aloud.

There was silence on the other end of the line. "If Mr. Hansen currently has employees, he must have procured private funding."

*Private funding.* It made sense.

Jack thought of Roy paying Diego Torres to continue working on his ranch. He remembered the shelves of history books, the framed documents, and antique maps. Roy would be interested in the archeology for its historical value. But Hansen had moved on. Why would Roy be paying him?

Jack thought about Frank Moran, and things made more sense. "Thank you for the information, Gloria. You've been a huge help."

"I have to say," she continued, "I wish more ranchers cared about archeology and the importance of preserving our antiquities. Most don't care much at all about what we do. But listen to me ranting. I should be grateful that at least *two* of you have shown an interest in the last month. "

"Two?"

"Yes," she said. "I had a call from another rancher three or four weeks ago. As a matter of fact, I think he was also from Val Verde County. Quite a coincidence, don't you think?"

No, Jack didn't think so. He didn't believe in coincidences. And, although he wasn't a rancher, he didn't correct her. She had piqued his interest. "Do you remember why the other rancher called you?"

"Of course. He had similar questions as you. *What types of artifacts are typically excavated in the Lower Pecos region? Were these worth anything? Where might they be sold?* Questions like that."

Jack stood motionless. The implication hit him like a

locomotive. Had someone else suspected Hansen of theft? He felt a bead of sweat trickle down his back.

Herrera had called the man a rancher. Had it been Roy? Or Frank Moran? Or had she been mistaken again? Maybe the caller wasn't a rancher? Jack wondered if it had been Diego Torres.

"Do you remember the person's name?" he asked.

"Hold on a minute," Gloria said. "I have it here somewhere."

Jack heard the computer mouse clicking again and held his breath. Another rivulet of sweat snaked down his back while he waited.

"Here it is," she finally said. "The other rancher was Thomas Rose."

# CHAPTER 50

THOMAS ROSE HAD called the state archeological society with the same questions. Now Thomas Rose was dead. It had Jack's mind spinning.

Jack was on the highway, headed again for the ghost town of Juno. The information from Gloria Herrera had him thinking, and he wanted to run a few more questions by Dr. Catherine Michaels.

The sun was rising in his rearview mirror, and he could already feel the heat radiating up from the pavement through the truck's floorboard.

Thirty minutes later, on the outskirts of Comstock, Jack saw a woman walking a dog. She was on the gravel road from the highway to the barn with the Texas flag painted on its roof. The woman had red hair and wore denim shorts with boots. There was a sidearm strapped to her hip. Jack turned his attention back to the road. Life in the wilds of West Texas was a different kind of living.

A few minutes later, he pulled into the parking lot of the Juno Archeological Center. It was early, and the center was still closed. But Jack pulled at the door, and it opened, and he stepped inside.

Catherine Michaels was arranging items in a display case. "Well, hello again, Mr. Martin," she said, sliding the glass door shut.

"If you've got a minute," Jack said. "I'd like to ask you a few more questions."

"Of course. We can sit in here."

Jack followed her into a small conference room. At its center was a table that sat eight. Timelines and posters of ancient art lined the walls. She pulled out a rolling chair and indicated for Jack to do the same.

She wouldn't like what he would tell her, but there was no way of saying it subtly.

"David Hansen is removing pictographs and selling them."

She pursed her lips but looked more angry than surprised. "I expected as much after our last conversation. So I did some research." She tapped her fingers rapidly on the table as she talked. "I called a colleague at the Museo Nacional de Historia in Mexico City. He said, as far as he knows, they've never had any pictographs from the Lower Pecos in their collection. But he's heard rumors of objects being in private collections."

"Do you know whose?"

"He mentioned a few names like I should have known who they were, but I didn't. They were businessmen in Culiacan and Tijuana, I think."

Jack knew the cities. "Cartel bosses."

She stopped tapping her fingers. "Well, I wouldn't know anything about that," she said. "But if David Hansen is defacing our treasures, he needs to be reported. I'll call the state—"

She started to rise, but Jack reached across the table, and she stopped. "Not yet," he said.

She sat back down slowly, and Jack held her stare.

"Hansen may be guilty of a lot more than stealing rock art," he said. "If we flush him out now, he could get spooked and run. I need a little time. *Then* you can report him to who-ever you want."

She looked doubtful, and Jack knew that she was debating what to do next. She began drumming her fingers again, and Jack settled back in the chair.

"Okay," she said. "I'll wait. But not for long. We have to stop him."

Jack nodded slowly. "We will," he said. "But first, I need your help."

# CHAPTER 51

CATHERINE MICHAELS SPENT the next twenty minutes answering Jack's questions and punching holes in several theories.

She insisted no one at the state agency would help Hansen fence stolen pictographs. There was no market for them in the United States. American museums wouldn't touch them, and European museums already had plenty of antiquities of their own.

After Jack left, he ran through what he knew as he drove south toward Comstock. The art was likely being smuggled into Mexico. And almost certainly being fenced to corrupt businessmen or high-ranking members of the cartels, men obsessed with the perception of power and success.

Jack had seen photographs of many of their compounds during his time with the FBI. Some were massive haciendas. Others were more contemporary, modern-looking compounds. But all of them had one thing in common—breathtaking art.

Jack had seen photos of Picassos and Chagalls, even Warhols hanging in the homes of drug lords. There were antiquities and works by Asian artists. After the arrest of El Chapo, authorities confiscated a hippopotamus skull plated in gold displayed in one of his safe houses.

Despite their proclivity to violence, the cartel bosses were an unusually patriotic bunch. Many had collections of antique

Spanish and Mexican weapons. Jack had even seen engraved silver swords encrusted with jewels.

They had a particular affinity for antique firearms. One boss in Tijuana had a gold-plated pistol once owned by the famous bandit Pancho Villa.

But what Jack remembered most were the Mayan and Aztec artifacts, the ancient ceramics and objects carved from stone. Alongside them, the stolen pictographs would look right at home.

Catherine Michaels had shown Jack a map of the Lower Pecos Canyonlands where the indigenous tribes had lived. The area extended from southwest Texas well into northern Mexico. "Much of the land is inaccessible," she had said, "but we've heard rumors there aren't many pictographs left on the Mexican side. It makes our preservation work in Texas all the more vital."

There was a black market in Mexico for practically everything. The drug lords would likely see the Lower Pecos artifacts as Mexican and thus their heritage.

But how were the pictographs getting into the hands of the cartels? It was the question Catherine Michaels couldn't answer. The logistics would be sophisticated. Smuggling it across the border would be only the first step. There would be facilitators to manage transportation and storage and others to handle sales.

Jack suspected that David Hansen wasn't sophisticated enough to fence goods to the cartels. Someone was helping him.

If Diego Torres was involved, could it have gotten him killed? But even with connections in Mexico, Diego couldn't have done it alone. Jack thought of Rooster Borden. From his drug smuggling activities, he would have plenty of connections. Borden would be more than capable of moving pictographs.

Jack wondered next about Roy. Was Roy also involved in the scheme? Something about their last visit didn't feel right.

The idea that Frank Moran was entangled in the crime was a given. Moran could be funding the whole operation. And since he owned thousands of acres of Mexican land, he would likely have adequate connections for smuggling.

At the intersection in Comstock, Jack hung a left on Highway 90 and almost immediately saw Hansen's truck in the parking lot of the local diner.

Jack parked next to Hansen's Ford, got out, and peered into the truck's cab and then the camper. No pictograph. Jack hadn't expected to see one, but it was worth a shot.

The notebook with the word *Inventory* scrawled across the cover was resting again on the dash. Jack glanced over his shoulder and tried the driver's side door, but found it locked. He wanted a glimpse at Hansen's "inventory," most of it now probably across the border.

He started across the parking lot for The J and P, a restaurant he knew well. It was a local joint that served area ranchers and people traveling cross-country. Although it had been years since Jack had been there, he wasn't there to eat. It was time to confront a crook.

And Jack had an idea.

He strolled over to Hansen's table. It was early, but he was eating a burger.

*"A quién le vendes las cosas en* México?" Jack asked. Who are you selling the stuff to in Mexico?

Hansen looked up and knit his brows together. "You again?"

Jack repeated the question.

"You'll have to speak English. I don't talk Mexican."

Hansen had just confirmed Jack's suspicions. Hansen was a two-bit thief incapable of handling the logistics of smuggling ancient art into Mexico. And he sure as hell wasn't responsible for selling it to members of the cartels. The question now was, who was helping him?

"Who's trafficking the stuff for you?"

"What are you talking about?"

Jack pulled out a chair and sat.

"Help yourself," Hansen said. "You want my breakfast, too?" He slid his plate over, then pulled it back.

"I know what you're doing."

Hansen dipped a French fry in ketchup. "I'm eating," he said. "And you're interrupting my meal." He stuck the fry in his mouth.

A waitress approached the table and offered Jack a menu. He shook his head and waited for her to leave. "You're cutting the pictographs from the shelters and selling them into Mexico."

Hansen blinked, and food caught in his throat. He coughed, pulled a napkin from his lap, and wiped his mouth. "I don't know what you're talking about, but I'd like you to leave. I'd like to finish my meal in peace."

"You can drop the charade," Jack replied. "I've seen the evidence for myself, and there are three things I want answered."

Hansen glared at him with a mixture of anger and fear in his eyes.

Jack continued. "I want to know who's funding your smuggling operation."

"I-I don't know what—"

"And I want to know if Diego Torres was a part of the operation. If it's what got him killed."

"Killed?" Hansen looked stricken. He fidgeted in his chair. "Now hold on there a minute. I hadn't seen Diego in months. I don't know anything about what happened to him. And I *sure* as hell didn't have anything to do with it."

Jack stared longer without speaking. "I know Frank Moran is involved."

Hansen blinked. "You don't have proof for anything you're saying."

"I do." Jack didn't tell him about the photographs he'd taken with his cell phone when he snuck out to Moran's place. "Now tell me again, when did you last speak to Diego?"

Hansen's face went flush. "What you're accusing me of is slander. And I'm going to take it up with my attorney."

"Nice bluff," Jack said. "But I'm not buying it. However, a call to your attorney is probably a good idea. When this is over, you're going to need their help. Now, if you won't tell me about Diego, tell me about Thomas Rose."

Hansen's jaw fell open, and Jack knew he had the little man's back to the wall. He was exactly where Jack wanted him. Jack knew that when criminals are scared, they make mistakes.

Jack rose from his chair and slid it back under the table. "I'm onto you, Hansen. And neither of us will rest until I nail your lousy hide to the wall."

Jack turned and left and felt Hansen's stare as he made his way to the door.

In the parking lot, he tried the passenger side door of Hansen's truck. Like the driver's side, it was locked, and Jack was disappointed. He wanted the notebook on the dash. It could have names, dates, or even phone numbers in it. Maybe even something tying Hansen to the murder of Diego Torres. Or to Thomas Rose.

There was a decent-sized rock at Jack's feet. He bent and picked it up just as the door to The J and P swung open. Jack nodded to the two cowboys who stepped out, then discretely let the rock fall to the ground at his feet.

He was fuming by the time he got back on the road. David Hansen was defacing ancient art and involved in its smuggling. But what ate at Jack's gut worse was wondering whether or not Hansen was also a murderer.

# CHAPTER 52

FRANK MORAN SLAMMED his sweaty fist on the desk. "Calm yourself down," he growled into the phone. "If you don't pull yourself together, you'll make a mistake. A *grave* mistake."

He could hear David Hansen breathing shallowly and fast on the other end of the line.

"Did he mention anyone else by name?" Moran asked.

"Like who?"

"Like anyone, you idiot."

"No."

"And you didn't tell him anything? Let something slip you shouldn't have?"

"No."

Although Hansen hadn't hesitated, it wasn't reassuring. David Hansen was an amateur. A half-witted fool. It was a mistake to trust him with as much information as they had.

"Alright," Moran said. "Let me think."

Things were complicated. Moran was taking money from the state to let the idiot archeologist dig on his land, and he'd been making a small fortune secretly selling the stuff into Mexico. If the state got wind of them smuggling pictographs, things would go south quickly. Moran would be sued. Or worse, he could go to jail. But he wasn't going to let that happen.

"What are we going to do, Frank?"

"Calm down and let me think."

Moran picked up a silver letter opener from his desk with a horse head mounted at one end. He had inherited it from his father. He ran a meaty finger over the blade's edge, wondering what the old man would do.

Jack Martin was trouble, a burr under Moran's saddle he needed to dispose of. Hansen must have let something slip. How else would Martin know he was involved? But more importantly, how much did Martin know?

*But I'm not in this alone*, Moran reminded himself. There was someone else who had even more to lose, someone who was going to take care of this problem for the both of them. Or else.

Moran studied the horse head on the end of the letter opener and pushed his thumb against the blade's tip, drawing a bead of blood before he let up the pressure.

He heard Hansen take in and release a ragged breath and it reminded him that the idiot was still on the line.

"Frank?" Hansen repeated.

"Shut up."

"What are we going to do?"

Moran slammed the letter opener down on the desk. "You just get your ass back out there and finish the job," he ordered. "Jack Martin is about to be someone else's problem."

# CHAPTER 53

JACK DECIDED HE wouldn't put Henry off any longer. But it wasn't answers Jack had for him, it was questions.

Kate answered the door. "Good morning, Jack. Come in."

"Thank you." Jack wiped his boots on the mat and stepped inside. "I was hoping to talk to Henry if he's around."

"Yes, he's——"

"Where's Ado?" Henry interrupted, stepping into the foyer and rubbing his head with a towel. His hair was wet like he'd just showered. "I'm missing my favorite work shirt."

"We have company," Kate said.

Henry looked up and saw Jack. "Well, it's about damn time."

Kate answered his question. "Ado went to San Angelo to visit her mother. She'll be back tomorrow."

"Flying around on her broomstick again."

"Henry."

"Just kidding." He laughed and kissed the top of his mother's head, then tossed the towel over a chair and tucked his shirttail in his jeans. "What are you doing here, Jack?"

"I'll leave you boys alone," Kate said.

Henry waited for her to leave the room. "I need a beer to clear my head. You?"

"No. It's early."

Henry pulled his phone from his pocket and checked the time. "But it's not *too* early."

Jack followed him into the living room and to a walk-in bar. Henry pulled a bottle of Tecate from an under-counter refrigerator and tipped it in Jack's direction. "Sure you don't want one?"

"No, but thank you."

Henry popped off the bottle cap and ran his fingers through his wet hair. He was nervous and trying to hide it.

Jack watched him take a draw of the beer. "Do you usually take a shower after lunch?"

"I do when I get sheep shit kicked all over me." He wiped his mouth with his shirt sleeve. "You don't return my calls."

"Sorry, I've been busy."

Henry set the bottle down. "I'm tired of being leashed like a dog. Odell has warned me not to cause any trouble, but nobody is telling me anything. Hell, you won't even return my calls."

"Odell's right, Henry. If you go off half-cocked looking for revenge, you won't be helping anybody. And you'll probably end up like Diego Torres. How's that going to help your mother?"

Henry stood tense.

"I don't have answers for you yet," Jack said. "I'm getting close, but I need your help."

The muscles in Henry's face relaxed. "I've been waiting for you to ask," he said. "What do you want me to do?"

"Don't *do* anything," Jack told him. "But I've got some questions."

"Questions? And here I thought you needed me to bust a confession out of somebody." Henry drained the rest of the beer and set the empty bottle on the bar. "Alright," he sighed. "I can answer your damn questions. But mind if we head outside first? I've got to shoe a horse."

Henry took a straw cowboy hat from a hook at the back

door and stuck it on. He then looked at Jack and shook his head. "As long as I've known you, Martin, you've never had a hat. You're going to fry in this sun." He grabbed a second one and tossed it to him. "Keep it."

As they walked toward the barn, a warm breeze stirred the dust at their feet. Halfway there, Henry stopped. He shielded his eyes from the sun and squinted at the northern horizon. "Storm's coming."

Jack turned to look. The sky was blue, with only a few wisps of clouds floating in the distance. He hadn't seen any evidence of the coming rain that had the whole town talking. He was beginning to suspect that people living in West Texas had a sixth sense about forecasting the weather. He would wait and see before he passed judgment.

"You know," Henry said, still looking at the sky. "Out here, we get roughly fifteen inches of rain a year. And I think tomorrow's gonna be the day we get it."

He smiled, slapped Jack on the shoulder, and the two started again for the barn. "Now, what questions do you have for me?"

"I want to ask you about Roy."

Henry stopped again, sending a small cloud of dust swirling at his feet. "Roy? Why?"

There was no easy way into the conversation. "He's tied directly to both deaths."

"Whose?"

"Diego Torres's and your dad's."

Henry shook his head and frowned. "Two completely different situations. Dad had an accident. And the Torres kid was murdered."

"Roy's hiding something. And he doesn't have an alibi for either death."

Henry stuck a finger in Jack's chest. "You just stop right there. This conversation is way out of line. There's no way

Uncle Roy had anything to do with Dad's death. It was an *accident*."

"Are you sure?"

Henry stared at him, and Jack could see it in his eyes. Like Kate, he had doubts Thomas's death was an accident.

"I've got evidence David Hansen is smuggling rock art into Mexico."

"The archeologist?"

Jack nodded. "Diego Torres worked for him before he was killed." He let it sink in. "On Roy's place."

Henry screwed up his face. "Shit, Jack. You sure know how to ruin a guy's day."

"Sorry."

"No, you're not." He poked Jack in the chest again. "And you listen here. Family is family. You might not know anything about that, but I do." It was a hit below the belt, but Jack let it go. "And there's no way Uncle Roy had *anything* to do with Dad's death. It was an accident. Pure and simple."

Henry shook his head and started for the barn again. A bay mare was tied to a hitching post, waiting for him. He said something in Spanish to one of the ranch hands, who quickly disappeared inside. Then Henry stood with his hand on the mare's back, his chest rising and falling heavy with each breath.

"What other questions do you have for me?" he asked. "Because I want you to find who killed the Torres kid and who has been stealing my sheep. And do it quick. Or I'm going to start looking for them myself again. And it won't be pretty when I find them."

Jack was running out of time. Henry was on the verge of doing something rash. It was like holding a bull in the chute. You could only do it for so long before you had to open the gate.

"I'm getting close, Henry," Jack said. "Just give me a little more time."

The ranch hand returned and set leather chaps and a worn-out canvas bag at Henry's feet. "*Aquí estás, patron.*"

"*Gracias.*" Henry buckled on the chaps, then dug into the bag and came out with a curved knife. He ran a hand down the mare's backside, then lifted a rear hoof, stuck it between his knees, and started digging, cleaning the underside.

"David Hansen has been cutting pictographs from the rock shelters."

"Not my business."

"He's smuggling it into Mexico and selling it."

"Still not my business." Henry continued to clean the hoof.

"It might be," Jack said. "It could be what got Diego Torres murdered."

Henry tossed the knife into the bag and stood up. "How does that make it my business?"

"Hansen had been excavating on Roy's place. But he's not sophisticated enough to smuggle and sell the stuff on his own. The guy can't even speak Spanish." Jack looked away momentarily, deciding how to say what he needed to next. "Someone is funding the smuggling ring and getting the stuff across the border for him."

"And you think that someone is Uncle Roy?"

"I'm just trying to connect the dots."

"Well, it's not him."

Henry wasn't budging. It was time to change the subject. "I've got another question."

"Lucky me." Henry bent to the bag and took out a set of clippers that looked like an instrument of torture. He pulled the horse's hoof up again, settling it in the leather chaps between his knees.

"What are those?" Jack asked.

"Pincers."

He winced as Henry clipped off part of the side of the hoof, expecting the horse to jump, but it didn't move.

"Have you heard the story of Maximilian's treasure?"

"What?" Henry stopped clipping.

Jack repeated the question.

Henry shook his head and chuckled. He began clipping again. "Yeah, I've heard it. It's an old wives' tale."

"You don't believe it."

"No, I don't."

"I think Diego Torres did," Jack replied. "I think he was looking for it when he was murdered."

"On Roy's place?" Henry laughed again. "If only we were that lucky." He shook his head at the absurdity of it. He worked some more, then said, "If you want a more educated account of Maximilian's story, you should ask Gretchen."

"Gretchen?"

"She's a history professor at the junior college."

A professor? Jack knew she was a teacher but always imagined her in a classroom full of kindergarteners. Not lecturing to college students.

"I might have to do that," he said, still surprised. He thought for a moment. "Just one more thing."

"Yeah, what is it?" Henry asked without looking up.

"If you were going to smuggle something into Mexico—

"Here we go again."

"Just hear me out."

Henry sighed, then pulled the largest file Jack had ever seen from the bag and began working it against the horse's hoof. "Alright," he said. "If I was going to smuggle something into Mexico, what?"

"How would you do it?"

"What do you mean?"

"You'd need help of some kind, right? Somebody to handle logistics and transportation."

"I guess."

"Del Rio is a small town. Who would you go to for help?"

Henry stopped filing a moment, and Jack thought he saw his body tense.

"What is it?" Jack asked.

"Nothing." He filed at the hoof again. "I just remembered something I need to do tomorrow."

Jack watched Henry's back and shoulders work faster than before. "I guess I'll get going."

Henry dropped the horse's hoof to the ground and tossed the file into the bag. "Answer me one question first."

Jack hesitated. "Sure. What is it?"

"How close are you really?"

"In finding out what happened to Diego?"

Henry nodded once.

"I told you," Jack replied. "I don't have any answers yet, but I'm making progress."

Henry held his stare. "You need to make progress faster. I've been sitting on the sidelines for a week. I don't like someone murdered on Rose land," he said. "Or stealing my sheep."

"I'm working on it," Jack said. "But these things take time. Criminals don't have the word 'psycho' tattooed across their foreheads."

Henry raised a brow. "Well maybe they should."

# CHAPTER 54

HENRY LEFT THE horse at the hitching post and walked with Jack to his truck. A small cloud of dust appeared in the distance, swirling just over the horizon.

"We've got company," Henry said.

Jack turned and watched a truck clear the rise. "You expecting someone?"

"No." There was a concerned look on Henry's face.

It was as if nothing had changed since the days bandits and outlaws roamed the area. In such remote environs, the arrival of a stranger was often cause for concern. Usually, the visit would be friendly. But what made locals anxious was the chance it was hostile.

Jack noticed Henry's right hand drift to his hip, where a sidearm would be if he wore his gun belt instead of chaps. He had been in a bad mood since Jack brought up Roy. And Jack hoped there wouldn't be trouble.

It was a sheriff's office cruiser, but the sun glinted off the windshield, obscuring the driver. "Bert Lynch?" Jack asked.

Henry started for the truck as it rolled to a stop. "No," he said over his shoulder. "Danny Ochoa."

It took a second for the dust to settle, and then Ochoa rolled the window down. "Howdy, Henry," he said, pulling off sunglasses.

"Danny. What can I do for you?"

The deputy nodded at Jack. "Martin." He turned back to Henry. "Have you seen Deputy Lynch today?"

"Bert?" There was surprise in Henry's voice. "No, I haven't. Should I have?"

Ochoa hesitated. "It's his day off. The Sheriff's looking for him, but we can't get ahold of him."

"He's probably in Sonora with that girl he's been bragging about. Can't imagine any woman giving him the time of day without him holding a gun to her head. Probably ugly as a mud hen."

Ochoa grinned, but there was something besides humor in his dark eyes. Something about the deputy's story didn't add up. Jack wondered what he was really doing there.

"If he shows up," Ochoa said. "I'd appreciate it if you'd let him know we're looking for him."

"Will do," Henry said. "But before you go, what's the progress on the investigation? You guys any closer to finding out who's been stealing my sheep?"

"We're working on it."

"Well, I sure as hell hope so. Joey Sutton told me that a dozen more were taken off their place last night. When Odell's ready to get serious about finding these guys and he wants to deputize me, y'all let me know."

Ochoa stuck his sunglasses back on. "Like I said, Henry. We're working on it." He rolled up his window and gave them a two-finger salute.

They watched the truck clear the rise on the way back to the highway.

"What's his story?" Jack asked.

"Whose?"

"Ochoa's."

"Danny?" Henry turned to look at Jack. "He's one of us."

"What do you mean?"

"He's from here. Grew up in Del Rio."

"You like him?"

"Sure, I like him. He's a great guy. Jordan and I went to school with him."

Jack thought about it for a moment. "What about Lynch?"

"Bert?" Henry blew out air. "Bert's a Yankee." He'd said it like there was no need for further explanation.

"Where's he from?"

"Chicago."

Jack decided not to mention that Illinois was well west of the Mason-Dixon Line. Henry likely considered anyone from east of the Red River a Yankee—including Jack. It probably explained the cool reception Jack had gotten when they met years ago.

Henry opened the truck door for Jack and held it. "If you're not too busy tomorrow evening, come out. You can help me with a special project."

The stern look on his face made Jack nervous, and he wondered what Henry was planning.

"And don't even bother asking what it is," Henry said. "Cause I'm not saying."

Jack worried Henry had reached his breaking point. He thought of Kate and Jordan. Then Gretchen's face appeared in his mind. The family had suffered enough tragedy. They didn't need Henry causing more.

Jack slid into the driver's seat. "I'll be here."

Henry pushed the door shut.

Jack started the truck and wound down the window. "What time?"

"I'll call you tomorrow," he said over his shoulder on the way back to the barn. "Maybe this time, you'll answer."

# CHAPTER 55

JACK SET THE cowboy hat on the passenger seat. He wondered what Henry had planned for the following evening and felt another stab of concern. The last thing Jack wanted was trouble.

Jack used the GPS on his phone to find the junior college and hoped Gretchen would still be there.

The route took him near the airport. A small plane took off, and Jack watched it gain altitude. It had him thinking about smuggling rock art into Mexico. He wondered if the smugglers were flying it across the border. Maybe on a plane similar to the one he saw.

But there would be complications in smuggling the stuff by air. The more practical way to get it across the border was over the international bridge, probably hidden inside legitimate cargo. Or *illegal* cargo.

Whatever the method being used to get the art across would require a sophisticated operation and include some unsavory players. Jack thought of David Hansen in his cargo shorts and faded t-shirts. Hansen was only a minor player. Someone else was funding the operation. But who? Roy? Frank Moran?

Maybe it was Rooster Borden. With his connections to the cartels, he could easily handle the logistics of transportation and sales of the pictographs.

Jack wondered again if Diego Torres had been involved.

He squeezed the steering wheel, watching the plane disappear in the distance. Although his gut was saying he was making progress in the case, his head was screaming he was no closer to the answer than the day he'd shown up in Del Rio.

Jack found the main entrance to the junior college and fought his way through a crowd of students to a woman behind an enclosed reception counter. She was shuffling paperwork and never looked up when Jack asked for directions. Her answer was brief but efficient. Professor Gretchen Rose has just finished a class in Room 116, down the hallway to Jack's left, then down the last corridor to the right.

Jack threaded through more bodies as he made his way to Room 116. The door was open, and he peered inside. Gretchen was wiping something off a giant whiteboard behind a podium.

Jack stood outside the classroom and watched her. She wore a fitted navy dress that fell just below her knees. It was conservative, but something about it was sexy as hell. She had pulled her auburn hair into a bun at the nape of her neck.

As she cleaned the board, Jack noticed the gold college ring, a smaller version of his own, on her right hand. His gaze drifted to her left hand hanging at her side and came to rest on her diamond wedding band.

He stood there a moment longer, then cleared his throat.

She turned and smiled. "Jack. What a nice surprise again." She placed the eraser on the podium and came toward him. "What are you doing here?"

"I was hoping you'd still be at work," he said. "I have a couple questions, if you have time."

She was still smiling. "I've always got time."

Something inside Jack clenched. He cleared his throat again. "Mind if we sit down?"

They took two chairs in the front row. "I didn't know you were a professor."

"I wasn't always," Gretchen said. "I taught at the high

school for several years while I took night classes. I got my master's degree seven years ago."

"In history."

She nodded. "You know I've always loved it. It was my undergraduate degree at A&M. But I'm sure you remember that."

He hadn't, and it surprised him. He thought he had remembered everything about her. There was a tiny scar over her left brow; he didn't remember that either. Had it been there before? Too much time had passed, and things changed. But he wouldn't think about that now.

"I've got a history question for you."

"Okay. Shoot."

"What can you tell me about Maximilian's treasure."

"Emperor Maximilian?" She was surprised by the question. "Well, that wasn't the question I was expecting. You want the whole story?"

"If you don't mind."

She twisted her wedding band on her finger as she pulled the story from memory. "Well, if I remember correctly, Maximilian was an Austrian archduke appointed to serve as emperor of Mexico. He reigned for three years, from 1864 to 1867.

"The legend of the treasure is that, in 1866, fearing he would be overthrown, he smuggled his wealth out of the country. Most versions of the story say he sent fifteen wagonloads of gold and silver, along with jewels and other treasure, north out of Mexico. Some accounts have the wagons crossing the border west of El Paso into New Mexico. But most say they crossed somewhere near Presidio, not far from here."

"Was Maximilian with them?"

"No. He stayed in Mexico City and was executed by firing squad in 1867. His wife, Empress Carlota, had already escaped back to Austria when he was killed. She later went insane. It's really a tragic story."

"Who traveled with the wagons?"

"The wagons were supposedly escorted by a group of Austrian and Mexican soldiers who were still loyal to Maximilian."

"What happened to the treasure?"

She shifted in the chair and tucked a foot behind the opposite ankle. "Several versions of the story have the wagons reaching Castle Gap. That's an area south of Crane, about two hundred miles northwest of here. Anyway, the group supposedly encountered a small band of former Confederate soldiers, and one of them overheard the Mexicans talking about the treasure. So, the Confederates killed them. But the treasure was too much for them to haul out at once, and so they buried it. They planned to come back for it later. Which they never did."

"Why not?"

"On their way back to San Antonio, they came under attack by a band of Comanches, and all but one of them were killed." She stopped. "Are you sure you want all this?"

Jack sat on the edge of the seat. "Please, go on."

"All the accounts I've read say the lone survivor confessed to the doctor treating him on his deathbed and even helped him draw a map for where to find the treasure."

"But it was never found."

She nodded. "Right. Some stories have the doctor searching around Castle Gap, but he never found anything."

"The survivor was probably lying."

Gretchen shrugged. "Maybe. Or maybe he was delirious from fever before he died."

Jack leaned back in the chair and dropped his gaze to the floor. "End of story," he said, processing the information.

Gretchen chuckled. "Don't tell that to the hordes of treasure hunters who've looked for it ever since."

"Around Castle Gap?" She had Jack's attention again.

"Castle Gap, Big Bend, New Mexico. From what I under-stand, they've searched all sorts of places."

Jack thought about it. "What about closer to Del Rio?" he asked. "Does anyone think it could be in Val Verde County?"

She shook her head. "Not that I've heard."

The story was intriguing. Jack had read enough accounts of fortune seekers to know that the quest for hidden treasure could drive men mad.

But crazy enough to commit murder?

# CHAPTER 56

*Tuesday, May 31*

JACK WAS AT Benny's Cafe early the following day. There was already a crowd, but the corner booth at the back was empty.

On Griner Street, he parked in front of Jordan and Gretchen's, then crossed the road to the Moran home and knocked on the door. A few seconds later, a petite woman in a black dress and apron answered it, her dark eyes searching his face for recognition. When it was clear Jack was a stranger, she closed it back a little, obviously afraid. *What had the help so skittish?* Jack wondered.

"I'm looking for Frank Moran," he said.

The woman nodded once without speaking and then shut the door on him. Had the nod indicated she would fetch her boss? Or was it her way of saying *adios* and *hit the road?*

The door was solid wood with no sidelights or adjacent windows. There was no way to see what was going on inside.

Jack turned and looked down the street one way and then the other, wondering how long he should stand there.

Then, the door swung open again. But more forcefully this time.

"I don't have anything to say to you." Frank Moran filled most of the doorway. He started to shut the door, but Jack stuck his boot against the jamb, keeping it from closing, and Moran startled.

"I think you're going to want to hear what I have to say," Jack told him.

The heavy man pursed his lips together, and his beady eyes went hard. He looked like a cartoon character. It was easy to imagine steam coming from his ears.

Jack was surprised to find he was enjoying himself and left his boot in the door.

"What do you want?" Moran asked.

"I want to talk to you."

"About what?"

"About smuggling pictographs…and about a dead kid."

Moran looked down both sides of the street, then leaned out and dropped his voice to a growl. "What you're accusing me of is slander," he said. "And you give me no choice but to call my attorney."

"Funny," Jack said. "David Hansen said the same thing."

"I could call the cops."

"Yes, but you won't."

Moran leveled a hard stare, a pathetic attempt at intimidation.

"It's not going to work, Frank. So you might as well let me in, and we can get this over with."

The old man's lips twitched. He checked the street again, then pulled open the door. "I'll give you five minutes. Not a single more."

Jack stepped inside and scanned the foyer that rose two stories. The woodwork was dark and heavy. An iron chandelier the size of a Volkswagen hung from the center of the ceiling. He saw the housekeeper disappear through a doorway off the balcony above them.

Moran shut the door. "This way."

It was dark in Moran's study. He had the blinds shut tight, blocking the view to the yard. Or, more likely, blocking the view from the outside in.

Moran flipped on the lights, and Jack pulled up inside the

doorway. Hanging above the fireplace was a nearly life-size painting, done in oil, of the man in all his corpulent glory. Jack wasn't a connoisseur but knew enough to recognize the artist wasn't a master. In the painting, Moran stood next to the elaborate staircase they had just passed in the foyer on the way to the study. He had one hand on the banister. He wore a suit and alligator boots, and his free hand held a lit cigar, a lace of smoke trailing above it. There was an insipid look of self-importance on his face. But what struck Jack the most was that Moran wore his cowboy hat inside. It was a faux pas in West Texas, something a self-respecting rancher would never do. But Jack didn't need to see the painting to know Moran wasn't a gentleman.

Moran settled his bulk into a chair behind the desk and stuck his thumbs under his silk suspenders. Although several empty chairs were scattered around the room, he didn't offer one to Jack.

"Get on with your business," he said. "My wife is at her weekly bible study meeting, and I want you gone before she gets back."

Jack stood in front of the desk. "You weren't at Benny's this morning."

"I was busy."

"How about the Broken Arrow? Ever eat there?"

"On occasion." Moran laid his palms on the desk and studied his manicured fingers. "But I know you didn't come to ask about my dining habits. So get on with it."

"How well do you know Rooster Borden?"

"I don't."

"He owns the Broken Arrow."

Moran lifted his hands. "Well, good for him," he said, then dropped them on the desk again.

The conversation was going nowhere.

*"A quién le vendes las cosas en México?"* Jack asked. Who are

you selling the stuff to in Mexico? It was the same question he had asked Hansen.

Moran didn't hesitate with his answer. "I'm not selling a damn thing to the Mexicans except cattle."

Moran had revealed he spoke Spanish. Given the size of his holdings in Mexico, Jack had expected him to. But he had unintentionally revealed something else. He had answered the question too quickly. It was as if he had been expecting it. He had talked to David Hansen.

It could explain why Moran had altered his morning routine and not gone to Benny's. Frank Moran was nervous.

"Hansen has been removing pictographs from your land," Jack said. "And I'm pretty sure that's against the terms of your lease with the state."

"To hell with the state," Moran replied.

"So you don't deny he's doing it?"

"I don't deny or admit to anything he might be doing on my ranch."

"I'm surprised, Frank. I would have expected a man like you to keep better control of things your ranch."

Moran began sorting through a stack of mail on his desk, pretending to be busy.

Jack continued. "Hansen is stealing the rock art. And I think that you not only know about it, but you're also smuggling it into Mexico."

Moran set the mail down hard and shoved it to a corner. "Let me guess. The Roses put you up to this." He thumped his stubby fingers on the desk. "Who was it? Roy?"

Jack remained silent.

"Nah," Moran continued. "Roy's not right in the head. It must have been Jordan or Henry. But my money's on Henry. He's always been the degenerate of the two boys. I always suspected he'd end up in Huntsville one day. Still might," Moran said, referring to the Texas state prison.

"I think you underestimate the danger you're in," Jack

said. "International smuggling is a federal crime. That means hard time. Then there's the civil suit with the state. That'll hit you in the wallet. But what does it matter if you're broke when you're stuck in federal prison?"

Moran's eyes flashed. "You can't prove a damn thing."

"Oh, but I can."

Jack took a moment to let it sink in and took the opportunity to scan the room. The oil painting was just the beginning. There were photographs of Moran everywhere, including one sitting on a bookshelf that Moran had taken with the former Governor, Buckley Bailey. Jack picked it up. The two men were wearing tuxedos.

"You know Buckley?"

"I can know anyone I want in this state," Moran replied smugly. He reclined his bulk in the chair. "I've thrown more money at political campaigns than you'll make in your lifetime. And you think you can come in here and threaten me like some junkyard dog. All I have to do is pick up the phone and ask one of them to get you off my back."

"Including Buckley?"

"If I needed his assistance, he'd help."

Jack set the photo back on the shelf. "Not if I told him not to." What Moran didn't know was that Buckley Bailey was a friend of his from Telluride.

Jack scanned more photographs. There were pictures of Moran taken on the ranch, on horseback, and one standing in front of a stock tank. There were photos of him as a much younger—and thinner—man. Some were with other prominent politicians.

Jack came up short when he noticed a photo near the back. It was of a high school basketball team. The handwritten caption at the bottom read *Wildcats Senior Varsity Basketball* and listed the boy's names in the picture. Frank Moran, Harlan Baker, Benton Wallace, Roy Rose, and Thomas Rose. All five were smiling.

Jack stood staring at the photograph, making sure he wasn't seeing things. He scanned the boys' faces and recognized Thomas immediately.

So Moran had been teammates with Thomas and Roy. Had they also been friends?

He turned back to Moran, who had pulled the stack of mail back over in front of him. Jack saw him snatch a letter opener from the desk. It was unusually large. Silver, with a horse's head awkwardly mounted at one end. The force Moran used to grip the opener had turned his knuckles white. Jack thought of the movie *The Godfather* and the severed horse head found in the bed of one of the characters.

"Time's up," Moran said without looking up. "You can show yourself out." He sliced open an envelope with ease, like he was cutting through warm butter. The opener was sharp.

"One last question," Jack said, watching Moran work.

"One more. And then get out."

Jack pulled his gaze from the letter opener. "Where were you the morning Thomas Rose died?"

# CHAPTER 57

THE ENCOUNTER WITH Frank Moran left Jack unsettled. He drove around for nearly an hour, thinking about the conversation.

Moran had said he was with his wife in San Antonio the morning Thomas died. "A birthday weekend for the Missus, not that it's any damn business of yours," he had said. It was an alibi that would be easy to check—hotel records, credit card receipts—if Jack felt the need, which he didn't.

Without realizing it, he turned left onto 2nd Street from North Main and a few blocks later entered Westlawn Cemetery. Thomas's grave would be there.

Jack had been to the cemetery twice with Jordan, both times during their winter break from school, when they took poinsettias to Thomas's mother's grave. Jordan's favorite grandmother had died at Christmas years earlier.

Jack was surprised to find himself in the cemetery again. He drove slowly, reading names until he found the right plot. The granite monument was massive and gray, with the name ROSE carved in the center. Two rows of headstones laid flush with the ground in front of it. Jack parked the truck and got out.

Thomas was easy to find. The dirt over his grave was still mounded, and a small paper marker sheathed in plastic served as a temporary headstone. Jack walked over and read the name. Thomas Everett Rose.

He stood there a moment, missing the man who had once treated him like a son and regretting he would never see him again.

Jack's thoughts turned darker as he sifted through images of the family and the ranch in his mind. Then, the rocky hillside where Thomas had fallen and died. He stared down at the paper headstone and made a silent vow to find Thomas's killer.

The noise of a semi downshifting somewhere in the distance broke into Jack's thoughts. He pulled his phone from his pocket and glanced at the time, then got into the truck and started for the south side of town.

Several minutes later, he snagged a parking spot across the street from Our Lady of the Holy Rosary as another car pulled away. Cars lined both sides of the road.

A hearse blocked the view of the church doors, but Jack knew there was nothing to see. Except for a solemn-looking fellow in a black suit leaning against the passenger side door, everyone else was inside.

Jack checked the time on his phone. Diego Torres's funeral had started a half-hour earlier.

A warm breeze swayed the palm fronds on the trees that lined the street, and he watched their shadows swing on the side of the building in the morning light.

Jack had rolled down the truck's window, and the cab was getting hot. But he left the engine off, preferring the quiet. He could hear music playing inside the church.

He wasn't sure why he was there. It was never his intention to come. He didn't want to intrude in Miguel and Sabina's grief any more than he already had. Or in Elena's.

Jack rested his arm on the open window and thought about the case. There was no evidence Diego was selling drugs again. And, according to the sheriff, there were no signs of narcotics in his bloodstream when he died. Although Diego Torres was involved in drugs in the past, it wasn't the reason he was murdered. Something he was doing while working for David Hansen or working alone on Roy's had gotten him killed.

Jack thought about the facts that he knew. Hansen and Frank Moran were in cahoots in the smuggling ring. Hansen supplied the ancient art, and Moran helped get it across the border. But someone else was involved, someone providing the logistics of transportation and sales. Borden, maybe? There wasn't evidence to connect Borden to Moran. But there was plenty to connect Moran to Roy Rose.

Jack saw the church doors finally open, and watched as pallbearers carried an oak casket down the steps. Sabina and Elena Torres led the crowd that followed closely behind. Fernanda, Elena's sister, was among them. There were hugs and tears as the coffin was slid into the hearse.

Jack watched as the mourners dispersed. When the hearse pulled from the curb, many followed in the direction of the cemetery.

When the church's exodus reached a trickle, Jack started the truck. And, at a break in traffic, did a U-turn. There was more work to do, and he was more determined than ever.

Diego Torres and Thomas were dead, and Jack wasn't going to rest until he found their killer.

# CHAPTER 58

THE AFTERNOON SUN painted the landscape an eerie orange. Jack wondered if it was the impending storm and searched the horizon north of the highway, but there still wasn't a cloud in the sky.

Anticipating Henry's mysterious plans had made the day seem interminably long. Jack only hoped it wouldn't involve anything illegal or end in bodily harm. He tightened his grip on the wheel, wondering what he was in for.

After Diego's funeral, Jack had spent the afternoon back at the library, digging through old news stories again, and searching for any that connected Frank Moran to Rooster Borden. But he hadn't found any.

The sun was shining brighter by the time Jack reached the hacienda. He grabbed the cowboy hat from the passenger seat and headed for the front door when it opened.

Ado stood silently just inside the threshold and ushered him inside.

"I'm here to see Henry."

"I will tell him," she said in her thick accent, then started from the room.

"Can I ask you something first?" Jack asked.

She stopped and pivoted back. Her dark eyes studied him suspiciously before she finally nodded.

"Do you prefer Ado or Adoncia," Jack asked, realizing he'd never called the woman by her given name.

It took a while for her to answer. "*Prefiero Adoncia*," she said, still watching him.

"Adoncia," Jack repeated. "It's a beautiful name."

She was silent a moment. "In English, it means sweet like the honey." She continued staring at him, almost daring a comment. She had undoubtedly gotten several from Henry before.

Jack simply nodded. "I like it," he said and saw her blush.

A faint grin curled the corners of her mouth before she turned away. "I am too busy for talking," she said, then muttered something else in Spanish as she hurried from the room.

A few seconds later, Henry appeared in the hallway. "I thought you were going to stand me up."

"Not a chance," Jack replied and meant it.

"I see you finally came prepared." He nodded at the cowboy hat Jack held at his side.

"I wasn't sure I'd need it, but I brought it just in case."

Henry snatched a hat from the hall tree and jammed it on his head. "You're going to need it," he said. "Let's go."

They walked to the barn, where Henry grabbed a small metal toolbox and filled an old plastic Thermos with water from an outside spigot. Next, they headed back toward the house.

"What are we doing?" Jack asked, relieved he'd grabbed a toolbox and not a gun.

"You'll see." Henry shot him a wry smile.

Jack followed him around the side of the house and was surprised to see several piles of wood sorted by size. Next to them was a giant roll of wire.

Henry set the toolbox down and opened it, drew out two pairs of leather work gloves, and threw one to Jack. They were going to be doing manual labor. But Henry would have already put in a full day's work.

"You don't take evenings off?" Jack asked.

"Not when the boss wants a chicken coop."

"Chicken coop?"

"Yep," he said, pulling on the gloves.

"You could have told me."

"If I had've, you might not have come." Henry took a sheet of notebook paper from his back pocket and unfolded it.

"What's that?"

"The plans."

Jack looked over the various piles of wood and wire, then back at the single sheet of paper. He shook his head. This was going to be a disaster.

"We're just prepping today," Henry said. "Getting it all lined out." He must have seen the look of relief on Jack's face because he laughed. "You didn't think we could build it in a day, did you? Not *this* chicken coop."

He turned the paper around so Jack could see the diagram. It was hand-drawn but looked surprisingly professional. And the coop looked remarkably large.

"The chicken Taj Mahal," Henry said. He looked at the sky. "The sun's going to dictate how much we get done today. But if you're not busy tomorrow evening…" He let his voice trail off and grinned at Jack expectantly. "Besides, I've been told manual labor calms anxieties. Might keep me from killing somebody." There was a mischievous glint in his eyes.

They spent the first half hour measuring and marking locations for post holes and apologizing to each other. Henry said he was sorry for the comment on family. And Jack apologized for having to ask questions about Roy.

Jack set the post-hole digger aside, and Henry checked the depth with a tape measure.

"Perfect," Henry said. "Want me to dig the next one?"

"I'll do it a while longer. Then we can switch."

Henry nodded.

Jack's shirt was soaked through, but the physical labor

was satisfying. He moved to the next spot. "Who are Benton Wallace and Harlan Baker?"

Henry was surprised by the question. "How do you know them?"

"I don't. That's why I'm asking." Jack rammed the shovel into the ground, pulled the handles apart, and lifted out the dirt.

"Benton and Harlan were friends of Dad's," Henry said. "Benton was killed in Vietnam. But Harlan is still living."

"In Del Rio?"

"Yep. He's an attorney. Retired, I think. But still does work for old friends. Why do you ask?"

Jack leaned on the handles of the shovel. "I saw an old photograph of them with Thomas and Roy. They were with Frank Moran."

Henry frowned, then remembered. "The old basketball team. Dad has that same photo somewhere."

"I didn't know he was friends with Moran."

"He wasn't. He couldn't stand Frank. Even back then. But believe it or not, the guy used to be a decent basketball player."

"Roy ever like him?"

Henry scoffed. "Never. Nobody has ever liked Frank Moran."

Jack kept digging. He was relieved that neither Thomas nor Roy had been friends with Moran. It put to rest the theory that Roy and Moran were involved together in the smuggling ring. At least for now.

Henry took the shovel from him. "My turn," he said, then started digging. After a while, he asked, "You ever miss Texas?"

Jack thought about it before he answered. "Sometimes."

Henry nodded. "I would." He then dug some more.

Jack measured the depth, and they moved to the next spot.

Henry tipped his hat back and wiped sweat from his brow with his forearm. "Tell me something," he said, digging again. "Whatever happened to that old Airstream you bought off Dad? Jordan thinks it's in some Louisiana landfill by now. But my money's on it being drug around with some two-bit carnival."

Jack smiled to himself, thinking about his trailer parked at the Telluride campground. "You're both wrong."

They talked about old times.

When they stopped for a water break a while later, Jack changed the subject. "I went to see Gretchen. I asked her about the story of Maximillian's gold."

Henry wiped water from his chin. "She know anything?"

"She knew a lot."

"I thought she would."

"It's an interesting story."

"Everyone out here's heard it," Henry said. "Bunch of malarky if you ask me. I'd be the first one searching if I thought there was any truth to it. There's another story that regularly gets folks stirred up. It's about a lost gold mine somewhere outside of Alpine. I think it's called the Haystack Mine. Anyway, they say…"

Henry was still talking, but Jack let his mind wander. Could Diego maybe have been searching for a lost gold mine? The ranch was littered with rock shelters and caves of various sizes. Maybe one held more secrets than Henry knew.

Jack let the warm breeze cool the sweat on his skin. The sun was approaching the horizon, and he realized they wouldn't be able to work much longer.

Despite his earlier anxieties, the evening had been surprisingly pleasant. Peaceful even. And he was looking forward to working again the next day.

As Henry continued to dig, Jack brought up Rooster Borden.

"Borden's trash," Henry shot back, stabbing the ground

with the shovel. "It doesn't matter how many overgrazed acres he buys north of town trying to look respectable. He'll always be trash."

Henry finished the last hole and stood studying the sky. "It's a rustler's moon tonight." Jack didn't know what he meant, so he explained. "Enough light to go thieving, but dark enough not to get caught."

There was a menacing frown on his face. Something was churning inside him, and it made Jack nervous. He shuddered to think of what would happen if Henry caught the rustlers red-handed.

Henry tossed the shovel on one of the wood piles. "But the moon won't be out for long. The storm's hitting later tonight."

Jack searched the sky and noticed a thin bank of clouds hovering above the northern horizon. Maybe the locals were right.

Daylight faded behind them as they started for the house.

"There's one thing I don't get," Henry said.

"What's that?"

"I know that Jordan asked you to come check on things after the Torres murder. But why are you so hell-bent on finding out who killed him? It's not your job."

Jack searched himself for the answer. After a few silent steps, he said, "I guess finding killers is the only job I know."

# CHAPTER 59

BY THE TIME Jack left the ranch, the cloud bank he'd seen earlier had grown and was approaching fast.

He pulled through the gate and paused long enough to let a sheriff's cruiser speed past on the highway, headed west. The cruiser's lights were off, but it had been going close to a hundred. Jack didn't recognize the deputy but wondered what had them in such a hurry.

He sat idling on the side of the highway and watched the taillights of the speeding Tahoe recede in the distance. He was going to turn east toward town, but the conversation with Henry had him thinking. And now, there was one more thing Jack needed to do before he would call it a day. He turned west instead.

At Roy's, Jack got out of the truck and immediately shielded his eyes from the wind, now howling through the mesquites and sending grit from the ground airborne. He turned and watched the last sliver of sun drop below the horizon, then drew in a deep breath and smelled rain.

It wouldn't be long before the storm hit. Jack hoped he had enough time to make it back to town before it started. From what he could tell, it was going to be a whopper.

Jack started for the gate, walking bent against the wind. He wasn't looking forward to another visit with Roy. Their last encounter had turned fiery when Jack asked about his alibi the morning Thomas died. But the truth was, Roy didn't have one. He also didn't have one for the night Diego Torres was murdered. But after the conversation with Frank Moran, Jack had more questions.

Roy's house was strangely dark in the dying light. Jack opened the gate and stepped into the yard. He took the sidewalk to the porch, but something didn't feel right. It was the first time Roy hadn't been outside to greet him.

He took the steps to the porch, knocked on the screen door, and listened, but heard no sound other than the wind. He knocked again and waited, then stepped to a window and peered inside. But the house was dark.

Where was Roy? Had the man who never left home decided to run an errand on the eve of a storm?

Jack retreated to the yard and stood wondering what to do next. The sun was gone, and although there was still enough light left to see, it would soon be dark.

He walked around the side of the house, glancing in windows. The wind was howling like a freight train by the time he reached the back, where he noticed a three-sided lean-to in the corner of the yard shuddering with each gust. It was obscured by shadows, but Jack's heart skipped a beat when he noticed movement inside. With no time to react, the furry animals crossed the yard and were upon him.

Roy's goats.

Jack relaxed.

They brayed furiously at his feet. One pressed the top of its head hard against Jack's knee. They were scared.

"Y'all get back in there," he told them over the wind, turning one toward the shed and giving it a gentle shove. But it was no use. They followed him to the back door. Jack knocked. But again, there was no answer.

He left the goats in the yard and went through a back gate to the barn. It was weathered a deep gray and twice the size of the house. If Roy were home, his truck would be inside.

Jack rolled one of the doors open a few inches and saw that, except for old tools and saddles, the barn was empty.

He rolled the door shut, and the storm suddenly exploded in the sky. Lightning flashed, illuminating the countryside with jagged bolts of electricity.

Jack saw that the goats had taken shelter in the shed and, not bothering with the gate, dashed around the yard for his truck. But before he could reach it, the sky opened. Sheets of water rained down, soaking him within seconds.

In the truck, Jack's wet clothes and the drop in temperature had him shivering. He squinted, studying the house through the storm as raindrops the size of quarters hit the windshield like bullets. There was nothing more to do. He started the ignition and headed for the highway.

On the way to town, the windshield wipers swiped furiously in vain, trying to clear the rain. Visibility wasn't much over fifteen feet. Jack drove, squinting into the torrent and fighting to keep the truck on the road.

He spent the entire trip to town wondering. Roy Rose, the man notorious for never leaving his ranch, wasn't at home. So, where was he?

# CHAPTER 60

*Wednesday, June 1*

JACK HEARD A siren in the distance and thought he was dreaming. He lay motionless, letting the bed envelop him in its feathery cocoon. But the wailing grew louder, eventually bringing him fully awake.

He opened his eyes long enough to see a band of sunlight through a gap in the curtains and realized it was morning.

He had spent the night before lying awake, listening to the storm rip through town like a hurricane. As the winds lashed the old buildings around him, he had rehashed everything he'd learned since arriving in Del Rio. He sifted through stories of drug running, rock art, old bones, and lost treasure and had tossed and turned for hours, trying to fit the pieces together. Sometime before dawn, he had finally fallen asleep.

He listened to the siren fade in the distance, then pulled himself up and sat on the edge of the bed.

The unanswered questions from the night before still gnawed at him. And although he'd only gotten a couple hours of sleep, it was time to get up and find the answers.

A half hour later, Jack was back in the truck headed across town. Except for downed tree limbs and signs, small water puddles collected in parking lots and at the curb; it was as if it had never rained. To his amazement, the ground already looked dry, the arid soil of West Texas having soaked up the rain like some supernatural sponge. He switched on the local radio station and heard a report that parts of the county had gotten golf-ball-size hail, and some areas had as much as eight inches of rain. There would be mud for days if Colorado had seen the same amount.

Jack pulled open the door to the Val Verde County Sheriff's Office and found the place buzzing with activity. When he told the receptionist he needed to see the sheriff, she hesitated. She made a call that lasted several seconds and then pointed to the door that led to Odell's office.

"He said to go on in," she told him. But there was something in her eyes that had Jack worried.

Odell was slumped over his desk reading. When Jack walked in, he looked up and sighed. "It's not a good morning, Martin," he said, shaking his head. "I can only give you a couple of minutes."

"That's all I need." Jack wondered what was going on. He took a seat facing Gardner. "Anything I can help you with?"

Gardner crumpled the paper he was reading and threw it at the wall. "Not unless you're a wiz at public relations."

Jack was confused. He watched Gardner drag his hands down his face, then drop his palms to the desk. "We caught the rustlers last night."

Jack frowned. It should have been good news, but the sheriff acted like it was anything but. "Congratulations," Jack said hesitantly.

Gardner shook his head. "One of my guys was in on it."

Jack immediately thought of Deputy Ochoa, who he had seen at the Broken Arrow, but kept his mouth shut. "How'd you catch them?"

"Border Patrol called it in. Said there was suspicious activity on a ranch north of Comstock." He shook his head again. "The idiots got their trailer stuck in a rockslide."

Jack leaned back in the chair. Gardner was right. The optics weren't good. Not only was one of the thieves on his payroll, but a call from Border Patrol finally broke his case.

Gardner was still talking. "We were already onto them. We probably only had a couple more days before we had enough evidence to bring them in." He threw his weight back in the chair and sighed. "At least we finally got Rooster."

"Borden?"

Gardner nodded.

Jack thought about it. "Your wife's third—"

"Cousin," Gardner finished for him. He looked utterly defeated. The sheriff's public relations nightmare was getting worse.

"Borden wasn't with them, but they didn't take long to spill the beans. Every single one of them fingered him in their interrogation." Gardner chuckled without humor. "How's that for employee loyalty?"

"At least you got them," Jack said, trying to put a positive spin on things. "It should get the ranchers off your back."

"I sure as hell hope so," Gardner replied.

Jack couldn't stand it any longer. "Who did you have in on it?"

"One of my deputies."

"Ochoa?"

Gardner pulled up and frowned. "No. Bert Lynch. Caught him red-handed with a couple of local boys that have been on our radar for months."

Jack processed the information. He had immediately suspected Ochoa, whom he had seen at the Broken Arrow. It had been a knee-jerk reaction on Jack's part. And a mistake.

"Did the same guys kill Diego Torres?"

"Lynch and them?"

Jack nodded.

"No. We've been surveilling Rooster for weeks. They were all at the Broken Arrow the night the Torres kid was murdered—including Bert."

There was a knock at the open door. "Excuse me, sir."

Gardner glanced up, and his body sagged. "What now?"

Jack turned and saw a uniformed woman with a slight build standing there. Like everyone else in the office that morning, she had a long face.

"We just got a call from Del Rio PD." She hesitated.

"And?"

"There's been a murder." The woman paused again. "It occurred on Griner Street. It's within city limits, but they thought you'd want to know."

"And why is that?" Gardner was growing impatient.

"The victim is from an area ranching family."

Jack remembered the siren and his chest clenched. He thought first of Kate and Henry. Then wondered if Jordan was back in town. But Roy was the one missing the night before.

Next, he thought of Gretchen, and he felt the color drain from his face.

Gardner dropped a fist on the desk. "Shit. Who was it?"

The woman flinched at her boss's reaction.

"Spit it out, Adriana," Gardner said. "Who was it?"

Jack held his breath, watching her intently, his heart pounding against his ribs.

The woman fidgeted. "It was Frank Moran, sir," she finally said.

Jack exhaled and felt his body relax.

"Frank Moran?" Gardner repeated. "What happened?"

The woman took a tentative step into the office. "They said his wife found him this morning at his desk. He was stabbed in the chest with what appeared to be a letter opener."

Jack's mind was spinning. He thought of Moran and the silver letter opener with the horse's head, then remembered the study—the portrait and the photographs. The shrine Frank Moran had created for himself was the scene of his murder.

The ideas came at Jack fast—the stolen ranch in Mexico, the business ventures gone sour, and the defaced pictographs.

Moran was universally disliked. But who hated the man enough to kill him?

One name immediately came to mind.

Roy.

# CHAPTER 61

BACK IN THE truck, Jack started the engine and cranked up the AC. He sat in the cab, letting it cool and putting the pieces together.

Everything pointed to Roy. He wasn't home the night Frank Moran was murdered. And, according to the deputy, there were no signs of forced entry. Moran had opened the door for his killer.

Jack remembered the old photograph, Roy and Moran on the same team all those years ago. Despite what Henry thought, the two could have been friends—and partners in a smuggling ring. But what had gone wrong?

Roy also didn't have an alibi for the night Diego Torres was killed. It didn't matter that law enforcement never found the murder weapon. Roy owned an arsenal of guns and would know better than to bring one used in a murder back to the house. And there were thousands of places to hide a rifle on the ranch. Gardner could assign an army of deputies to search for the gun and never find it.

Jack thought of the stolen pictographs, the old bones, and the story of lost treasure, and wondered how all the pieces fit together. Had Diego found something incriminating? Did he discover David Hansen was stealing pictographs and made the mistake of telling Roy? Diego could have been killed to keep his mouth shut permanently.

Although everything pointed to Roy, there were still too many questions. It was time for answers.

Jack put the truck in gear and swung it out of the parking lot and onto the highway. When his thoughts turned to Thomas, his knuckles went white, squeezing the steering wheel.

He was sure Thomas was murdered. Henry's insistence on the sanctity of family now rang hollow. Roy had the means and opportunity to kill Thomas that Saturday morning. But what was his motive?

Jack remembered his conversation with the director of the Texas Archeological Society. Thomas had uncovered the smuggling scheme. But had Roy killed him to keep defaced rock art a secret? It hardly seemed possible. But Jack knew from experience that people often murdered for less. The news would devastate the Rose family.

Jack kept one hand on the wheel, then pulled his phone from his pocket. He scrolled through his contacts and found the one he wanted but hesitated. The realization of what he was about to do weighed heavily on him.

But Jack drew in a deep breath and made the call. He started to speak but was immediately interrupted.

"Jack! You wouldn't believe the storm we had last night. We had a couple roads wash out that we need to clear. And filled in the damn post holes we dug."

"Henry—"

"But it's not like we'll have to dig them out fresh. They'll be easier to dig a second time."

"Henry, Frank Moran is dead."

There was silence on the other end of the line.

"What'd you say?"

"Frank Moran is dead," Jack repeated. "He was murdered last night."

"What happened?"

Jack told him what little he knew. "Listen, Henry. I'm on my way to see Roy, but I need you to go with me."

"Roy? Why?"

"I'll explain after I pick you up. Are you at the house?"

"The barn," Henry replied. "I've got the guys cleaning up after…" His voice trailed off. "What do you want with Roy?"

"I'll explain when I get there." Jack glanced in the direction of the Broken Arrow as he flew past. The parking lot was empty. "Gardner caught the thieves stealing sheep last night," he said, hoping to change the subject.

"How do you know?"

"I just left his office."

"Well, it's about damn time. Who'd Odell say it was?"

Jack swerved to pass a semi. "They caught three guys on a ranch north of Comstock. Bert Lynch was one of them."

"Bert?" Henry practically spat the name back at him. "I told you I never liked that guy. Sorry son-of-a—"

"They also took Rooster Borden into custody. Gardner said he was behind the whole thing."

"Well, I'll be damn." Henry took a moment to think about it. "I guess they're the same ones who murdered Torres."

"They're not."

"Well, of course they are."

"They're not, Henry. Gardner had the rustlers under surveillance the night Diego was killed. They didn't do it."

There was silence. "Then who did?"

"Listen, I'm just hitting the edge of the lake. Meet me at the highway in twenty minutes. You can ride with me to Roy's."

Henry started to ask another question, but Jack cut him off. "I gotta let you go, but I'll see you in twenty," he said and clicked off the phone.

The call probably had Henry's mind reeling. *Let him stew on it*, Jack thought. It could help convince him his uncle was a murderer.

# CHAPTER 62

ROY SAT IN a rocking chair on the porch, thinking about his trip into town the night before. Nothing had gone as planned. He rocked the chair slowly back and forth, turning the gold coin over in his calloused hand and pulling at the side of his mustache with the other. He was worried he might have made a grave mistake.

It was one reason he rarely left the ranch anymore. Too many things could go wrong.

He had gone into town to see Harlan Baker. He hadn't seen Harlan in well over a year and thought the visit could kill two birds with one stone—he would catch up with an old friend and take care of some neglected business.

Harlan was an attorney. And, although he was retired, he kept a small office at home and did occasional work for friends and a select few old clients. Through the years, he had handled all the legal work for Thomas and Roy.

For the first twenty minutes, Roy had let Harlan talk, catching him up on local gossip and news Roy didn't care about. When Roy couldn't stand it any longer, he changed the subject and got to the point of his visit.

Roy spent the next half hour telling Harlan everything he knew that had happened to Diego Torres and Thomas. At first, Harlan had resisted, not believing the deaths could be related. But Roy had been relentless in pointing out how they were, confident he was right.

It hadn't been a pleasant conversation. Roy had told Harlan everything. Harlan had listened closely, then promised to help. Although his old friend was prone to gossip, Roy knew from experience that he would be discreet. There was too much at stake.

But now Roy was having second thoughts. He worried that his confessions would come back to haunt him. He drew in a breath of air redolent of sage made more pungent than usual because of the storm.

Charlotte and Cecilia appeared from around the side of the house and seemed surprised to find him sitting there. They clambered up the steps and onto the porch.

"Morning, girls."

The goats bleated. Cecilia pushed the top of her head against his shin, and Roy stroked her neck.

"Hungry?" He rose slowly from the chair, favoring his right knee. He stuck the coin in his pocket. "You girls stay here while I get your breakfast."

A small dust cloud on the horizon caught his attention as he pulled open the screen door. Staying on the porch, he let the door close behind him and watched as the billowing cloud finally crested the rise in the road.

Roy recognized the truck immediately. He stuck his hand into his pocket and squeezed the coin, and felt his pulse quicken.

# CHAPTER 63

"THAT'S A BULLSHIT theory, Jack." Henry's voice was hard with anger. "Roy's family."

The conversation had been heated and gone worse than Jack imagined. Although he had laid out the facts, Henry refused to believe Roy was capable of murder.

Jack fidgeted on the seat, trying to keep the Glock from pressing against his lower back. He had grabbed it at the last second when Henry insisted on driving, and secretly tucked it into the waistband of his jeans and pulled his shirt out over it. He hoped to hell he wouldn't need it.

"Watch Roy when I confront him about Diego and Frank Moran," Jack said. "Study his eyes and body language. And watch him when I ask him about Maximilian's treasure."

"He didn't do it," Henry insisted again. "And you're going to owe the family a huge apology when this is over. Then I want you gone. You get the hell out of here and never come back."

They drove the rest of the way in silence.

As they cleared the last rise before they reached Roy's, Jack noticed a whirlwind of dust in the distance on the ranch, a small dirt devil kicking up grit. It amazed him again how quickly the signs of the storm had disappeared.

The road dipped as they dropped toward the house. Everything looked quiet. Except for Roy's truck parked in the barn, there was no sign anyone else was there.

"You're going to regret this," Henry said, getting out of the truck at Roy's.

Jack followed him as he crossed the yard and took the porch steps in a single leap.

Henry pulled open the screen door and knocked, then opened the front door and stepped inside. "Uncle Roy, it's Henry."

The house was quiet.

"Uncle Roy?"

Jack went in behind him but pulled up at the sight of Henry frozen at the threshold to the study. His face had gone white, and his mouth hung open.

"What is it?" Jack asked, stepping closer. Then he saw it, too.

The body was slumped back with its head hung to the side. The eyes were still open. There was a crimson bloom in the center of the dead man's chest, and he clenched his fists in his lap. It was as if he had seen the end coming.

"He's been shot," Jack said.

"Uncle Roy!" Henry ran around the desk and checked for a pulse Jack knew wouldn't be there. When he withdrew his hand from Roy's neck, he took a step back from the body with a look of disbelief and confusion on his face. "Who would do this?" His voice was barely audible.

Questions came at Jack furiously. How could he have been wrong about Roy? Or had there been more than one killer? Why was Roy dead? And who killed him? Once again, Jack had more questions than answers.

He turned his attention to the room. What had been neat and orderly the times he'd been there was now in disarray. Desk drawers were left open, and books had been pulled from the shelves and laid on the floor.

It suddenly dawned on Jack that the killer could still be there. He left Henry in the study and raced through the house, opening closets and looking under beds. There was no one there, but the other rooms were in the same condition. Someone had emptied bathroom and kitchen cabinets, leaving them open. And they had overturned mattresses and cushions to the couch. Chests of drawers had been emptied, and clothes were pulled from shelves.

Jack called the sheriff's office and reported the crime, then went back into the study and found Henry still standing in the same spot.

"The killer was looking for something," Jack said. He glanced at the gun cabinet. As far as he could tell, the guns were all there. He then glanced at the desk and realized the Colt revolver was missing.

He studied the wound on Roy's chest. One shot. Downward trajectory. The size of the wound was appropriate for the caliber. Roy Rose had been killed with his own gun.

"What would they want?" Henry asked. His voice was full of emotion. "What does Roy have worth killing him for?"

"I don't know."

"A bunch of old books?" Henry kicked one aside that was lying on the floor.

"I don't think it was a thief."

"How can you say that? Look at this place." Henry swung an arm over the room.

Jack shook his head. "A thief would've taken the guns. As far as I can tell, his Colt is the only one missing." He then noticed something on the desk. "And a thief wouldn't have stayed long enough to have coffee."

Henry's gaze went to where Jack pointed at the half-empty mug of light brown liquid.

"Roy took his coffee black," Jack said as he took a step closer and stuck his finger in the cup, careful not to touch the sides. "It's still warm."

Henry stared into the coffee, processing the information. His face went taut with emotion. "Who could have done this?" he asked, reaching out for his uncle.

"Henry, don't—"

But it was too late.

Henry had laid his hand on Roy's shoulder, and the dead man's arm rolled off his lap and fell to the side, sending something clattering to the floor. Henry stood like a stone, staring down at it.

Jack came around the desk.

Roy's fist had opened, dropping a large coin he'd been holding. The coin had come to rest atop one of several advertisements for local houses strewn across the floor.

"Don't touch anything else," Jack said. They had contaminated too much of the scene already. Without touching it, Jack bent toward the coin for a better look. He squinted and couldn't believe what he saw. "It's gold," he said, straightening up slowly. "And it's Mexican."

"Mexican?" Henry was quiet, taking a moment to think it over. "Is there a date?"

"1864."

Henry stooped for a closer look. "Well, I'll be damned. Couldn't possibly be…" His voice trailed off, and he shook his head.

Both men stared at each other, secretly considering the possibility.

Henry was the first to break the silence. "Do you think the coin was what the killer was looking for?"

"It could be." Jack laid a hand on Henry's arm. "But we need to get out of here. I called the sheriff's office, and they're on their way."

They went out of the house and into the yard.

"Why?" Henry doubled over and rested his hands on his knees. "First Dad, now Uncle Roy."

Jack gave him time to grieve and paced the sidewalk, thinking. If someone murdered Roy for the gold, they must have known about the coin. But who? Diego would have known—he probably found it. But Diego was dead.

"Elena," Jack said, thinking aloud.

"What?" Henry rubbed his eyes with his palms.

"Diego told his sister about the treasure. He could have told someone else."

"I'm not following you."

"Diego was likely the one who found the coin, then gave it to Roy." Jack was fitting more pieces together. "It's why Roy paid him to stay on the ranch and keep digging."

"What are you talking about?" Henry was growing frustrated.

Jack's gaze drifted to the horizon as he pieced together a new theory.

The bones. No one had been interested in them. Not David Hansen. Not even Catherine Michaels at the Juno Center. But Roy knew the legend of the treasure and would have realized their significance when they were found with military regalia. Roy had grown close to Diego. He could have convinced him to stay when Hansen and the others left.

"What are you talking about?" Henry repeated.

"The old bones Hansen dug up—their carbon date. And they were found with things a Mexican soldier would have had. Roy knew all about the legend. He would have known."

"Known what?"

"That the bones were those of a Mexican soldier who could have been escorting wagons loaded with—"

"Treasure," Henry finished for him. He fell silent a moment. "But it's only one coin. If it's part of Maximilian's lost treasure, where's the rest of it?"

"That's what Diego Torres was looking for."

"So, there's more out there?"

Jack thought about it. It was an improbable theory, but the pieces fit. "Maybe."

"That archeologist did it."

Jack shook his head. "Hansen would never have left the ranch if he'd known about the coin. He'd still be here looking for the rest of the treasure instead of removing pictographs on Moran's place."

Henry frowned. "Removing what?"

Jack stood silent with his hand on his hips, thinking. There was the problem of Frank Moran. It wasn't a coincidence that Diego, Frank Moran, and now Roy were all dead. Somehow, all of the murders were connected. But how?

Jack ran through the possibilities. If Diego and Roy were killed for the treasure, why kill Moran?

Maybe there was also a connection with the smuggling ring.

Jack took several minutes, struggling to connect the dots, then whispered, "Carter."

"What?"

He remembered the maps of Texas and Mexico on the walls of Carter's office, the elk mount that stared down at him, and his client who owned an international manufacturing plant. He looked at Henry. "What type of law does Carter practice?"

Henry frowned. "Customs stuff mainly. Why?"

"I should have known."

"Speak English, Jack."

Jack talked slowly and methodically as he thought out loud. "Roy must have told him about the gold." He remembered the real estate flyers from the top of the desk and on the floor. "Carter wanted him off the ranch."

"What are you talking about?"

Jack was still thinking. "But why kill Moran?"

"What does Carter have to do with it, Jack?"

"Carter killed them."

"Killed who?"

"Diego, Frank Moran…and Roy."

"You think *Carter* killed Uncle Roy? For what, the gold?"

"Roy must have told him about it. Or maybe Diego did."

"You're talking crazy again, Jack."

"Am I? Hear me out." Jack paced the sidewalk as he told Henry about the stolen pictographs. "Assume Carter's the one handling logistics for the smuggling ring. He kills Moran when something goes wrong between them. Moran could have somehow found out about the treasure and wanted a piece of it—I don't know. But it could also have something to do with their partnership smuggling pictographs into Mexico. Maybe I leaned on them too hard."

"But why kill Uncle Roy?" From the tone of Henry's voice, it was evident he was coming to terms with the idea Carter could be a killer.

Jack shrugged. "He could have done it for any number of reasons. The treasure, for one. When Carter couldn't get Roy off the ranch, he took him out of the picture—for good."

Jack thought of Moran. "He could have killed him after something to do with the smuggling ring went wrong. Maybe Roy *wasn't* in on the smuggling, but he figured out what was happening. Maybe Diego Torres told Roy about it." His mind was racing. "Or maybe Thomas did." Jack's voice trailed off when he realized what he had said.

"What about Dad?"

Jack looked at Henry but didn't know what to say. Of course it had been Carter. Thomas's murder had occurred on a Saturday morning when Carter knew Thomas would have coffee with Roy. He could have lain in wait on the highway, then lured Thomas onto the ranch and to his death.

"What did you say about Dad?" Henry demanded.

Jack hesitated, then said, "Your father found out about the smuggling ring."

It took time, but Henry's eyes widened with realization. "Carter killed him, didn't he?"

Jack shook his head. "It's just a theory."

But it was too late. Henry's face was crimson and contorted with fury. "I should have shot the son-of-a-bitch years ago." He stormed into the house and came out seconds later carrying Roy's sniper rifle that he kept propped against the hall tree.

"What are you doing?" Jack held up his hands, but Henry pushed past him. He threw open the gate and headed for the truck. "Henry, stop! Let's wait for the sheriff."

"To hell with the law." Henry jerked open the driver's side door. "I'm gonna kill that son-of-a-bitch myself."

# CHAPTER 64

JACK SCRAMBLED INTO the passenger seat as Henry kicked on the ignition. The situation was getting more volatile by the minute, and Jack didn't like it.

"Henry, this is crazy," he said. "We need to wait for the sheriff. Even if we find Carter, you can't just shoot him."

"The hell I can't."

Henry swung the truck away from the house. Instead of turning toward the highway, he went in the opposite direction, heading deeper into the ranch.

"Where are you going?" Jack asked.

"We didn't pass Carter on the way in. And you didn't see him on the highway, did you?"

"No."

"Me neither. And I was there waiting ten minutes after you called. It's a hunch, but he must have seen us coming." Henry accelerated, sending the truck bouncing violently over the gravel road. "He went this way."

Jack remembered the whirlwind of dust on the horizon. Henry might be right. It could have been dust from Carter's truck and not a whirlwind. But too much time had passed. Henry would never catch up to him. Carter would circle the far side of the ranch, where the road connected into one that would take him past the hacienda on the way to the highway.

"Turn around," Jack said. "We need to get to Kate."

"Carter can't get to the house. He doesn't know the

road up ahead was washed out in the storm. We've got him trapped."

The truck hit a rut and jerked to one side. Jack braced a hand on the dash. If what Henry said was true, a confrontation with Carter was imminent.

"Carter doesn't know we're on to him," Jack said. "Let's wait for Odell."

Henry didn't reply. A look of crazed determination on his face had Jack worried.

Despite the rough ride, Jack pulled his phone from his pocket and found the sheriff's number. The call was immediately picked up on the other end. "Odell, you've got to get someone out here *now*," Jack insisted.

"I'm already on my way. And I've got two deputies behind me." He sounded concerned but not concerned enough.

"You're going to be too late. We think Carter McConnell killed Roy, and he's still on the ranch. I don't know what Henry will do if we find him before you guys get here."

Jack heard Odell curse and switch on his siren.

"Listen to me, Jack. Henry can be a live one. You've got to do whatever you can to keep him away from Carter."

A few miles further, the road dipped into an arroyo and ran alongside a dry creek bed. Jack looked out the passenger side window and up at the sloping hillside. There were rock escarpments that capped the ridge line above them. There were countless places where someone could hide.

Henry was speeding. When the road turned sharply to the right, he slammed on the brakes, sending the truck into a sideways skid.

Jack's heart lurched as they became engulfed in dust and rock. The tires on the passenger side lifted from the road. The truck was about to flip.

Jack threw his hand up, trying to grab the handle over the door, but there wasn't time. He flew forward, slamming his head into the windshield and cracking the glass.

The truck bounced and skidded for what seemed like an eternity before finally coming to rest after one last bounce.

Although he never lost consciousness, Jack sat stunned while the debris settled around them. The warm drip of blood down his forehead snapped him from his daze. He checked for the Glock, found it still there, and left it alone.

"Shit," Henry exclaimed. "I thought we were going to roll."

Jack wiped the blood collecting at his brow with a shirt sleeve, then saw the reason for Henry's hard brake. The truck had stopped inches from where the road had washed out the night before. Huge stones and uprooted trees covered its surface. Jack shuttered to think what would have happened if they would have hit it.

"Well, I'll be damn," Henry said. "Look there."

Before Jack could turn to look, Henry had opened the door and gotten out. Then Jack saw Carter's truck partially hidden in the trees and scrub brush bordering the creek bed.

"Shoot," he muttered, shoving the passenger door open and scrambling out. "Henry," he hollered. "Wait here. Odell's coming."

But Henry was already at the truck and peering inside. He slammed a hand down on the hood. The truck was obviously empty, and Jack was relieved.

"Carter's not going anywhere," Jack said. "Now, let's do this by the book and wait for Odell."

"He's out here somewhere," Henry said, storming past Jack. He grabbed Roy's rifle from the truck's floorboard, where it had settled after the skid, then stood in the middle of the road, searching the countryside. He raised his face to the heavens and roared, "Car-ter!"

A bevy of quail fluttered out of a nearby mesquite, and the name echoed off the cliffs in the distance.

Jack turned in the direction of the highway, praying for a

miracle. But even driving top speed, Odell would be another twenty minutes.

There was a clamor of stone in the distance, and Jack turned to looked.

"Did you hear that?" Henry asked. His voice had dropped to a growl. "He's up there."

Jack shielded his eyes from the sun and searched the slopes around them. He saw movement in the distance. Something had ducked behind a mesquite.

Jack felt his chest tighten. *God, let it be a deer.* "I don't see anything," he lied.

Henry was looking in a different direction. "Car-ter!" he roared again.

Jack was running out of ideas and needed more time.

Henry turned to him. "What are you carrying?"

Jack frowned, surprised by the question. "How'd you know?"

"Your shirttail. It was in when you got out of your truck. And out when you got in mine."

Jack was secretly impressed. He pulled the Glock from his waistband.

Henry frowned. "Cop gun." He dug into the truck again and came out with another bolt-action rifle. "Take this," he said, tossing it to Jack. After a pause, he added, "But take the Glock, too."

"Henry, let's wait for Odell," Jack pleaded again. "Carter is armed. In situations like this, you *always* wait for backup," he said, omitting the fact he'd never let waiting for backup stop him before. But this time was different—this involved family. And Jack was no longer a lawman.

Henry fidgeted, shifting his weight from foot to foot as he considered Jack's request. He shook his head. "This is bull-shit," he said. "I'm going."

Jack reached for his arm, but Henry was too quick. He started up the embankment beside the road.

Jack twisted in the direction of the highway, then back again. He watched Henry clamor over rock and cactus like a wild man, Roy's sniper rifle resting in the crook of his arm. Dammit. Odell would take too long.

With the Glock back in his waistband, Jack gripped the rifle with both hands. He turned toward the highway again, wondering what to do next.

"Ah, hell," he said and started up the mountain.

# CHAPTER 65

HENRY HEARD JACK struggling behind him, trying to catch up. But he wouldn't be able to.

Henry had grown up on the ranch and could scale its rocky hills like a mountain goat. Jack would never catch him.

Henry climbed fast but was careful with each step. It was easy to misstep in the rocky terrain, twisting an ankle or worse.

After several minutes, he stopped, shielded his eyes from the sun, and searched for movement. Where was he?

"Car-ter!"

A hawk circling overhead screeched in protest.

There was movement high and to his left. Carter was darting between boulders and trees, taking cover as he struggled to climb higher. He was trying to make it to the ridge line, where he could hide in the rock outcroppings or caves. He had a rifle with him.

Henry turned around and saw that Jack had fallen further behind. *Just as well*, Henry thought. *He would only try to stop me.*

Beyond Jack, a small dust cloud swirled near the highway. Odell. He was still several miles away, but Henry knew he was running out of time.

He turned and scrambled higher.

After a few minutes, he caught another glimpse of Carter and realized he was heading for a keyhole in the ridge that falsely promised a path down the other side. But there was a chasm there, a deep scar in the earth like the one Thomas had fallen into. Carter wouldn't know he was climbing to a dead end. Or that Henry had him trapped.

Jack hollered from somewhere below. "Carter, it's time to give up. Odell will be here any minute."

"You're bluffing," Carter yelled back. He had reached the chasm and stopped.

Henry watched him take cover inside a nearby cave. *Rookie mistake*, he thought. *Now I've got him.*

Henry started climbing again.

A minute later, a rifle shot boomed. At nearly the same instant, a bullet ricocheted off the ground a few feet to Henry's left, sending up shards of rock and debris.

Henry dropped to the ground. "Son-of-a..." He hadn't seen Carter sight the gun on him. He twisted and saw that Jack had taken cover behind a rock. He was relieved Jack was alright, but it only intensified Henry's anger.

He crawled on his stomach, ignoring the pain of thorns and rock, his eyes never leaving the cave while he positioned himself behind a nearby ocotillo. The spiny stems wouldn't stop a bullet, but he was counting on Carter being a bad shot.

"Why'd you do it?" Henry yelled up at him, wanting to start a conversation and draw him out from cover.

"I didn't have a choice," Carter hollered back. He was crying. "I begged him to leave."

Leave what? Henry didn't understand what Carter was saying but he didn't care. Carter had moved inside the cave and revealed his position.

"If he just would have moved off the ranch," Carter cried.

"What about my father?" Henry hollered up the mountain, hearing his voice shake. "Why'd you have to kill *him*?"

The following silence spoke volumes. Jack had been right.

Henry's body quaked with grief that he shoved aside. He

wiped sweat and tears from his eyes, then raised the rifle and squinted through the scope.

There was no other way.

Henry forced his thoughts aside. And the world around him slowly dropped away.

Carter was still calling out, but Henry was no longer listening. Everything was happening in slow motion. He had fallen into a sniper's trance.

Relax.

Breathe in.

Distance to target. Check.

Wind. Check.

Breathe out.

Heart rate, slow.

Recalibrate scope.

Breathe in.

Finger to trigger.

To resistance.

Target identified.

Breathe out.

Sight center-mass.

*He killed Dad.*

Breathe in…hold.

Trigger pressure.

"Henry, don't!" Jack hollered from behind him.

But the rifle exploded.

# CHAPTER 66

*Thursday, June 2*

JACK SAT ON a park bench in Brown Plaza, letting the warm breeze ruffle his hair and cool the sweat on his back. The day before had been a whirlwind of interrogations and interviews, helping the Val Verde County Sheriff's Office tie up the loose ends in the case of Henry Rose shooting Carter McConnell, his distant cousin by marriage.

The incident caused quite a stir in the close-knit border town, where both family feuds and family ties ran deep. When word got out that Roy had died, neighbors from miles around converged on the hacienda. Women brought casseroles and condolences. Men talked of the tragedy of losing Thomas and Roy in the same year. Their antipathy to Frank Moran's demise was unspoken but apparent.

After Jack had finished at the sheriff's office, he joined them at the hacienda.

Henry had been taken into custody and then released several hours later. His homecoming at the ranch was mixed. Although Kate and Adoncia embraced him heartily, several of his mother's friends seemed nervous by his presence. Their husbands, however, had welcomed him into their conversation, one even ribbing him on the inaccuracy of his shot.

Carter McConnell had been taken from the ranch directly to the hospital, where a uniformed deputy would sit outside his room until he was healthy enough to be released and immediately taken into custody, then escorted to the county jail.

Jack still couldn't fathom how Carter was still alive. Henry was an expert marksman, a former sniper in Afghanistan. And he had taken the shot from less than a hundred yards from his target. With Roy's old sniper rifle, Carter should have been blown to bits. Instead, the bullet hit low and to the right. Carter was taken down by shrapnel—slivers of rock and thorns embedded in his left side and face. Jack would always wonder if Henry had missed on purpose. One day he would ask him.

"We can never repay you for what you have done for us." The voice was gentle and filled with compassion.

Elena sat next to Jack on the bench. The subtle rose scent of her perfume and the warm breeze could have lulled him to sleep if he had let it. But the day was early, and there was still too much to do before he left town.

"Will you thank your friend who found Diego?" Elena asked, referring to Henry. "If he hadn't, we might never have known what happened."

The sheriff's office had confiscated a rifle and ammunition from Carter's home that was the same caliber as the one used to kill Diego. Although ballistics hadn't been completed, when confronted, Carter had confessed to the murder.

Instead of showing remorse, he had been caught on a recording device in the interrogation room, regretting not having buried the body immediately. After shooting Diego, he had planned to return at daylight and bury him, but Henry beat him to the scene.

"I'm sorry about your friend's uncle," Elena said. "I knew Diego liked him, but I didn't realize how close they were. For him to leave my parents so much money…" Her voice trailed off for a moment. "And to our church."

When news of Roy's murder spread, Harlan Baker called the sheriff's office and went in and made a statement. He explained how Roy had come to see him the night before, insisting on meeting despite the impending storm. They had spent several hours discussing Roy's suspicions that Carter was involved in something illegal. He confessed to never having fully trusted his nephew and had even hinted he could have had something to do with Thomas's death.

Baker had agreed to rewrite the will. And while the storm raged outside, Roy sat patiently until the document was finished, not leaving until Harlan's wife, Janice, dressed in a nightgown and robe, had witnessed it. The new will bequeathed two hundred thousand dollars to Diego's parents, Miguel and Sabina Torres. The remainder of Roy's investments went to the primary beneficiary, which the new document changed from Carter McConnell to Our Lady of the Holy Rosary Church.

As was designated in the original will, Roy left the ranch to Jordan and Henry, which, upon Kate's death, would be combined with Thomas's land, restoring the Rose Ranch to its original size, once again making it the largest property in Val Verde County.

*How sadly ironic,* Jack thought, *that Carter had mistakenly assumed he would inherit the ranch when Roy died.* If Carter had known it would go to Jordan and Henry, he never would have killed his uncle.

"Roy was an interesting old guy," Jack said. He was lost in thought for a moment. "I wish I had known him better."

Jack had a slew of questions. He wanted to learn more about the enigmatic Roy Rose, the young man he had once been, and the things in his life that had shaped him into who he was when he died. Now, Jack wouldn't be able to ask the man himself. But he would ask Jordan and Henry. And Kate.

"Father Nieto told me to tell you thank you," Elena said.

"I don't think he likes me."

"He does now," she said with a chuckle. "He was suspicious of you at first—like I was. He had done so much to help Diego turn his life around and was worried you would hurt us somehow. Father Nieto is very protective," she said. "But he is also very grateful."

Jack nodded, then got up from the bench and smoothed the front of his jeans. "I guess I better get going," he said. "I just wanted to say goodbye."

Elena stood and took hold of his arm. "Thank you for everything, Jack." She smiled at him gently, then remembering something, dug into her pocket. "Before I forget, my mother wanted you to have this."

She held out a fist, and Jack laid his hand under it. When her fingers opened, a silver necklace dropped onto his palm.

Jack looked closer and noticed a small crucifix was attached. He looked up at Elena.

There was a hint of sadness in her eyes. "It was Diego's," she said. "My mother wanted you to have it."

Jack shook his head and held it out to her. "I can't—"

But she closed his fingers over the necklace. "Take it," she said softly. "It will make her happy to know that you have it. You have been a blessing to our family."

When she released his hand, Jack opened his fingers and looked down at the necklace. He began to put it on, but Elena took it and helped him.

"There," she said, holding him at arm's length. "It looks good on you."

Jack studied Elena's face, fascinated by her. Her warm, dark eyes had seen so much pain yet still exuded strength and compassion. He wouldn't forget the kindness of the Torres family and promised to visit them when he returned to Del Rio.

They said their goodbyes, and Elena started for home.

"Don't wait another ten years to come back," she said over her shoulder.

"I won't," Jack whispered.

But she was already gone.

# CHAPTER 67

JACK FOUND HENRY saddling the bay he had put shoes on days earlier. Although the mare stood patiently, Henry's movements were quick and rough. A ranch hand came out of the barn and offered assistance, but Henry waved him away.

"I still don't understand it," Henry said, grabbing the cinch strap under the mare's chest. "Killing family for what? Some old legend of lost treasure?"

"There are lots of people who've killed for less," Jack said.

Henry shook his head. He stuck the strap through the buckle and yanked it tight, causing the horse to step sideways. "I never liked Carter. But I never saw this coming." A hint of regret or guilt mixed with the anger in his voice.

"No one could have predicted what Carter did to Roy," Jack said, trying to reassure him.

"Well, Roy suspected something, or he wouldn't have written him out of his will the day before it happened."

Jack stood watching him work until Henry broke the silence.

"Odell said Carter broke under pressure in the interrogation. Son-of-a-bitch admitted to pushing Dad off that cliff. Did you know that?"

"I heard."

"And for what?" he said. "To hide a smuggling operation?" His tone was incredulous.

"Your father figured it out and was going to tell Roy."

"But he made the mistake of confronting Carter first." Henry took the stirrup from where it was hooked on the saddle horn and let it drop to the mare's side. "Dammit. Why did he have to do that?" Henry looked at Jack, his eyes full of pain and anger, wanting answers no one could give him.

"I'm sorry," Jack said. There was nothing else to say. If only Thomas had confided in law enforcement or one of his sons before he confronted Carter, he would probably still be alive.

But Thomas had been a private man—and a fair one. It was easy to assume that he was giving Roy's nephew the benefit of the doubt by asking him about what he had uncovered before mentioning it to anyone else. The loyalty to family had likely cost Thomas his life.

Greed had cost Frank Moran his. When the city police bluffed and told Carter that fingerprints on the letter opener used to kill Moran were his, he had confessed to killing Moran as well, claiming it was self-defense. Moran had threatened to expose Carter's role in the smuggling ring if Jack Martin became a problem. Instead of doing something about Martin, Carter killed Moran. Carter felt the smuggling had run its course, and he no longer cared about making money selling the pictographs into Mexico since it was only a matter of time before he found the rest of Maximilian's treasure. In Carter's mind, with Roy out of the way, he would soon become a very wealthy man. He never knew the ranch would go to Henry and Jordan.

Henry shook his head and untied the reins from the hitching post. "I'll walk you to the house."

The two men fell into step with each other, and the mare trailed slightly behind them.

"Danny Ochoa told me to tell you thank you," Henry said. "I don't think he ever bought into Odell's theory that the Torres murder was a cartel hit."

"I had doubts about him for a while."

"Who? Danny?"

Jack nodded.

Henry scoffed. "Danny's sterling. He's liable to have Odell's job one day."

Jack agreed. "How's Kate this morning?" he asked. Although she had suspected Thomas's death wasn't an accident, the confirmation that it had been murder would have hit her hard. Especially when she found out Carter was responsible.

"She's getting through this like the rest of us," Henry said. "One day at a time."

They walked several steps in silence.

"What's going to happen to that archeologist?"

"David Hansen?" Jack replied. "So far, Odell doesn't have any evidence he was involved in any of the murders. And I doubt he finds any. The guy's a crook, but I don't think he's a killer."

"I bet his digging days are done though."

"They definitely are."

Earlier that day, Jack had called Catherine Michaels at the Juno Center. When he confirmed Hansen's involvement in the smuggling ring, she had wasted no time reporting him to the state archeological society. Hansen's career was over. Jack thought of Sherry and Bryan and wondered what would happen to them. He would probably never know but wasn't sure he cared.

Kate was outside when Jack and Henry reached the house. She gave Jack a long embrace. "How can we ever begin to thank you for what you've done?" she asked, releasing him. "Are you sure you won't stay? Jordan will be home tonight. I know he wants to see you and thank you in person."

Jack was tempted to stay, but there were too many reasons to go. He wanted to get back before Otto left for the mountains. But mostly, he felt the Rose family needed private time to grieve. His presence would only be a reminder of what had happened.

Jack shook his head regretfully. "Thank you, Kate, but I need to get back."

"Mother, let the poor man go home," Henry said, trying to lighten the mood. He stuck out his hand, and Jack shook it. "Thank you, Jack."

"Anytime."

Adoncia stepped out of the house carrying a small paper sack. She hesitated, then handed it to Jack. "Tamales," she said. "For when you are hungry."

Jack thanked her, and she nodded shyly, her eyes moist with tears.

Henry put a boot in a stirrup and swung up onto the horse. "What about me, Ado?" he asked. "I'm riding pasture today."

"For you, no." Ado's face went stern. "You lose the weight first." She wiped her face with her apron, then turned and waddled back to the house.

Henry laughed and shook his head. "Thank God some things never change." He pulled something from the breast pocket of his shirt and looked at Jack. "When you get tired of the snow, come on back. I'll be busy on the weekends for a while and could use the help."

With a sly grin, Henry flipped what he held into the air, and Jack saw a shimmer of gold.

Henry caught it and stuck it back in his pocket.

The coin.

Henry touched the brim of his hat, still grinning. "See you, Jack." He then wheeled the horse around and loped from the yard.

Jack stood for a moment, watching him ride away.

"What was that all about?" Kate asked, stepping closer.

Jack grinned, still watching him go. "I think he's found

a new hobby." Henry Rose was quite a character, and Jack would miss him.

"Did you tell Gretchen goodbye," Kate asked.

Jack drew in a long breath. "I was hoping you'd do that for me."

Kate laid a hand on his arm and smiled up at him knowingly. "I'll tell her."

Jack realized now why he had stayed away so long. Gretchen. But seeing her again, so happy and with the boys, something inside of Jack changed. He no longer felt the need to stay away. Part of him wanted to remain in Del Rio, to stay with the people who had become like family. But the pull of the mountains was strong.

"There's so much I want to say," Jack told her. "To thank you for…" His words fell away when he heard his voice quiver.

Kate shook her head and took his large hand in hers and squeezed it. "Just remember that you have a home here on the ranch anytime you want it."

Jack leaned in and gave the woman who had become like a mother to him a hug.

He then got in his truck and drove away.

# CHAPTER 68

*Going home…*

SOMEWHERE ON THE long, stretch of highway between Lubbock and the Texas-New Mexico border, Jack checked the weather on his phone. He saw that it had been unseasonably warm in Telluride and knew the remaining snow would be melting fast.

He had the radio tuned into a country station, and when Willie and Merle started in with "Pancho and Lefty," Jack thought of Otto—and then about Crockett. He tightened his grip on the wheel and accelerated, hoping he wasn't too late.

He spent the night in Albuquerque but was on the road early the next day. As he cleared the rise in the highway outside of Aztec, New Mexico, the sun broke the horizon, giving Jack a view of the sawtooth outline of the Rockies in the distance. Something inside him fluttered. He would miss Texas. But he knew now that he was going home.

Several hours later, he pulled through Telluride and into the campground. But Otto was gone. His army surplus tent was zipped tight. There was no sign of Crockett, and Jack's heart sank.

He immediately went to the Pandora Café, where Judith Hadley greeted him with a warm hug.

"He left several days ago," Judith told him. "Sometimes he'll make a trip down to town mid-summer, but there's no guarantee. He could be up there till September."

"Can I get a message to him?"

She shook her head sadly. "I'm sorry, Jack. There's no way to reach him unless you send a message via radio that he happens to pick up on the scanner. But that's a long shot."

"And he's never told you where the mine is?"

"As far as I know, he's never told anyone." She chuckled. "And we've all asked. Around here, the location of Otto's mine is as big a secret as what's behind the fence at Area 51."

Jack sighed. He knew what he would have to do next but couldn't do it on an empty stomach.

Judith sat with him while he downed a bowl of chicken and dumplings. She asked questions and listened closely as he recapped everything that had happened in Del Rio.

When he finished talking, she asked him, "So what's next? What are you going to do this summer?" She raised her brows as Jack told her his plans. "That's mighty ambitious," she said.

"It's the only option I've got left."

She stared at him a moment. "Well, don't leave just yet. I'm going to give you something."

Jack watched her disappear through the swinging door into the kitchen. She emerged several minutes later, holding a large paper bag. He stood up as she approached the table and took it from her.

"Provisions to get you there," she said.

Jack opened the bag and peered inside. "Thank you, Judith."

"Just promise you'll come see me as soon as you get back," she said. "I want to hear all about it."

An hour later, Jack had changed out of jeans and cowboy boots into pants and hiking shoes and had carefully stowed the food Judith gave him into the backpack with his other provisions and survival gear. He checked the GPS location on his phone again, locked the Airstream, and set out.

He spent a cold night at just over 12,000 feet and woke

early the next morning covered by a thin layer of frost. Every muscle ached as he crawled out of the sleeping bag and rolled it up.

The climb the day before had been long and grueling. By mid-afternoon, there was no longer a trail. He had pushed himself harder than he ever had before.

The morning trek was painful but glorious. Deep patches of snow still clung to the rocky summits of the peaks directly above him. The cloudless sky was a brilliant shade of turquoise, offering panoramic views that stretched for miles. Jack looked east into the heart of the Rockies and marveled at the snow-capped ranges beyond the San Juans. He then turned west and could make out the mountains of Utah.

As he walked, he saw the early buds of wildflowers pushing their way up through the grass. By July, he was sure the high Alpine meadows above Telluride would look like heaven.

He kept hiking. A few hours later, he finally saw what he had been searching for.

He stopped and stood a moment, watching as two dogs played in the distance. One was brown, the other one red. An old man sat in a canvas folding chair, watching them.

Nearby, a small wooden shack not much larger than a tent hugged the southern side of a rocky outcropping. Just beyond it, Jack caught a glimpse of gold soil tailings that spilled from the side of the mountain. The entrance was hidden from view, but Jack knew immediately that it was Otto's mine.

Jack started forward. The dogs saw him and stood alert, studying the advancing stranger. A few seconds later, Jack's heart lurched when the brown dog barked and loped toward him.

"Hey, Crockett," he said, laughing and rubbing the dog furiously.

The old man watched as they came closer. A small propane stove was on the ground at his feet, heating a blue speckled coffee pot. Crockett still danced and whined in delight, and Red ran out to meet them.

Otto sipped from a tin cup as they approached. "Howdy, Jack." There wasn't even a hint of surprise in the greeting.

"Otto."

"Looks like you could use some coffee." His voice was low and scratchy. "I only got one cup to drink from. But we can share."

The two men talked for a while, passing the tin cup and refilling it several times. Otto never asked how Jack found his campsite. And Jack didn't mention the tiny GPS tracker he'd slipped onto Crockett's collar before he left for Texas.

At a lull in the conversation, Otto set the cup down on the frosty ground. "We're burning daylight," he said. "Gold doesn't get itself out of the mountain." He scratched his gray beard and then struggled to stand.

Jack stood and helped him.

There was a mischievous twinkle in Otto's eyes, and Jack realized what he was suggesting. "The mine?"

"Seems it ain't a secret no more." He clapped Jack on the shoulder. "Wanna see it?"

Jack smiled at his old friend. "I'd love to."

\* \* \*

# ACKNOWLEDGMENT

*Death in a Harsh Land* depicts several real locations in and around Del Rio, Texas, but all events and characters are entirely fictional. Anything negatively portrayed is done so purely for literary effect.

This was an especially meaningful story for me to write. I am, in fact, a descendant of the Rose family who moved to Del Rio in 1888 via covered wagon. And I enjoyed adding bits of our family history to the novel. Although all of the Roses in the story are fictional, I no doubt have family members who will recognize the characteristics and personality traits of several of the characters.

I particularly enjoyed setting the story in Del Rio and hopefully giving the reader a taste of life in my hometown. It's a town steeped in history, with warm and inviting people—something rarely portrayed in the plethora of news stories regarding the current border crisis. I hope my affection for the land and the people is evident despite the slew of questionable characters that writing a murder mystery requires!

I have included several of my favorite local establishments in the story. Although the Broken Arrow is fictional, Benny's Cafe, The Brown Bag Deli, and Mesquite Creek Outfitters are very real, and should be on your list of places to visit if you're ever in the area. The bed and breakfast above Mesquite Creek, where Jack stays in town, is also an actual location. Yes, you can sleep where Jack Martin slept!

For interested readers, three books were of great assistance in deepening my knowledge of Lower Pecos Valley archeology and the indigenous tribes that created the magnificent pictographs. They are *Pecos River Style Rock Art* by James

Burr Harrison Macrae, *Ancient Texans, Rock Art & Lifeways Along the Lower Pecos* by Harry J. Shafer, and *The White Shaman Mural* by Carolyne E. Boyd. These are beautiful books with a wealth of information on the subject. It's a shame I could only use a fraction of it in the story.

As always, I want to thank my fabulous editor, Kristen Weber. She consistently helps make the stories better than I can make them on my own. And for that, I am once again immensely grateful.

Thank you to my sister and best friend, Kim Cauthorn, for spending several days with me early last spring scouting possible scene locations in and around Del Rio. Your prowess as a tour guide was instrumental in helping shape ideas for the story. The numerous meals we enjoyed together—most including heaping piles of chips and salsa—were a highlight of the trip. Life is more fun because you're in it!

Thank you also to my friend Shawn Ella Creamer. The barn with the Texas flag painted on the roof that Jack sees from the highway is Shawn Ella's. But more importantly, I can't begin to estimate the number of hours I spent pouring through posts on her blog, *The Lone Star Barn*, and her Instagram account for depictions of ranch life in West Texas. I highly encourage you to check them out for yourself!

Thank you to my husband, Chris, for continuing to encourage me to follow my lifelong dream of writing a novel. First, there was one; now, there are five! I will be forever grateful.

And mostly, to you, the reader. Thank you for spending a few hours reading another one of my stories. I hope you enjoyed it. And a million thanks for your messages, letters, comments, and reviews. I appreciate each one of you more than you know!

37532342R00176